To
Darren Mark
From Gran and Grandad
Hindle
With lots of love
Xmas. 1984.

Exciting Stories

of fantasy and the future

Exciting Stories

of fantasy and the future

Illustrated by Oliver Frey

Hamlyn
London·New York·Sydney·Toronto

Falcon Fiction Club

Titles in this series you will enjoy

First published 1982
Third impression 1984
The Hamlyn Publishing Group Limited
London · New York · Sydney · Toronto
Astronaut House, Feltham, Middlesex, England

© Copyright The Hamlyn Publishing Group Limited 1982

ISBN 0 600 36677 4

Printed in Yugoslavia

Contents

THE TROUBLE WITH PARADISE
by Alan A. Grant

COLONY ORGANIZER'S LOG: P-day minus One.
TOMORROW MORNING AT DAWN, our one-year voyage through hyper-space will be over. Our transport ship, the Toyu Maru, will set us down at last on the Planet Epsil-14. Already, we are calling it by the name Mo Oliver gave it – *Paradise*.

Hope amongst our two hundred-strong group of colonists runs high. After the claustrophobia of the polluted, over-populated Earth from which we are fleeing it will be joy itself to set foot on our new, lush, green world – 'a planet of clear air and fresh water, where real fruit hangs from every tree', as Mo Oliver described it.

Mo first saw Paradise back in her days as a solo scout with the 4th Spaceborne Division. She spent a whole day flying over it on the way back from a reconnaissance mission, and came away dreamy-eyed. This was a place where a person could settle down, she told me thirty years later, as she prepared to lead out the first batch of colonists.

'I've given you the coordinates, Kris – but keep 'em to yourself,' she warned me. 'When you and your colonist group have raised enough money for your trip, follow us out there. It's Paradise, Kris, believe me.'

That was in 2418. Now, two years later, here I am – Kris Blake, 57 years old, ex-pilot, late of Earth, bound for a new life on a new world. As Colony Organizer I haven't had much time to join in the pre-landing celebrations. But everything is ready now. Tonight, I'll drink to Paradise.

COLONY ORGANIZER'S LOG: P-day!

At dawn, Captain Igiyatsu brought the Toyu Maru in over Paradise. He made three sweep-searches in and around the coordinates Mo had given me, but could see no sign of the first colony.

'There too much trees, Mr Blake,' he said with his sing-song Japanese accent. 'I set you down on flat bit here, okay?'

I agreed, and the Toyu Maru set down in a wide, fertile valley.

The colonists gathered in an excited group around the exit ramp. I tried to organize them into orderly lines, but all I got was abuse, so I gave up.

The hatch slid open and pure, fresh air gushed in. I sucked it deep and long. It was like nothing I'd ever tasted before. It was . . . beautiful.

At least the others had the decency to allow the young Walker girl the privilege of being first out. (She won the raffle at the party last night.)

They gave her about two seconds, then they stampeded out.

They were absolutely delirious – leaping in the air, shouting, bending and kissing the ground. Old Mrs Fogerty was running round in circles waving what looked like a bandage above her head, yelling, 'We're here! We're here!' until I thought she'd have a fit.

The three Sutherland boys plunged straight into the clear blue river that meanders through the valley. I knew for a fact only one of them can swim! Just as well their father, Mike, ran after them.

I must confess I myself felt a trifle overcome by the sheer purity of it all. Mo Oliver was right – this *is* Paradise.

But Colony Organizers can't spare too much time for personal pleasure. Captain Igiyatsu was waiting. There was a ship to be unloaded.

I tried to calm some of the colonists down and organize

them into a work detail. Abuse again!

I had to unload almost a hundred tonnes of supplies more or less by myself. Full marks to the Fergusons and their family, who pitched in and did their share.

It was well into the afternoon before I was finished. By now some of the elation had dissipated, and my colonists were at work establishing our base camp. Paradise-2, I've called it. I think the name might well catch on.

Just before nightfall we all assembled to bid farewell to Captain I. and his ship. There were a few tears, a few heavy hearts as our final link with Earth was severed. We are on our own now. We will never see Earth again.

Fatigued by my efforts of the afternoon, I am having an early night. It is cool and comfortable here in my plasti-tent. The stars are very bright in the sky. From the other side of the valley I hear the screech of some creature – shrill, but somehow relaxing.

Morgan's son spotted some earlier. He says they look 'sorta kinda like apes'.

No doubt we will find out about them tomorrow – and much more.

Now, my camp bed beckons.

COLONY ORGANIZER'S LOG: P-day plus One.
Wakened early, feeling glorious. The colonists were cheerful, too – easy to see that they are feeling the benefits of Paradise already.

I organized work parties – very surprised with the generally cooperative response. It augurs well for the future.

I appointed May Ferguson as my deputy organizer and left her in charge of the construction of Paradise-2. I selected a search party, twenty in all, and set out to see if we could locate Mo Oliver. I was surprised, frankly, that she hadn't observed our landing yesterday and come to greet us. Perhaps her colony had found a better site and moved to it en masse. Only one way to find out – go and look!

We forded the stream and set off at a brisk pace across the valley floor. The vegetation began to grow thicker, and then we were at the tree-line.

A cry echoed through the trees and we all looked up. Swinging through the upper branches came a troupe of the creatures young Henry Morgan saw yesterday.

Fantastic creatures – apes for sure, but no species I've ever come across. Many of them were almost as tall as a human, but with elongated arms and short stubby tails. Their long glossy pelts varied in hue from a rich dark ochre to an almost dazzling white. Their fuzzy faces had an almost human quality which was quite endearing.

Imagine my surprise when one of them uttered a strange cry – 'Cobek! Cobek! Cobek!' – and hurled a large piece of fruit directly at me.

I had no time to duck. It spattered its purple juice all over the clean white pith helmet I'd bought in the Colonists' Emporium back on Earth. What a mess!

And then they were all at it – fruit, branches, even a stone or two. And all the time they were screaming 'Cobek! Cobek!' like a mob of demented monkeys.

Rhydderch, the big metalsmith, put a shot through them and they turned and fled. He was all for going after them and slaughtering them for food, but I put him firmly in his place.

'We haven't come to Paradise to start murdering its native species,' I rebuked him. 'That's just the sort of thing we're trying to get away from.'

There was a murmur from the others, and Rhydderch looked sheepish.

I felt quite proud of myself as we moved off. I think I've gone up in the others' estimation.

We searched all day, but the only trace of Mo's group we

Imagine my surprise when one of the fantastic creatures uttered a strange cry and hurled a large piece of fruit directly at me.

found was an empty Heinz plastipak. At least I know they were here!

There was only one other minor incident – Jon Forbes bent to sniff one of the peculiar red and white-spotted flowers that garland the bushes. It exploded in his face!

No harm done, of course – although Forbes couldn't stop sneezing for an hour. That'll teach him. I ordered the others to give the spotted flowers a wide berth.

We're camping for the night on a low ridge. Again I can hear the far-off cries of the Cobek-beasts, as I have called them. Behind me, the occasional sneeze issues from young Forbes' tent. Silly boy.

COLONY ORGANIZER'S LOG: P-day plus Two

This morning we found Paradise-1, Mo's camp – and my heart sank. There were almost a hundred wooden cabins, overgrown with weeds and creepers. Many were decayed and crumbling. There were signs of human habitation – implements, unopened store-boxes, a hoverskip lying rusting on its side where it had crashed.

But of Mo and her people, there was not a sign.

Everyone was quick to put forward theories, of course. Rhydderch's seemed to be the most popular.

'It was them Cobeks,' he snarled. 'They killed 'em and ate 'em! You should've let me go after 'em and slaughter 'em like I wanted, Blakey!'

The others murmured in agreement, and I fear I have lost some of the respect yesterday's bold stand won me. I couldn't let that pass. I pointed out the lack of any bones or remains.

'Probably carried 'em off to their secret lair and scoffed 'em there,' Rhydderch mocked. I thought it best not to pursue the matter.

It was evening when we got back to Paradise-2. Not as much had been done as I'd have liked – May Ferguson had obviously allowed the other colonists to slack.

I called an immediate meeting and told them of our expedition's discovery. The news broke the mood of euphoria that has been all-too-rampant since our arrival.

Now, as I write, a certain despondency pervades the camp. Perhaps it is a good thing. It will keep our minds on our tasks.

Whatever happened to Mo Oliver's group needn't happen to us. As Colony Organizer, it is my job to make sure it doesn't.

COLONY ORGANIZER'S LOG: P-day plus Three.
A busy day. Spent most of the morning walking amongst the colonists, boosting morale wherever I could. I fancy I did quite a good job – they're looking more cheerful again, and the cabins are beginning to take shape. May Ferguson called me 'boss' twice; I allowed myself a little tingle of satisfaction.

Spent lunch-time in my tent with a tin of stain remover, scrubbing at my helmet. No good! That purple fruit stain will be with me for ever.

By late afternoon, everyone was looking a little fed-up with working. Rhydderch suggested he lead a hunting party to kill Cobeks, and I stepped in right away. I wasn't convinced of the Cobeks' guilt, and I defused the situation by suggesting a game of football. The whole camp joined in. Result: Rhydderch's Wanderers 49, Blake's Rangers 50. That should keep R. in his place! I have a feeling that man wouldn't mind at all replacing me as Colony Organizer.

I asked Dr Paton to have a look at Jon Forbes. He was still sneezing occasionally and his nose had swollen somewhat. The doctor agreed there was nothing to worry about. A happy diagnosis.

COLONY ORGANIZER'S LOG: P-day plus Four.
Not such a good day. Wakened this morning by a fearful racket from the Forbes family's dome-tent.

I hurried over, to find Dr Paton outside, nursing a bleeding lip. Evidently the Forbes boy had been acting strangely during the night. His father had called for the doctor.

'I don't know what to make of it,' Dr Paton told me. 'He's calmed down now, but for a while there he was acting like a madman – raving and screaming and thrashing about like an animal.'

Jon Forbes was huddled, panting, in a corner. 'I wan' go out play,' he growled at his mother.

'You're going nowhere until you learn to behave yourself,' Mrs Forbes threatened.

I'd never noticed before quite what an odd-looking specimen young Forbes was. His limbs were too long for his body and his back at times looked almost hunched.

'His speech and behaviour are quite peculiar,' I remarked to the doctor. 'I'd never realized that young Jon wasn't quite right . . .' I tapped my head meaningfully.

'I gave him a medical before he left the Toyu Maru. He was perfectly all right then,' the doctor replied – rather testily, I thought. 'We can only assume it's some effect of that sneezing plant.'

It was rather a depressing day in other respects, too. Work went badly, and May Ferguson even had the cheek to suggest to me that I resign in favour of Rhydderch. 'Rhydderch,' she said, 'is all for fun. All work and no play – you know what I mean, Blakey?'

I didn't deign to answer.

COLONY ORGANIZER'S LOG: P-day plus Five.

A most extraordinary feeling on wakening! I wanted to say – 'Away with work. Let this be a day of play!' I had to fight hard to control myself – but I needn't have bothered. Apart from myself not a jot of work was done all day by a single colonist.

About forty of the men and a good few women had gone off

with Rhydderch to hunt Cobeks. They took all our weapons with them!

Dozens of youngsters were running wild, and their parents didn't raise a voice to stop them. In fact, the parents were no better.

Mr and Mrs Walker were having a stand-up battle by the rubbish pit. They both ended up *in* it, and with gleeful shrieks began pelting the other colonists with refuse. The others, of course, joined right in.

I must admit, it did look like fun. A strange urge came over me to get involved, but I resisted it. I had noticed that some of the women around the pit were wearing garlands of the red-spotted flowers I'd expressly forbidden the camp to touch. I began to remonstrate with them, but they drove me off with abuse and handfuls of muck. (It is truly amazing just how much rubbish the colony has accumulated in only four days!)

Went back to my tent – to find young Jon Forbes sitting on my bed, crushing fruit in my pith helmet. I snatched it from him and went to cuff his ear. But he bit my hand quite severely and ran out, laughing.

I shut myself in my tent and spent the rest of the day there, cleaning my helmet.

It's dusk now and the Cobeks are howling again. Somehow, their cries seem to carry an eerie note of warning.

There is trouble in Paradise. As Colony Organizer, it is my job to find the source – and stamp it out.

COLONY ORGANIZER'S LOG: P-day plus Six.
This morning I resolved to find the cause of the madness affecting my people.

As I left the tent, the gangling figure of Jon Forbes leapt from a nearby tree, bowling me right off my feet. 'Gimmy hatty,' he roared. Before I could recover he was shambling off with my pith helmet clutched firmly between his teeth.

I don't know what came over me. I threw a stone, and hit him on the back of the head. He fell unconscious. As I replaced my helmet, I vowed that never again would it leave my head.

Blood ran down over the Forbes boy's hairy face, and I considered going for the doctor. But I had other things to do. Anyway, I was sure he'd be all right.

I suspected that the red-spotted sneezing flowers might have had something to do with all this strangeness. I went down along the valley where the flowers grow in profusion, and sure enough they were in full bloom, pop-pop-popping, shooting their tiny spores into the clean air. Quite a pleasant odour, really. Could these spores be causing the trouble in Paradise-2?

I decided to talk to the doctor and old Bill What's-his-name, one of our resident boffins, about it. But later.

Spent the rest of the day swimming and gambolling along the valley. I found an excellent mudpool where I whiled away a pleasant hour or two, squelching and oozing about.

Back in camp now. Still haven't spoken to Paton or What's-his-name. Well, tomorrow's another day.

COLONY ORGANIZER'S LOG: P-day plus Seven.
Blake not write today. Not feel like it. Played instead.

COLONY ORGANIZER'S LOG: P-dya plos Nine or tEn.
Have to write one time more time. Say – something bad wrong happen with us. Colonnists changingg. Not sure how, but look diferent. What we becom Blaik no know. Blake no care.

Hard write. Fedup write. No write no more. Paradise she call.

It was 2426 before another group of colonists chanced upon Planet Epsil-14. From their ship it looked perfect, and a scout-pod was despatched to carry out a close-range inspection.

Its two-man crew touched down in the verdant valley that had once attracted Mo Oliver and Kris Blake.

'It's beautiful here,' one scout breathed. 'Like some kind of fairyland. Just taste that air!'

'This is the place for us, Georgie-boy!'

From the trees nearby came a series of guttural cries. The two men turned. High in the trees, swinging towards them, came a troupe of fabulous creatures. Their glossy pelts ranged in hue from dark ochre to a dazzling white.

They perched in the branches only thirty metres away. Suddenly, one leapt, grabbed a branch, swung . . . and a piece of heavy fruit hurtled from its hand.

It hit the man called George square in the face.

'Cobek!' it shrieked. 'Cobek! Cobek! *Cobek!*'

Then just as suddenly, the whole troupe was gone again, scattering back into the trees.

'Did you see that?' one of the men gasped. 'I could've sworn that beast was wearing a pith helmet!'

'I didn't see anything, did I?' George snapped. 'I had a face full of fruit!'

'And that noise it made – it sounded like *Go back*. You think they're trying to warn us, George?'

'You're letting your imagination run away with you, sunshine.' He reached for the pod radio and put it to his lips. 'Come on down, skipper. We've made it. We've found Paradise!'

BLUE MAX
by John Wagner

THEY DIDN'T WARN THEM in advance that Max was coming.

Les 'Lofty' Wadmore, A-Wing Commander, had just brought his fliers in from a hair-raising phase-up over New Glasgow. The enemy had attacked in force, filling the sky with the shark-like shapes of their interplanetary bombers.

Lofty's was the only fully operational wing left in Number Four Squadron now. His eighteen Bowtell Boomerang Starfighters – 'boomers', the men called them – had to handle things almost on their own. A few ageing Starblasts had managed to flap over from Number Three Squadron, but too late to be of any effective value.

Lofty's boys had made the Nyabu alien raiders run for home, but not before phosphor bombs had turned New Glasgow's entire dock area into an inferno. A-Wing paid a heavy price for their bold defence. Four boomers didn't come back.

So the men weren't in the best of moods when Squadron Leader Rory Edson – 'the Skipper' – brought Max in.

'HQ have sent us a new pilot,' he announced. 'Men, I want you all to say hello to Max.'

The men just stared. At last Lofty burst out: 'What is this, Skipper – some kind of joke?' He laughed bitterly. 'We're not in the mood for it. We just lost a few good pilots up there . . .'

'I know, and I'm sorry,' the Skipper told him. 'That's part of the reason why Max is here.'

'But he's a *robot*!' Pilot Officer Phil Anka exclaimed.

'Yes, he's a prototype model from Iveson Robotics. I've volunteered to try him out.'

Through all this Max just stood there. His face was incapable of expression, just a silvery ovoid of burnished aluminium. Where his eyes should be was a pair of bionic receptors, like barrels of an old Remington thwup gun. He had no nose. Instead of a mouth there was a rectangular speaker grid. On top of his head, looking slightly ridiculous, perched a peaked blue flier's cap.

His slender body frame had been cast in the shape of a Pilot Officer's uniform, and painted regulation blue. On his upper arm were welded a P.O.'s distinctive double chevrons. The overall impression could have been one of absurdity, like some overgrown child's toy put into a man's uniform. But the moment was too serious for humour.

The robot extended its hand. Its metallic voice rasped: 'Hi there. My name is Max. Pleased to meet you.'

Lofty ignored it and spat with disgust. 'Come on, Skipper! What use is a robot in the cockpit of a boomer? This is a war we're fighting – not a kids' game!'

Squadron Leader Edson was renowned for his hot temper, but now he patiently kept it in check.

'Max is no toy, Lofty. His specifications are impressive. He has a sensory-linked neuro-computer capable of reacting a thousand times faster than a man. His limb speed and co-ordination are twice as good as yours. He has separate motor and function controls in his five main body parts, capable of independent action should he receive a direct hit to his main computer.'

The Skipper put his hand on Lofty's shoulder. 'We've been taking heavy losses, Lofty, but the Nyabu don't seem to be getting much weaker. The new pilots aren't coming through fast enough. Max here, and others like him, could be our only hope of saving Terra Nova from the Nyabu torture camps.'

'Yeah, Skipper, we need pilots – but *men*, not robots,' Lofty said. He waved his hand contemptuously at Max. 'Oh, your tinman might have all the specifications – he might have daisies growing out his ears for all I know – but I'll tell you what he can't have.

'He can't have a sinking feeling in his gut when he sees a city ripped apart by Nyabu fire bombs. He can't get the blind hate that hits you when you see your best friend ripped apart in the boomer next to you.' Lofty smacked himself on the chest and thrust his chin out. 'He hasn't got emotions, Skipper, and that's what you need up there. That's why he'll never fit in.'

For a moment it seemed as if Lofty were going to strike the Skipper, but then he was striding past him to the wall of the squadroom where several rows of cap badges were pinned beneath the squadron crest. Forty-seven in all, the badges of fliers who never came back. The names of the Wing's four latest victims had already been added to the Roll.

Not a man spoke as Lofty tapped the wall. He was speaking for them, putting it better than they ever could.

'That's why your robot will never replace men like these, Skipper – because he'll never know anything worth dying for!'

The Skipper had heard enough. 'Max flies with A-Wing, and that's an order. Is that understood, Wing Commander Wadmore?'

Lofty saluted stiffly, staring straight ahead. 'Yes, sir!'

'Good.' The Skipper turned and walked to the squadroom door. 'I'll leave you to get acquainted.'

As the door closed behind him, Max again extended his hand towards the assembled men.

'Hi there. My name is Max. Pleased to meet you.'

But the men turned away.

There was a slight scare that night, when A-Wing was alerted to intercept a possible Nyabu raid on a supply convoy coming in from Old Earth. Lofty Wadmore scrambled all but one of his fifteen available pilots. Max was left behind. 'Backup duty', Lofty called it.

In fact, two days passed before Max was given his opportunity to fly with the Wing, and then it was on the direct order of Squadron Leader Edson.

'You're not getting away with it any longer, Lofty. Max flies – or I'll have you on a charge!'

Lofty couldn't argue. 'As you wish, sir!'

The next scramble came in the early hours of the morning. Max was already standing by his boomer when the rest of the Wing reached the launch pits. As Lofty passed Max, he paused reluctantly.

'We fly the Triple-V formation,' he snapped. 'You know that much, do you?'

'Yes, Lofty,' the blue-painted robot replied. 'The Triple-V formation is an advanced level combat stance involving the synchronization of three strategic flight elements –'

'Don't tell me about it – just do it!' Lofty was already running towards his lead boomer, calling back over his shoulder: 'And when you speak to me, you call me sir!'

The VTO Starfighters rose into the air and streaked spaceward. When they cleared Terra Nova's atmosphere, they had assumed the complicated Triple-V formation.

Up ahead, fifteen thousand miles out in space, an armada of several hundred Nyabu strike craft had been intercepted by units from several other squadrons, and a fierce, wide-spread dogfight had flared. Now every available Terra Novan fighter had been despatched to the scene.

The war had begun less than six standard months before, when the Nyabu attack fleet first appeared in the Alpha Centauri system – a system that had been at peace for over a hundred years, ever since the first colonists from Earth had arrived in the year 2279.

The original colony had started on the fourth planet in the system, Terra Nova – or 'New Earth' – and had prospered. By 2360 Terra Nova's population had swelled to over fifty million, and a sister colony had blossomed on Haven, the system's fifth planet.

It was at Haven the Nyabu first struck. No warning was given and no mercy shown. Haven numbered by then only five million inhabitants, and their flimsy defences were no match for the Nyabu shark-bombers and sleek, well-armed attack craft.

The giant troopships came in the wake of the first assault. Within thirty standard hours it was all over. Those who had survived the ferocious attack were imprisoned in the rigidly organized Nyabu torture camps.

There was no hope of mercy from the savage aliens. Two and a half metres tall, with scaled skin and sharp-hooked upper jaws that resembled nothing so much as a vulture's beak, their physical appearance was mirrored in their character. Ruthless, cold-blooded, their greatest delight was to witness the pain of their victims.

Terra Nova had mounted a rescue mission to their sister planet. It was beaten back by overwhelming firepower.

Now the Nyabu had turned their attention to Terra Nova. Their intentions were clear. Not a single human being would be left alive in this system.

'Wing Leader to all boomers!' Lofty Wadmore's voice crackled through the formation. 'They're coming up on scan now, boys. Maintain formation until I give the word!'

The fifteen A-Wing Starfighters powered in at over twenty thousand miles an hour. Seconds later, they were on the fringe of the battle. Three or four individual Nyabu ships made the mistake of coming for the tight-knit boomer formation, and were blown apart for their foolishness.

Then they were in the thick of it, and Lofty Wadmore was shouting: 'Break! Break! Independent targets!'

The formation split as human fought with Nyabu, their craft winding and twisting frenetically in a high-speed game of death. The Terra Novan Starfighters were not known as boomers simply because of their flattened boomerang shape. The banks of Xtern Phasers ranged along their leading edge boomed out like controlled volcanoes, sowing destruction where they struck. Their four Rolls Royce Meso-engines gave them the edge in speed over their alien opponents.

The battle lasted thirty minutes. Though heavily out-numbered, the Terra Novans gained the upper hand and finally the surviving Nyabu broke and ran for their well-defended bases on Haven.

A-Wing headed for home. Four ships had received damage, two serious – Phil Anka's starboard wing had been sliced in half, and Jimbo Johansen had to limp back on only half an engine. Nobody knew how he made it.

Bruce Lennie, the Wing's popular practical joker, had not come back at all.

Max had acquitted himself well. His flying control had been faultless, his reactions miraculously fast. He had destroyed three enemy craft, and seriously disabled another. The pilots had to admit he'd not done badly for a first action. But as T. C. Rudd said: 'In a scrap like that, you either get lucky or you don't.'

The men agreed with him. They all felt as Lofty did. Max was a machine; somehow his very presence was an affront to the names on the wall beneath the squadron crest. There were forty-eight of them now.

The men's attitude gave Max much cause for thought. He had been programmed to make himself liked, the better to gain acceptance from the men with whom he had to live. But though he had proved his flying ability and always been polite, he was still the pariah, the unwanted outcast.

Over the following days he redoubled his efforts to ingratiate himself with the A-Wing fliers. He took on all the squadron's unpleasant duties and performed all manner of helpful tasks for the men.

'I do not need sleep, sir,' he suggested to Lofty one evening. 'I will take night duty from now on to allow the men more sleeping time.'

'You'll do what you're told,' Lofty retorted, 'and I'm telling you to shut up and get out of my sight!'

To the men, Max's efforts at friendship looked pathetic, and only made them dislike him all the more.

Six days after he'd joined the squadron, Max went to see Squadron Leader Edson. 'I am requesting a transfer, sir.' His metallic voice made whatever he said sound dull and matter-of-fact.

'You *what?*' To Edson, the idea of a robot seeking a transfer seemed ludicrous. 'But why? I know the men have been giving you some stick, but surely you're not unhappy here?'

'It is not in my programming to be happy or unhappy, sir. But I feel my presence here has begun to negatively affect the performance of the wing.'

Edson could see the logic of Max's argument, but he was determined that this experiment would succeed. For the sake of Terra Nova, it had to!

'Request denied, Max,' he said. 'Keep trying. That's all.'

It was the following day when Lofty was called into the Skipper's office.

'I've got a mission for you, Lofty. This is it, the big one. Sit down.'

At last the Terra Novans were taking the war to the Nyabu. On the wall was a map of the section of Haven known as the

Tiger River Valley. It was here, in deep underground caverns, that the alien weapons factory had been located.

'We've got to stop the flow of attack craft that factory is churning out, or we're finished,' the Skipper explained, and Lofty nodded. 'A direct assault is out of the question – the whole area is too well guarded. But HQ have come up with a plan . . .'

He pointed at a wide river meandering through the valley. 'The factory is located some twelve miles below this point here. HQ computers have calculated that if an explosive device of sufficient strength to breach the riverbank is detonated here, the resulting flood will completely wash out the factory.

'A bomb has been constructed – it will arrive this afternoon.'

Lofty's eyes lit up with anticipation. 'Ruddy good show, Skipper! I've been hoping we'd take the offensive.'

'I knew you'd feel that way, Lofty. Here's the plan: only three pilots will fly the raid – one in the bomber, the other two as escorts. That way, it will appear to the Nyabu like a normal reconnaissance flight. At this point here –' Edson indicated a map vector, 'you will leave orbit and make all possible speed for the planet's surface – and your target. The Nyabu will have less than three minutes' warning.'

'It will be a dangerous three minutes,' Lofty mused, 'but I'm game. I'll fly, of course, and Colin Kirk will take the other escort. T. C. Rudd can pilot the bomber.'

'Rudd's fine, but Kirk stays here.' Edson paused for a moment. 'Max flies the other escort.'

Lofty shot to his feet. '*What?* The most important mission of the war, and you're sending that tinman! You're crazy!'

'On the contrary, Lofty.' The older man's eyes stared into those of his Wing Commander without wavering. 'It's the sanest decision I ever made.'

They left early next day, Max and Lofty in their boomer escorts and a swift Milward Pi-Bomber with T. C. Rudd in the hotseat. Their flight would bring them in over the target just before dawn.

In his cockpit Lofty was still fuming – but he was a better pilot than to let his emotions interfere with his duty. 'All the same,' he promised himself, 'when I get back I'm going to personally dismantle that metal mess . . . that's *if* I get back.'

By contrast, Max felt no emotion at all.

They came in bang on schedule. Four hundred miles out a half-dozen alien strike craft appeared to investigate – and the two escorts streaked ahead to engage them.

The battle was fierce but short. The Nyabu craft were disintegrated by the boomer phasers; Lofty and Max shared the honours equally.

Then they were in orbit around Haven, and their scanners showed an entire alien squadron blasting upwards on interception course.

'We should reach cut-off point before they're on us,' Lofty barked into his mike. 'But all the same, watch your rear, robot!' The Wing Commander missed the familiar presence of Phil Anka on his tail.

The Nyabu didn't expect the sudden dive towards the planet's surface. They streaked past, overshooting by thousands of miles.

The three Terra Novan craft dived planetwards, the leading edges of their wings white hot with friction. A stray alien attack craft came in from the side, aiming to sneak into the raiders' slipstream. In the rearmost boomer, Max's reaction was instantaneous. In a mere fraction of a second he had aimed and fired his four back-mounted phasers. Behind him the Nyabu ship blew apart.

Max heard Lofty's grudging voice crackle: 'Four to you, robot!'

26

They swooped into the target at speed, avoiding the massive barrage thrown up by the ground defences around the concealed factory. Then their retros locked on and they were slowing, slowing, until the blurred ground below took on features.

Along the high banks of the river, mobile Nyabu defence units had stopped, and their rapid-fire ground-to-air tracers lit the pre-dawn sky. Neat holes were punched in Lofty's wing, and he altered course a fraction of a degree.

'Target's dead ahead. Let her go!'

T. C. Rudd's bomb-bay sprang open and the huge cone-shaped bomb dropped towards the ground, and buried itself in the compacted soil of the riverbank.

'Dammit! It hasn't exploded!' T. C. Rudd cried as the three craft screamed over the river – then his voice was lost as a tracer bolt slammed into the bomber's engines and the whole ship exploded.

Behind T.C., Max veered instantly as a massive chunk of shrapnel shattered his cockpit. His aluminium finger hit the COCKPIT EJECT and the smashed plasteen dome was whipped away in his slipstream.

'A dud bomb! That's bloomin' torn it!' Lofty swore.

Then Max's calm voice cut in: 'I compute a ninety-one per cent probability that the detonating mechanism is jammed. It will require a sudden jolt with a force of approximately fifteen kilograms per square centimetre to set it off.'

'A direct hit from a phaser should do it!' came Lofty's reply. 'Turn 'em round, Max – we're going in again!'

Lofty spoke as if to one of his men. In the heat of the moment they were comrades in war at least, not man and machine.

The air around them was thick with tracer flak as they circled and came in for a second run. Max was lead boomer now. He dived with all sixteen front-edge phasers blazing.

But the enemy fire was an impenetrable curtain. Before

The air around Lofty and Max was thick with tracer flak as they circled and came in for a second run, front-edge phasers blazing.

28

Max could get within striking distance, a series of mighty explosions sent his ship crashing to the ground in flames.

Lofty peeled off and twisted skyward. There was no way through. The mission was aborted.

Suddenly Lofty's radio crackled and a familiar toneless voice said: 'Continuing with mission, sir. Over and out.'

On the ground Max's twisted body hauled itself from the blazing hulk that had been his boomer. His visual receptors focused on the wide cone base of the bomb, buried in the ground not thirty metres away.

He began to stagger forward, dragging one twisted leg behind him. On the riverbank above, a Nyabu soldier laughed. This was how he liked his victims – easy! He squeezed the trigger of his tracer and watched the ridiculous blue robot's body split asunder.

Max had been but a bare metre from the unexploded bomb. His main neuro-computer lay in a thousand pieces. But Max's mission was not over.

There was a low 'pop' as the bolts securing his left shoulder to the shell of his torso blew away. Then the fingers of the arm clutched the ground, clutched and pulled, clutched and pulled, edging their way forward until the dismembered arm lay alongside the unexploded bomb.

Then the arm bent at the elbow, and the clenched fist came sweeping forward with a precisely calculated pressure.

The force of the blast that followed tore away a chunk of soil a hundred metres wide. The banks of the Tiger River folded inwards and the water flooded out, an horrendous torrent pouring down the valley.

Within minutes it was streaming through the cracks in the soil above the underground death factory. The last Nyabu strike craft had been made in that place.

In the sky high above, Lofty's boomer was tossed by the force-wave of the blast. Max had been successful. Lofty shook his head. You had to hand it to that robo-pilot – he never knew when to quit.

He dipped his wing in brief salute, then accelerated violently and was gone.

News of the mission's success reached the squadroom well before Lofty. When the Wing Commander strode in the men were waiting to congratulate him, but he brushed by them and walked to the wall where the forty-eight cap badges were pinned.

'Well, lads, we did it,' he said grimly, 'but we lost two good pilots in the process.' He turned and slowly, deliberately pinned two cap badges beneath the others. The names on them were 'T. C. Rudd' and 'Max'.

'Two of the best!'

The men stared in amazement. The long silence was broken only when a polite cough came from behind them.

Squadron Leader Edson stood in the doorway; by his side was another robot painted in regulation blue. It extended its hand to the men.

'Hi there. My name is Rex. Pleased to meet you.'

Lofty pushed his way through his unmoving pilots and grasped the robot's metal hand firmly in his own.

'Come on in, chum. I'll introduce you to the lads.'

THE ALIEN
by Kelvin Gosnell

HIGH ABOVE THE AZURE AND WHITE crescent of Earth, the spaceship was about to die. It was an alien craft from deep in the heart of the Galaxy. So alien was it that we would have great difficulty in recognizing it as a spaceship at all. The nearest thing that it resembled was a snail – a gigantic snail, many hundreds of metres across.

Their main propulsion units gone, the alien crew knew that their chances of surviving the inevitable crash were minimal. They had no choice but to sit at the controls and hope. The very most the commander could hope for was that they would retain control long enough to avoid crashing into any centres of population below. They knew that we were down here, but their mission hadn't included any contact with us. Now they resigned themselves to the fact that Earth was to be their last resting place.

The ship made its first contact with Earth's atmosphere and started to burn up, great chunks ripping off the blazing outer shell. The death of the vessel had started.

Deep in the heart of the ship, the creature stirred. It could see the pictures of terror in the minds of the crew. It reached out to them with its own mind, tried to soothe them but they were too far away, too busy at their tasks to hear its strange soothing soundless words . . .

Hundreds of miles below, the Cornish peninsula nestled under the normal grey clouds of an English summer. In a wood running alongside a secluded creek, two young girls played on a rubber tyre strung from the branch of a tree to form a crude swing. The tyre swung out over the creek and one of the girls squealed with delight and fright when it was her turn on the swing.

The other girl was enjoying herself just as much as her friend but she was unable to experience the delicious thrill of being scared, for she couldn't see the three metre drop that opened up when she swung out over the creek. Her name was Mary Tredinnick and she had been blind since birth.

She and her friend, Alice James, came from the nearby village of Mylor and both were aged twelve. Alice had just finished her first year at the big comprehensive school in the outskirts of Falmouth – so she was in very high spirits. Mary too had just broken up for the summer, but much as she would have loved to attend school with her friend, she knew that was impossible because of her blindness. She attended a special boarding school on the other side of the county where they catered for children with a wide variety of handicaps.

So Mary was especially pleased on that afternoon, not only to be released from the grind of school, but to be reunited with her friend again.

'Come on, Treddles.' Alice called Mary by her nickname. 'Get off! It's my turn again now!'

'Coming in,' Mary called as she swung back towards the land. 'Tell me when to jump!'

'Three – two – one – GO!' Alice shouted out to her and exactly on the word 'Go' Mary launched herself from the swing and landed perfectly on the bank. It was a system they had worked out for themselves and it worked perfectly, whether they were playing on swings or crossing busy main roads.

Mary walked over to the big willow tree that she knew was just along the bank. She leaned against the ancient tree and ran her hands over the rough bark. Perhaps it was an illusion but she could sometimes swear she could feel the age of the thing – without the power of sight, all her other senses were that fraction keener than those of someone who could see.

As Alice clambered on to the tyre, Mary heard a peculiar, familiar rhythmic swishing noise. It was almost musical in quality and she heard it come closer, growing louder and louder . . .

'Watch out for the ducks, Alice,' she called.

'Eh?' came Alice's startled reply. And then, 'Oh, you heard them, didn't you! Still trying to shock me with your "superpowers" are you?'

'They're not that and you know it, Al,' Mary called in her friend's direction – she always found it disconcerting speaking to a voice which was swinging back and forth. 'You can hear and feel and smell and taste just as well as I can. It's just that you never use those senses to the full, that's all. What can you hear now, for example?'

There was a short pause before Alice replied. 'I can hear rushing water. That's about all – oh, I can hear a bird singing as well.'

'There are at this moment,' Mary replied, 'well over twenty birds singing within our earshot. *And* there are two girls coming down the path.'

'All right, smartypants,' Alice said, 'tell me *who* are the girls coming down the path?'

Mary concentrated very hard. 'I don't recognize their voices or their footsteps,' she said. 'They must be new to the area. I think one of them is called Gobber or Godber . . .'

'Oh, good grief,' said Alice, 'let's get out of here and quick.' She landed back on the bank from the swing. 'If that's Godber from my new school we're in dead trouble.'

'But why?' Mary asked.

'They're third years from the comprehensive. And I have

just spent the last year keeping as far away from them as possible. They're horrid and spiteful. Come on, let's get away!' Alice said as she took Mary by the hand.

But Mary slipped her grasp. 'Don't be silly, Al,' she said. 'Even with you guiding me, I couldn't go fast enough to beat them. You run if you like, I can find my own way back . . .'

'No, it's okay, Mary.' Mary could hear the shudder of repulsion in her friend's voice. 'They'd only take it out on me next term. I'll stick around here.'

Mary heard the heavy footfalls of the two older girls approach and then Mary heard a gasp as Godber grabbed and twisted Alice's ear.

'Who's your friend, weed? Don't remember seeing her in your class of weeds last year – she new?' The voice was rough.

'N-no, Godber – let go of my ear, please – she's Mary Tredinnick, she's blind and has to go to a special school,' Alice said with the pain still in her voice.

'Blind, eh?' (The more Mary heard Godber's voice, the more she disliked it.) 'Hear that, Sturt?'

The voice of Sturt was even less likeable. 'Yeah, seen any good films lately, have you, Trednik?' The laugh that followed the cruel joke was cold and humourless. Mary understood why Alice was so worried by the girls. She had met the same type in her own school. There were only two ways to deal with them: fight them, and in doing so sink to their level, or let them have their way. Mary normally found it better to give in to them, let them make their cruel comments.

She was about to reply when she heard the familiar boom of an aircraft's supersonic bang. But this one sounded somehow different as though it came from a great deal further away; it was flatter, as though travelling downwards. And instead of the engine roar, a few seconds later, there was the most terrifying, heart-rending soundless scream. It seemed to fill the whole world!

34

Mary's hands flew by instinct to her ears in a vain attempt to shut out the noise, but it had no effect. It seemed to be coming from *inside* her head. It was a multi-toned high-pitched wail – but more than that, too. She felt as if she could reach out and touch the sound – whoever or whatever was making the noise seemed to have released all the pain and tragedy and stark horror ever experienced in the world.

Suddenly, Mary understood. She didn't know how, or why, but she understood what that sound meant – it was a lament, a lament for beings that were on the threshold of death.

'They're dying!' she screamed. 'Can't you hear them? They're dying. They're dying. They're dying!'

High, high above, the creature in the hold of the alien ship was watching the crew die. The vessel had finally hit the thick inner atmosphere of Earth and burned out of existence in a fraction of a second. The crew were vapourized where they sat and the creature experienced their deaths – it tried to comfort them in their last moments, but failed; all it did was pick up their mental pain and anger and re-broadcast it in a tight beam downwards. The creature was a telepath – it could read thoughts, and project its own thoughts into another's brain. That was why the crew had collected it. They thought their scientists might find it interesting. It was not a particularly intelligent creature, it just had the ability to do naturally what the crew and their race had to use machines to do. It was this amplified telepathic scream that hit Mary.

As the ship broke into a thousand pieces the cage in which the creature was kept broke off with a piece of the thick, rock-like wall. By a freak chance, the shape of the piece of wall was aerodynamic – it would not plunge straight down and smash into the sea like every other piece, it would generate lift and glide gently towards the land. The thicker air would slow it as it fell and provide a soft and survivable landing. The creature huddled on the back of its tiny unexpected survival capsule and waited.

It glanced out just before impact and saw a brownish river winding through a wood. There was a strange circular black thing hanging from one of the trees. It had never seen a thing like that before. There was a terrible bang and the creature fell head over heels again and again.

Mary had collapsed on the muddy bank when the mental blast wave hit her. She struggled back to her feet. The voices of Sturt and Godber were still there.

'What's the matter with her, Sturt? Did you hit her or something?'

'Never touched her, did I?'

Mary could hardly hear them. All she could hear were the simple, insistent calls for help that the creature was broadcasting: 'Help me – hurting – lost – frightened – help me.'

'Oh, please, please! Stop talking and help him or it or whatever it is!' she said.

'What are you talking about, Trednik?' Godber slurred at her.

Mary was confused. 'Can't you hear that voice? That awful cry?' she said.

'What are you talking about, girl? If this is some kind of trick to make us look stupid, why I'll . . .'

By this time Mary had had quite enough of the two brainless fools. She couldn't waste any more time on them. 'Oh, for heaven's sake, be quiet,' and they were so surprised that they were. 'Listen – there is someone or something in trouble just over the top of the hill and I have got to help it. Come on, Alice, help me get up to the top.' And with Alice leading her by the arm, she strode off up the path. Godber and Sturt followed.

36

The piece of flotsam which had crashed from the skies had carved a path through the trees. Some of the leaves still smouldered from its touch. Alice described all this to Mary, but she wasn't listening, she was following a homing signal, the insistent 'Here I am, friend' which was pulsing into her mind. She couldn't understand why the others couldn't hear it – she assumed it was because they had their sight and she didn't, but the signal was so strong that she didn't really have time to worry about it – she only had time to obey it and find it.

She was crashing through the undergrowth on her own now. Alice was shouting after in concern, but she couldn't hear. She was only metres away from the source.

When Alice caught up with her friend, she found her kneeling, quite oblivious, in the centre of a nettle patch, crouched over the strangest creature she had ever seen. It was about the size and shape of a small rabbit but there was a long bushy tail instead of a small white fluffy one. But strangest of all were the colours – the delicate mauve fur and the striking green eyes!

'Mary,' Alice called. 'Don't touch it. It – it's wrong!' She searched for a word to express the strangeness she saw in the creature. 'It's *alien*!'

But Mary took no notice at all. Her hand touched the fur of the creature's snout and it nuzzled into her palm. Then, without any warning, it scampered straight up her arm and on to her shoulder. It was then that Alice thought her friend was going to die. Mary gulped in a great lungful of air and a look of deep shock spread over her face.

'Mary, wh-what is it?' Alice gasped.

She was totally stunned when the next thing that Mary did was to laugh hysterically. 'Oh, Alice, Alice!' she cried. 'All the years we've played together and I never knew you had red hair!'

It was Alice's turn to be shocked. 'You – you can see? You

The strange, rabbit-like creature scampered straight up Mary's arm and on to her shoulder.

38

really can? But how . . .? Why . . .?'

'It's this creature. It can – uh – I can't describe it properly – but it can get inside my head. It can read my thoughts. And I can sense what the creature is thinking. It has understood that I am blind and so it's simply sending me pictures of what it sees.' She cupped her friend's face in her hands. 'It's so wonderful, I don't think I'll ever get used to it.'

'You won't get the chance, Trednik.' The sour voice shattered the mood as completely and violently as the spaceship had shattered. 'I'm taking this rabbit or whatever it is into my protection!' Godber grabbed the creature from around Mary's neck. The creature struggled in her grasp. 'We heard every word you said. If this thing can make blind people see it needs very special looking after. Doesn't it, Sturt?'

'Yeah – quite right, Godber. These two are too young. They don't know how to care for it properly – not like we do!'

Both of them backed away into the thick wood, leaving Alice and Mary in shocked silence.

After a while, they had recovered enough to start picking their way back down the slope of the hill the way they had come up. It was a good deal tougher going in that direction, since Mary did not have the driving force of the pleas from the creature to guide her. They were nearly back to the path when they met a badly bruised and dazed Sturt.

'Help her,' she sobbed, pointing away into the thickest part of the wood. 'Help her, help her.' And she staggered past them away down to the path.

Hot on her heels, the creature came running out from the undergrowth and settled up on Mary's shoulder again. She knew in an instant what had happened – Godber and Sturt had been so gloatingly proud of their prize that they hadn't even looked where they were going, much less cared. They had been passing over the site of an old tin mine shaft – the hill was honeycombed with them and Godber had gone down it without even knowing what was happening. The eyes of the creature guided Mary to the spot.

The shaft went down almost vertically. It let in enough light to make it clear that there was a shocking drop to the bottom and hardly any handholds in the crumbling walls. Godber was about seven metres below the top, clinging like a leech on to the side and whimpering like a baby.

Alice and Mary advanced to the very edge of the shaft. Mary's new found eyes showed her precisely the danger that Godber was in.

'Godber,' she called down to the pathetic figure, 'if you do exactly as I tell you, you'll be all right. Move your right hand upwards. There is a ledge just above you and you can . . .'

An increase in the whimpering interrupted her. 'Can't – can't move. I'll die if I move. Help, help, help me.' Godber had frozen – the fear of the unthinkable fall beneath her was so great that it had paralysed her.

Mary sensed that there was no chance of talking Godber round – there was no chance of her helping herself. Mary would have to do it for the trapped girl, since the fall could not frighten her. Slowly and so gently, using the creature's eyes and her own super-sensitive touch, she started to work her way down the crumbling wall. She felt a brick start to move under her fingers and instantly switched her hand to another location. The brick dropped away – it was a long, long time before it hit bottom.

Soon she was alongside the terrified Godber. Talking gently, confidently, as a nurse might to a frightened child, she persuaded the older girl to move one hand then another. Slowly, they edged their way to the top. Godber half jumped, half scrambled out. Mary was coming up behind her when Godber's foot caught Mary on the neck and dislodged the creature.

Everything went dark for Mary again. She had the presence

of mind to grab hold of the turf at the mouth of the shaft and hold on like grim death. A fraction of a second later, the mental scream of pain and fear from the falling alien creature hit her. She cried out in anguish and sympathy for the being that had given her such a fleeting glimpse of sight.

When the pain finally faded, she dragged herself up the last few inches to safety. Alice was beside herself, 'Oh, Mary. The creature, it's fallen – is it . . .?'.

'Yes, it's dead.' The sadness was still in Mary's voice, but there was resignation there as well – she accepted the creature's death. 'It's probably better this way – the creature could never have been happy here, so terribly far from its own kind. No matter how happy it made me it would have been lonely. Come on, Al – let's go home.'

The blind girl and her friend started to pick their way down the wooded slope. Behind them the pathetic and guilty figure of Godber lay on the earth – it was a long time before she stopped crying.

THE PERSISTENCE OF YESTERDAY
by Angus Allan

'I HAVE NEVER, NEVER SEEN ANYTHING LIKE IT!' Lieutenant Marvin McGann stared fascinated through the frontal screens of his Banshee fighter at the immense, sparkling city far, far beneath him. It was a glittering place of domes and spires, set in the perfection of a deep valley surrounded by lofty green mountains.

'It's – it's stunning. Incredible! Absolutely beyond description!'

The twin suns of the Orgal System blazed in the heavens above, and as he turned his craft to make a second pass over the city, McGann slid down his protective visor to shield himself from their glare.

'I see a spaceport. Just beyond the edge of the place. You know something? I'm going to land. I've got a feeling about this place. It's Paradise!'

The urgent voice of Central Control shrilled in the pilot's headset. 'Do not land. Repeat, do not land. You are hallucinating, McGann. Do you read me? Do you understand? You are hallucinating!'

Marvin McGann didn't seem to hear – didn't seem to respond at all. 'Oh, boy,' he laughed. 'It is out of sight! It is too much!'

Cutting thrust, he edged the nose up and began to settle on his approach run. Aware now of the feverish pitch of his controller's voice, and irritated by it, he deliberately switched off the communications link.

Central Control was located in the tallest of a group of ugly buildings set squarely in a barren valley on the desolate planet known simply as Orgal Beta. The windows of the buildings were gold-laminated to protect those within from the fierce brilliance of the twin suns that threw the entire landscape into harsh patterns of black and white.

The place was a relay station on the commercial space-route between other planets in the Orgal System, and Marvin McGann, half-way through a twelve-month tour of duty there, had been in flight somewhat less than an hour – his job merely to test out an engine correction that had been made to the Banshee fighter.

Central Control's senior officer, Colonel Dan Sefton, looked grim as the duty operator reported communication severed and asked, 'What's happening to McGann, sir?'

'I don't know, Charlie.' Sefton slowly shook his head. 'For him, the place he's seeing actually exists. That much is clear from the way he was talking. But you know – I know – that it cannot be there.' He turned to another of his officers, manning a directional ranging console. 'What's his position, Mary?'

Ensign Mary Chibwe bit her lip. 'Twenty out on the green sector, two-five-six degrees, closing fast. Banshee's in landing attitude.'

'He's not linked to an over-ride, sir.' Now it was the Second-in-command, Major Jules Couperin, who spoke. 'I'm afraid there's nothing we can do for him.'

'No. Nothing. Poor McGann . . .'

The eager pilot cut his power to zero, and waited for the light thump that would signal contact with the straight, smooth concrete apron stretching ahead of him. His finger closed on the trigger that would operate the billowing retro-chutes at his tail.

The landing gear touched ground. But it was no level expanse of concrete! Just a tumbled scatter of broken rocks in a valley wilderness not two miles away from Central Control!

The Banshee bounded drunkenly back into the air. It seemed to hang there for a moment, before it touched again, and this time the starboard absorbers collapsed with a sickening shriek of metal. A wingtip dipped and churned a rain of debris into the air – and the entire craft began to cartwheel! Even as it broke up, the ruptured fuel tanks spilled their contents on to the hot engines, and in one savage, spectacular moment, the fighter was totally engulfed in a massive, flaring fireball.

Slowly, the ugly black smoke-pall drifted away. Where man and machine had been, now there was nothing . . .

Abruptly, Colonel Dan Sefton turned from the window, and saw his own horror mirrored in the eyes of his staff. Military professionals, all were used to death. But this had been so startling. So unexpected. So baffling.

'Jules. Would you mind getting McGann's medical records up here for me? I'd like to run them through the computer.'

Couperin saluted and left the room, to return seconds later with the required reels. McGann's history proved entirely normal. There was nothing, absolutely nothing to suggest why he had witnessed the fantastic scenes he had described.

Summoned to Sefton's office, neither the Station Doctor nor his colleague from the Psychiatric Department could throw any more light on McGann's behaviour. 'Some kind of brainstorm . . .?' The psychiatrist spread his hands, sounding lame and apologetic.

'All right, gentlemen. You can go.' Dan Sefton pondered deeply. Then, at last, he got up and walked back into the control area.

'Jules. Have another Banshee fuelled up and put out on the pad, will you? And have – let's see – Lieutenant Nakamura report to me. He and I will fly this mission together.'

'What's your angle, Colonel?'

'I want to duplicate McGann's flight.' He turned to Mary Chibwe. 'Get a print-out of his exact course and manoeuvres, will you, Mary? Oh, yes. And Jules . . .'

'Sir?' The Major paused at the doorway.

'Better have *my* Banshee fitted out with a ground-control over-ride. Just in case.'

Twenty minutes later, suited up, Colonel Dan Sefton strapped himself into the pilot's seat of the sleek fighter. Beside him, in the seat that had been vacant on McGann's ship, sat a lean, relaxed and expert flier, Lieutenant Toshio Nakamura. But it was not entirely for his expertise that Dan had selected him as his companion. It was because Nakamura was reputed to be somewhat psychic.

'All set, Toshio?'

'All set, sir. Pre-flight prelims made and double-checked. Course computer has already been locked on to McGann's pattern. You could fly this one hands-off.'

'Could, but won't,' said Dan with a grim smile. 'I'm old-fashioned, kiddo. I respect computers. I live by 'em. But it doesn't mean I trust 'em with my life.'

The veteran cut in the motor relays, eased off the brakes, and let the Banshee roll forward for take-off. Clearance came from control, and the two men felt the familiar pressure as the thrusters slammed them down the pad.

A fraction of a second afterwards, they were pointing at the glaring sky, and their strange and unprecedented mission had begun.

Just forty-five minutes passed before it happened. They had made a long, curling turn, and far, far below them, the battered landscape of Orgal Beta was clearly visible through scatters of patchy cloud. Suddenly, without the slightest hint of warning, it all changed. Nakamura couldn't repress the shout of astonishment that rose in his throat. 'Look!'

Dan Sefton's jaw had fallen open. His eyes were bulging in his head. When he spoke, his voice sounded strange and strangled. 'It's there! Exactly as he described it! But – but how . . .?'

There, shimmering in the friendly sunlight far below and beyond, the spread of the beautiful city lay exposed. Tempting. Tangible.

Both pilots looked at each other, and as they did so, their minds were wiped clear of all memory of the purpose of their mission. Slow smiles spread over their faces.

In Central Control, Major Jules Couperin, seated squarely behind the communications console, said: 'Let's have it, Colonel. What can you see? Is it McGann's vision?'

There was no immediate answer. Then: 'Jules! My boy, you should see this! It's incredible! A magnificent place! Utterly astounding! Such architecture! Such splendour!'

'Come on, Colonel!' Couperin's voice had a thin edge to it now. 'Remember what you're there for! You're beginning to sound irrational.'

Abruptly, just as McGann had done, Colonel Sefton reached out and cut all radio connection with his base. Grimly, Couperin turned and met Mary Chibwe's eyes. 'Do we over-ride and assume control, sir?' she said.

The Major shook his head. 'Leave it for the present, Mary. But the instant – the very instant – the Colonel puts that Banshee into a landing attitude, take over.'

'Oh, oh!' The girl reached for the buttons. 'That means right now! They're attempting to go in.' Then her voice rose to an agonized shriek of dismay! 'It's not working! We have a systems fault!'

Smiling and relaxed, both Colonel Sefton and Lieutenant Nakamura watched the stretch of concrete apron come up to meet them. 'Here we go, Toshio. Cutting power – now.'

By some incredible fluke of chance, their landing gear settled on a relatively smooth expanse amidst the rocky wilderness of reality. The retro chutes billowed out and brought them to a juddering halt.

'Heck, that was kind of bumpy,' said Dan Sefton, testily. 'I must be losing my touch.'

Nakamura knew better than to comment on his commander's ability, and said, instead: 'Here comes a reception committee, sir.'

Dan threw back the cockpit screens of the Banshee as a pair of brightly-painted hover-cars flashed out towards them from the glass-and-mosaic buildings of what must have been the spaceport terminal. The cars stopped, and half a dozen tall men in metallic suits, their faces strangely elongated, their complexions of a greenish hue, got out of one of them. They looked like soldiers, and indeed, they lined up in a semi-circle facing the fighter, and held rifle-like weapons loosely in front of them. From the other car, an even taller being had stepped. Magnificently robed, he wore a strange head-dress that sparkled with precious metals and gems.

'What do we say, Colonel?' Nakamura stood beside his senior on the apron. 'I doubt if they speak English.'

'No, nor Japanese, Toshio.'

The impressive alien made a brief gesture with his long-fingered right hand. 'There are no communication problems. My brain will automatically translate what you say, and you will hear my words in your language. You will please identify yourselves.'

'Colonel Daniel Sefton, Lieutenant Toshio Nakamura. From the Relay Station on Orgal Beta. We – uh – come in peace, of course.'

'That much I sensed,' said the tall one. 'Otherwise your craft would have been blasted from the skies. You are not from

47

*Six tall men in metallic suits,
their faces strangely elongated,
got out of one of the cars.*

48

Manthir. Nor are you of any of the infernal races who are Manthir's allies.'

'Manthir? That means nothing to us,' said Dan Sefton.

'Your talk of Relay Stations, and of a place called Orgal Beta means nothing to me, either. I am, by the way, Kvesh, Regional Commandant of the City of Nedj, in the service of His Majesty Ttanshn, Lord of Lumiq.'

Dan inclined his head. 'We've no wish to intrude.'

'But you *do* intrude,' interrupted Kvesh. 'For years my planet has been embroiled in a long and wearying war with the Empire of Manthir. A truce was recently brought about, but all the time, we suspect that Manthir will attempt a sneaking assault upon us. It may be that you – beings unknown to us – have been sent to divert our attention . . .'

'Now look here! That's just not true! My bona fides are totally in order!'

'Enough,' snapped Kvesh. 'We shall find out in good time. For our own security, we shall have to place you under arrest.'

'So much for our visions of Paradise, Colonel.' Nakamura glanced uncertainly at his boss. 'What do we do?'

'I think we get out of here, Toshio!' Dan spun on his heel and he and his lieutenant dived back into the Banshee. A scatter of shots from the semi-circle of Kvesh's soldiers tore past the fighter as its engines fired. Again, the smoothness of the runway apron was a deception that covered the reality of jumbled rocks, but the craft lifted in the split-instant before it would have crashed to destruction. In a steep upward climb, it left the beautiful city far below.

Major Jules Couperin sagged in the passenger seat of the balloon-tyred vehicle that had set off from Central Control. With bated breath, he and his staff had seen the Banshee land, had seen Sefton and Nakamura get out. On the telescanner in front of them, he and his driver had witnessed the pilots

49

apparently talking to someone – someone invisible. Now they had observed them dash back and make rapid take-off, coming within an ace of doom!

Couperin said: 'Whee-ewww. Whatever's going on is beyond me, boy. Come on – turn round. Back to base. Full speed.'

Mary Chibwe bounded to her feet as the Major reappeared in the control room. 'We've located the fault in the over-ride system, sir! We've taken command of the Colonel's fighter!'

Sure enough, through the windows of the building, Couperin could see the Banshee again. Turning slowly, its power diminished as it dropped towards the safety of the pad.

Colonel Sefton snapped free of his strap restraints. He felt tired. Terribly tired. He looked at Nakamura, who seemed just as weary. Their eyes held, and Sefton let out a long, shuddering sigh. 'Do you remember – a vision? A city . . .? You know – like the one McGann saw . . .?'

'I-I think so, Colonel. I'm – not sure.' Nakamura rubbed his temples, like a waking man vainly attempting to recall the disintegrating fragments of a dream. 'There was a man. A tall man . . .'

Major Couperin, his face grave, was there to meet them as they got out. He found them barely coherent. The station doctor was with him, and said: 'I think I'd better give them something, Jules.'

Couperin nodded slowly. 'They witnessed something in that flight that neither they, nor we, are likely ever to understand. Perhaps – if your colleague were to subject them to deep hypnosis . . .?'

'Later,' said the doctor. 'Later.'

It turned out that they were destined never to remember a clear moment of that incredible mission. They would never know that, a million years in the past, the barren place they called Orgal Beta had been the planet Lumiq, ruled by His Majesty Ttanshn. Lumiq had indeed been embroiled in a long war with the Empire of Manthir. Yet somehow, by the strange forces that exist in Space, McGann, fatally, and then Sefton and Nakamura, had taken a specific flight-path that had broken into some astounding warp of time's own memory, into the same spot in the Universe where, long before the existence of trivial mankind, those events had once taken place.

Why had those on the ground seen nothing? Who can say? That it was no mere fancy was proved beyond doubt by the crashed Banshee. One dead pilot. And by the strange chips, that might have been caused by bullets, on the outer casing of Colonel Dan Sefton's fighter.

From time to time, at ever-decreasing intervals as they grew older, the Colonel and Lieutenant Nakamura had recurring dreams. It wouldn't have occurred to them to tell each other, but they both dreamed the same thing. Of someone called 'Kvesh', who came to them in the small hours before dawn and reproved them – as if for diverting his attention while his enemies made ready to attack and destroy his beloved city . . .

JUST LIKE HOME
by John Radford

WHEN THE PHOTOSENSORS on the nose of the ship had calculated that the luminosity of Fomalhaut had reached the pre-programmed level, a silent command was passed to a solid-state relay in the sleep-generator, and Margon woke up.

He was instantly alert, as if he had spent a few moments catnapping rather than several years in suspended animation. He didn't even yawn.

Fomalhaut was hanging huge in the control-room vidscreens as Margon eased himself into the only seat. The cyberpilot sensed his presence, and the screens blacked out for a moment, then lit again with a tape of the lined face and grizzled shoulders of Orban Gart, Prosecutor-General of the Terran Justice Secretariat. Margon groaned. He had seen that face too many times before.

'Jon-6 Margon,' the precise, measured voice issued from the speakers below the screens, making it seem for a moment as though Margon was surrounded in the small cabin by clones of the chief justice. He shivered. 'You are nearing your destination. I am required by the statutes of the Secretariat to read you your sentence before ConTransit 774 makes planetfall. You have been tried and convicted of multiple murder in the course of treasonable larceny, and it has been the judgement of this Secretariat that you should suffer the maximum penalty.' The sombre face paused and looked up for a moment, then continued: 'Death, by the prescribed methods, with the alternative that you may choose transportation to one of the outer planets. You have chosen transportation.'

Margon laughed sickly. 'You bet I have, you old fool,' he muttered.

'You have been assigned to the second planet of the Fomalhaut system, known as Torbanel. You are forbidden to return to the Terran system. That is all. Good luck.'

The screen blanked, then lit up with the great yellow ball that was Fomalhaut once more. Margon sniffed derisively.

'Good luck!' He sneered. 'They're so all-fired civilized on Terra!' What did they care if he had good luck or not, as long as they were rid of him? He stretched back in the comfortable padded seat of the robot ConTransit ship and smiled thinly. By now he had planned to be living in luxury on Elisium IX, the paradise planet in the eastern spiral arm. And he would have been, if a couple of stupid guards at the InterSpace depot hadn't got the idea they wanted to die like heroes.

He thought again of the rich cargo his informant had told him about. A shipment of Erg-crystals worth, at a conservative estimate, five or six million Stellars was hanging around at InterSpace waiting for a pilot to take it out to one of the industrial planets in Centauri. Margon had taken a job as a loader with InterSpace, had got to know the layout, and the routine, and had sorted out his plans. It should have been so easy. Then the two guards had showed up. Young, fresh kids, anxious for promotion. What they got was three kilovolts from Margon's plasmag. And what Margon got was the death sentence.

Terra was far too civilized to execute its criminals, that's why the alternative was always offered – transportation for life. It was always taken. You never knew where they were sending you, of course, until you woke up, but Margon had reasoned that there was an even chance of getting to some backward planet where the natives were harmless and you could set yourself up without too much difficulty and live like a lord. What Torbanel was like, he didn't know; but it couldn't be a whole lot worse than the polluted, overcrowded cities of Terra. And it could be a whole lot better.

As the ship cruised in a low orbit towards the spaceport, Margon scrutinized what was to become his new home. It was pretty barren for the most part, a rocky, mountainous landscape, with here and there clouds of ash and smoke hanging over the peaks, showing that there were active and semi-dormant volcanoes down there somewhere. There were cities with what looked like advanced industrial complexes, and occasional stretches of straggling grassland, sometimes wild and lonely, sometimes intensively cultivated by the latest artificial agronomic machinery. Torbanel, Margon decided, didn't look too bad.

The ship landed at the spaceport in Sorbat City, and there was a welcoming committee waiting for him. He'd half expected a squad of armed troopers, but what he found were two smiling Torbaneli, a man and a woman. As he walked down the ramp of the ship, the man came forward and introduced himself as the head of the Sorbat City Rehabilitation Service. Margon was surprised.

'We know how you come to be with us, Mr Margon,' said the man, 'but on Torbanel we have a rule. We don't ask any more about a man's past than he wants to tell us. We are a young civilization, and anyone who is prepared to help us and work with us to build it up is welcome without question.' He held out his hand. Margon shook it with a smile. This was better than he'd thought. What a bunch of suckers!

'I'm glad to be here,' he said. He meant it. The man led him towards the terminal building as the robot ship lifted off silently behind them.

'We've arranged accommodation for you, Mr Margon, and after you've had time to have a look round the city and get the feel of life on Torbanel perhaps you'd like to visit the Occupation Bureau,' said the woman, earnestly. 'They'll be only too happy to find you some kind of job that will give you satisfaction.'

Margon couldn't believe his ears. If he'd known about this place he'd have come here years ago. It was ripe for development! Margon's own particular style of development, that is. The woman was continuing – giving him a potted history of the planet.

'A century ago Torbanel was very primitive,' she said, apologetically. 'Not very civilized at all, I'm afraid. It consisted mainly of isolated groups of nomadic tribespeople who cultivated the greenlands where they could, and made war on one another sporadically. Then the ships came from Earth, or Terra, as you call it now. They taught our people how to mine for ores, smelt them, build factories, and develop technology. The people of Torbanel learned well, and quickly, and the result is what you see before you.'

She indicated the bustling city street into which they had stepped from the spaceport terminal. The man was at the kerb, flagging a hover-taxi. The people passing by were well-dressed in a sober-suited kind of style, and smiling happily as they went about their business. Along both sides of the street were brightly lit and well-stocked shops selling everything from synthifoods to roboservants. It could have been any medium-sized city on Terra, except that the air was cleaner. Margon breathed deeply.

'It's great,' he said. 'Just like home.' The woman smiled.

The flat that the Rehabilitation Service had fixed up for him was better than anything Margon had had on Terra. It was on the fifth floor of a high-rise block on the edge of the city and boasted a cyberchef, wall-width triholograph, ultrasonic shower and vidphone. The only thing wrong with it was the view from the sitting-room window, which gave on to a bleak, rocky plain with distant, brooding volcanoes. But Margon wasn't about to complain, especially when his companions pressed something into his hands as they left. It was a nice little welcoming note from the mayor of Sorbat, along with a thousand Stellars in cash, 'to help you set up home'. Margon laughed, loud and long.

He spent the next couple of days exploring the city. There was everything he needed in the shops, even fresh vegetables and real meat. Margon couldn't remember when he'd last eaten real meat. He laid in stocks of food and drink, and put a down-payment on a roboservant whom he christened Tinbee. Life was good, easy, and all set to get better still if Margon could open up the possibilities he saw all around him. He laughed to himself over an excellent dinner cooked by the cyberchef and served by Tinbee. 'There's one born every minute!' He chuckled as he tucked greedily into a vaq steak. 'Terra? Who needs it!'

By the fourth day, Margon's thousand Stellars were pretty well gone, so he went down to the Occupation Bureau in the city. It was staffed entirely by robos, and he seated himself in a booth opposite a machine with the plastiface of an attractive girl.

'Welcome, Mr Margon,' said the machine. 'We were told that you would be calling.' Margon was surprised. 'We are programmed to recognize all citizens,' the machine went on, by way of explanation. 'Please call us Zinta if you would prefer to think of us as human.'

This was an annoying thing about robos. There wasn't enough room in their tin heads for the circuitry necessary to make them android, so they were all linked to a giant central data-bank by microwave transmission. It worked well, except that the machines would talk in the plural all the time. It could be confusing, but Margon wasn't bothered. He grinned.

'How come you have an employment office for humans?' he asked. 'You robos do things much better.' The machine smiled. It was quite a good imitation of a human smile.

'At first,' it said, 'robos and cybs did all the work on Torbanel, but it was found that there are certain jobs where the personal, human touch is necessary. Also it was discovered that when humans have no work they become distracted and unhappy. So work is available to provide exercise for the human intellect. This has proved to be successful.'

Margon grinned again at the thought of work as a leisure activity. That was the sort of work that he was interested in. 'Right,' he said, evenly. 'What sort of jobs have you got on the books?'

'Your file is empty,' replied Zinta. 'We have no knowledge of your skills and accomplishments. Perhaps you would input some data and we can make a selection?'

Margon thought for a moment. There had been the looting in the riots of '98, then reform school, then some minor bank robberies, then the penitentiary on Staphos III, then the two bogus finance corporations who borrowed money from each other, then another spell on Staphos III, but he felt sure they didn't want to know about all that.

'Money . . .' he said, at last. 'I've always worked with money.'

'You are a qualified accountant?'

Margon shook his head. 'No, not quite that,' he said, 'more – well – banking, and that sort of thing.'

The machine smiled again. 'There is a vacancy for a clerk in the city branch of the Central Sorbat Bank. This is one of the jobs where humans prefer to deal with other humans. If you are interested in this we can vidphone for an interview appointment.'

Margon tried not to look too eager. He told the machine that he thought he might be interested in this.

The Central Sorbat Building was a mountain of tinted glass and concrete in downtown Sorbat, and Margon was conducted inside by the manager, who introduced himself as Toph Roman.

'I understand that you have experience in banking,' he smiled.

Margon nodded and confirmed that he knew quite a bit about banking, although he didn't say exactly what. The pay was four hundred and eighty Stellars a week, and Margon started work the following day.

One of the first things he learned was that the Torbaneli were the most trusting, honest bunch of dimwits in the galaxy. When he 'accidentally' dropped a hundred-Stellar note and shuffled it out of sight with his foot, the customers were always willing to agree that they had made a mistake in counting their deposits. Within two weeks Margon had paid off what he owed on Tinbee. As far as he was concerned, Torbanel was paradise.

After a couple of months, Margon tired of the small-time fiddles he had polished up to a fine art at the bank. He was lying on the sofa one night, watching a fifth-rate talent show on the triholograph, and turning the situation over in his mind. His gaze wandered through the window towards the sullen landscape with its distant volcanoes and mountains. There had to be an angle. A big-time angle. The Torbaneli were so stupid that getting away with it would be a doddle, but it would have to be worthwhile. He thought for a few minutes. One of the computer-room staff was leaving in a week or so. The comp-room handled every account that the bank held, and Margon had already taken the trouble to familiarize himself with the workings of the accounting system.

Suddenly, he had a brainwave. An evil smile flickered across his face. Now, if he could only persuade Toph Roman to promote him to comp-operator . . .

Roman didn't need persuading. Margon's record at the counter had been exemplary, and he quickly demonstrated that he knew all there was to know about operating the computers. He got the job there and then, along with a rise to six hundred Stellars a week. 'This is it,' he thought gleefully. 'This is where Jon-6 Margon gets into the big league!'

The comp-room had never run so smoothly. Nothing was ever too much trouble for the new operator. At the month-end when all the customers came to pay in their salary cheques, Margon demonstrated an obliging willingness to work late into the night, entering every transaction with meticulous care. He had taken the trouble to open an account for himself under a false name at one of the other banks in the city. Needless to say, the computer systems of all the banks were linked through a central data-store, and it was a fairly simple process to cream off a small percentage of the deposits and have them listed under his own, false name in the new account.

The statements the bank sent out to its customers were so detailed and long-winded that Margon had no difficulty in inserting deductions and listing them as 'charges' or 'transfers'. The secret was to take only a small amount from each account. If the customers noticed the entries on their balance sheets, they always assumed that the bank knew what it was doing, and so no one complained. Shortly, Roman gave him a rise to six hundred and seventy-five Stellars a week, such was the new efficiency of the department. Margon accepted it with good grace. He could afford to – he was well on the way to becoming a millionaire.

After eight months or so, Torbanel was beginning to pall. There was little or no night-life in Sorbat City, and the triholograph programmes were lousy. On top of that, the miserable landscape outside the flat was beginning to affect Margon. He found himself longing for the sight of green fields and flowers, hills and valleys untainted by clouds of gas and volcanic dust, and the sparkling freshness of a sandy coastline. All the things, in fact, that could be found on Elisium IX.

He made a decision. After a year at the bank, he would be entitled to a month's holiday. He would take it, but he wouldn't be coming back. Elisium IX, as well as being the most comfortable planet in the known galaxy, was rigidly neutral in its politics and law. Even if he were found out at some future date, there was no chance that Torbanel would get an extradition order for him to come back and stand trial. He set to work with a new sense of purpose. He came to despise the Torbaneli, with their smiling, trusting faces and their eternal goodwill towards their fellow citizens.

A week before he was due to take his annual holiday, which was officially to be spent on Cornal, a neighbouring planet much favoured by the Torbaneli, his private account was worth close to three million Stellars. His last job before leaving the office was to use the computer link to transfer his assets via an orbiting data-bank into a holding account in a neighbouring system. From there he would be able to extract the money when he was safely on Elisium IX. It was almost too easy. His whole stay on Torbanel had been one long breeze. He almost felt a twinge of guilt at taking money from these simple, trusting people. Almost – but not quite.

That night, he packed his things. He was travelling light, so as not to arouse suspicion. Tinbee offered to help, but Margon was as sick of the robo's helpful presence as he was of everything else on Torbanel, and banished the machine to the kitchen. The sky was heavy and black outside the windows of the flat, but Margon's heart was light. Within a few days' travel (as it would seem to him) he would be sunning himself at one of the luxury hotels on the equatorial belt of Elisium IX, and Torbanel and its idiot inhabitants could go and –

Just then there was a deep-throated rumble far below, and the building shook. Margon looked up sharply. Outside the window a blazing cloud of gas was belching out of the cone of one of the distant volcanoes. Then a second one, nearby, erupted violently. Margon watched as the glowing lava spilled down the side of the range and on to the plain. There was another minor quake, and he grasped the windowsill for support as a third and fourth volcano spat ash and fire into the now-red sky. Margon was glad he was getting out. If this happened every year Torbanel was obviously a good place not to be. He slammed the case shut and headed for the door.

Before he reached it, it flew open and Margon found himself confronted by three stony-faced men in floor-length grey robes. He recognized instantly the garb of Torbanel's priestly hierarchy. He had seen them often in the city, walking about, or collecting money for the church, that sort of thing. He had ignored them; but he couldn't ignore them now.

'The gods are angry,' said one of them in an expressionless voice, waving his arm towards the window where the mass eruption was really getting going in the distance. Margon stepped back in alarm.

'It is written,' intoned a second priest, 'that the voice of the gods will be heard when we have welcomed as brothers and sisters those who would do us injury.' Margon tried to laugh. He failed.

'This is a joke, is it?' he said, sweat breaking on his brow, but even as he spoke he knew that it was no kind of joke. He took another step backwards. 'Gods? I mean – gods? This planet's got more advanced technology than a dozen worlds put together and you talk about gods? That's a volcano out there. Don't you have any geologists? Seismographers?'

Two of the priests stepped forward and took his arms. He dropped the suitcase.

'You will come with us, Margon. You must pay for your

wrongdoing,' said the third man. It wasn't a request.

Margon's mind was in turmoil as they dragged him into the street. The cityscape was lit with the flickering red of the volcanic eruptions, and the street was lined with people, the same people Margon had passed on his way to work every day for a year, wearing the same subdued grey suits and the same sensible dresses. But their faces were no longer placid and smiling. They were alight with fervour, eyes staring, mouths open. They chanted one word as he was pulled towards a tall building in the city centre square.

'Sacrifice.'

'S-sacrifice?' Margon couldn't believe his ears.

'The gods must be appeased,' said one of the priests.

'The gods must be appeased,' murmured the other two as the grim procession neared the building. Margon was choking in the priests' vice-like grip. The building was plainly some kind of church – Margon had never taken much notice of it before. Wide stone steps led up to a great, double door. The crowd was gathered round in a semicircle, still chanting.

Suddenly, the doors flew open, throwing forth the glare of a hundred flaming torches, each in the hands of a priest. The robed clerics filed out of the building and lined each side of the steps, then bowed as a huge man wearing a black robe and a plumed headdress came out of the door, and slowly descended towards Margon, cowering at the bottom of the steps. He carried in his hand a scimitar-like weapon, a metre long at least. The flickering of the torches flashed and reflected from its polished blade.

Margon looked around desperately. In the chanting crowd nearby he spotted the man and woman who had greeted him that first day at the spaceport. They were chanting with the rest. Then he remembered something that the woman had said: this had been a primitive planet. The Terran mission had taught them science and technology, and maybe a lot of

62

*Margon cowered as the man with
the evil weapon advanced.*

other things, but one of them hadn't been religion. Just because they had hover-cars and roboservants, it didn't mean that their religious beliefs were any different from the ancient and barbarous cult of their tribal forebears, a mere century ago. Margon had been so careful to take every problem into account, or thought he had. But this was the one thing he had overlooked.

There was a mighty explosion of lava at that moment, lighting up the square with a blood-red glare as bright as the day. Margon looked up, his vision blurred with sweat, at the scimitar poised, flashing, above his head.

'Sacrifice!' chanted the crowd.

The scimitar fell.

THE DEPTHS OF FEAR
by Adrian Vincent

I WAS SWINGING GENTLY with the rolling of the waves in a cradle of darkness. A long swoop to the left, a shorter swoop to the right. My eyes were filled with oil, and I couldn't see a thing, but I could feel the water still bubbling under me, and every now and then my hands touched something that had come up from *Starlight*; a piece of wood, an officer's cap, a silent body floating past.

The waves kept carrying me slowly from left to right, and in panic I thought, 'They've all gone down with her, all my good friends and shipmates, and in a minute I shall go back and join them because I've no life-jacket; and the ship that sank us will never think of looking for survivors because the depth charges which burst in the side of our submarine should have sent us all down in our steel coffin. I'm going to drown.'

'You're there,' a voice said in my ear. 'Port Campbell.'

The elderly Scotsman who had shared the carriage with me all the way from Glasgow already had the carriage door open for me. Thanking him, I scrambled out on to the platform where a decrepit-looking porter was waiting to grab my bags.

'I can manage,' I said. 'Is it possible to get a taxi from here?'

'You'll not need one.' He was already shuffling away in disgust. 'There's another of you waiting outside.'

I went through an unattended gate into the country lane where a rather short, pleasant-faced man in lieutenant's uniform stood waiting beside a horse and trap.

'I'm Lieutenant Poole,' he told me. 'I've been sent along to meet you.' He took one of my bags and led the way towards the trap. 'I could have brought a car, but I thought you'd find this more pleasant.'

'Good idea,' I said. I clambered in beside him, and we went off down the road.

Neither of us spoke for some time. He said finally: 'I hear your submarine went down. *Starlight*, wasn't it?'

'That's right.' I could feel my hand shaking as I reached for my cigarettes. 'I was the only survivor.'

He was silent again, and then he said vehemently: 'Subs. I hate them.'

'Any particular reason?' We had started to go around a small loch. The ruins of an ancient castle reared up against a backdrop of mountains. The castle and the mountains reflected in the still waters of the loch, and it made a beautiful sight. But I could hardly bear to look at it. The sight of any expanse of water these days made me sick with fear. I smiled at Lieutenant Poole. 'It's dangerous work of course. But –' My voice tailed away.

'I've been in them from the beginning,' Lieutenant Poole said. 'But I've never got over the feeling each time I dive that I'm not going to come up again. I'm sure it's because I've spent so much of my life outdoors.'

'What did you do in civvy street?'

'I'm a forestry expert,' Lieutenant Poole said. 'Trees were my life before the war. There's not a thing I don't know about them.' He pulled the trap gently to a halt and pointed to a cluster of elm trees by the side of the road.

'Look at those elms.'

I looked at them. 'Yes?'

'Dutch elm disease,' Lieutenant Poole said gloomily. 'They haven't got a chance.' He seemed visibly affected.

For some reason I couldn't really define, I had a feeling that I was going to get on very well with Lieutenant Poole. 'I'll tell you something,' I said, acting on a sudden impulse. 'I'm scared of being down below myself now.'

Then it all came out in a rush and I told him of the end of *Starlight*. By the time I was almost at the end of it, I could feel the beads of perspiration gathering on my brow. '. . . The second depth charge split our casing, while we were still diving. Miraculously, the blast ejected me like a pea from a pod, and I was able to make it to the surface. I was picked up four hours later.' I stared across the loch, avoiding his eyes. 'Since then, I've never been the same. I-I have nightmares.'

'I'm not surprised,' Lieutenant Poole said. He gave me an encouraging smile. 'It seems we have a similar problem. So maybe we can help each other.' He reached for the reins and glanced at me enquiringly. 'Shall we go on to the camp now?'

'Yes,' I said. 'Let's do that.'

The camp was, in actual fact, a large hotel, which had once been used by the wealthy as a base to sally out on to the nearby golf-course. It was now a rest camp for any naval officers whom the Admiralty had decided needed a mental refit due to battle stress. There was a similar camp for ratings nearby.

I spent a month there, taking it easy and generally enjoying myself, mostly in the company of Lieutenant Poole. Neither of us spoke again of our particular problem, and I've no doubt we would have eventually left the camp with it unsolved, and been a general loss to the Service, if it hadn't been for a small clerical error on the part of someone at the Admiralty.

The error was a circular which obviously shouldn't have been sent to the camp. It read:

VOLUNTEERS WANTED
FOR X-TYPE SUBMARINES.
DANGEROUS BUT INTERESTING WORK.
ALL ACCEPTED VOLUNTEERS MAY
RETURN TO GENERAL SERVICE
UPON REQUEST.

67

Lieutenant Poole and I both stared at the noticeboard.

'Maybe,' Lieutenant Poole said slowly, 'we should volunteer.'

I thought about it for a moment. 'Kill or cure,' I said. 'Why not? That's if they'll have us.'

Knowing the solicitude of the Admiralty for our welfare, I decided it would be a waste of time to submit our applications direct. So I approached a relative who was an Admiral, and against his better judgement, he pulled a few strings for us. Within two weeks we were at Port Bannatyne, near Rothesay, having our first introduction to the X craft.

To give you some idea of what Lieutenant Poole and I had let ourselves in for, I'd better tell you what our X craft was like. She was a complete miniature submarine, designed for a crew of three plus one frogman. She was seventeen metres long, had four compartments, was one and a half metres in diameter, and had a ceiling that wouldn't permit a man of even average height to stand up. All in all, she was a perfect torture chamber for anyone suffering from claustrophobia.

Somehow, incredibly, we got through our training. But if we had hoped to come out of it cured, so to speak, we were due to be disappointed. The one thing that could be said in our favour was that not once did we show how we felt. I suppose the thing that kept us going was the knowledge that if we cracked up on a mission we would carry it as a burden of shame for the rest of our lives.

'Gently does it,' Lieutenant Poole said. We came up slowly until our periscope broke water. 'Hold it!' Lieutenant Poole remained quite still for some moments, his eyes glued to the periscope. Then beckoned me slowly away from the hydroplane controls. 'Come and have a look at this.'

I took the periscope away from him and looked through it at the great, grey shape of the enemy battleship, nestling like some complacent beast in the harbour. From the surface, a man with powerful lungs could have successfully hailed the sailors moving about on her decks. Lieutenant Poole said thoughtfully: 'It looks almost too easy to be true.'

Behind us, Tubbs, the third crew member, sat stolidly at the helm, waiting for his next instruction. He was a particularly welcome addition to our crew as he was an unimaginative man who seemed totally unconcerned at having to work within the suffocating confines of an X craft. Which was more than could be said of Lieutenant Poole and myself.

We were on our first mission, which was to sink the *Zeus*, which had gone into harbour for a refit. We were not carrying a diver, as we intended to try and get in under the hull of the battleship and drop our two explosive charges, which were mounted on each side of our X craft. Four tonnes of explosive amatol, working on a time clock, would be far more effective than a limpet mine.

'They're bound to have anti-torpedo nets up,' Lieutenant Poole said. 'But generally they only hang down to fifteen metres. We'll go in at twenty.' His face was dead-white as he looked at me. 'Are you all right?'

I nodded and went back to the hydroplane controls to adjust the trim for the dive. We went down smoothly and obtained our neutral buoyancy at twenty metres without any trouble. We nosed gently through the waters for some minutes, and then came to an abrupt halt.

Lieutenant Poole swore softly under his breath, 'We've fouled the nets!' He turned to Tubbs. 'Full speed ahead!'

The motors throbbed noisily as we went full ahead, driving deep into the nets until we had exhausted their slack.

'That's it,' Lieutenant Poole muttered. 'Now full astern.'

We repeated the operation several times hoping that we would gain enough impetus with one of our thrusts to push us through the nets. On the fifth attempt we weren't even able to go full astern.

'Lovely!' Lieutenant Poole said bitterly. 'Now we've got ourselves stuck between two layers of nets.' He rubbed a hand across his glistening face. 'We'll try diving to thirty metres.'

We started to go down slowly, with the nets audibly scraping our sides. I could feel the sweat pouring off me as I sat there, gazing blankly at the tangle of machinery in front of me. Even if the nets didn't reach down to the sea-bed, I knew that a low, swift running tide could tangle them at their base. If this happened, we would be completely trapped, like a small fish in a child's shrimping net. It was something that didn't bear thinking about.

At thirty metres Tubbs straightened us out, and we waited for further instructions. Lieutenant Poole took a deep breath. 'Let's try our luck. Full speed ahead.'

We went full ahead, expecting to feel any moment the familiar jar of resisting nets. Instead we went on . . . and on. I looked back at Lieutenant Poole, who was leaning limply against the attack periscope. 'We seem to be through,' I said.

Soon afterwards, we came up again to take a second bearing, only to find that the periscope had flooded, robbing us of our vision.

Lieutenant Poole sighed. 'How much air have we got?'

'Less than a bottle,' Tubbs told him.

'Then we haven't got enough time to try and repair it,' Lieutenant Poole said. 'Anyway, with the amount of explosives we're carrying, we can judge it near enough. Keep on the same bearing.'

We went in along the sea-bed, dropped our charges, and then set out to put as much distance as possible between us and the doomed battleship.

Lieutenant Poole said: 'We got in at thirty metres. We'll go out at the same depth.'

A few minutes later we came to an abrupt halt. 'The nets

again,' I said. 'How did it happen?'

'We came out on a slightly different course,' Lieutenant Poole said, 'and we've run straight into another set of nets hanging at a lower level.' He glanced at his watch. 'Full astern, and then take her down another ten metres.'

We went down and then tried to straighten out, only to find we couldn't move.

'We seem to be in a pocket,' Lieutenant Poole said calmly. 'It doesn't help, does it?' We looked at each other, and I knew we were both thinking the same thing. The charges had been set to go off in an hour. If we weren't away from the area by then, the force of the explosion could easily finish us off. Even if that didn't happen, we would suffocate as soon as the air ran out. Either way, we had less than an hour.

'Let's start manoeuvring,' Lieutenant Poole said.

We wriggled around desperately for fifteen minutes, and only succeeded in getting ourselves more helplessly entangled. Sitting there, I could hear, in my imagination, the time clock ticking our lives away.

Tubbs said quietly: 'Is there anything else we can do, sir?'

'Not a thing,' Lieutenant Poole said. 'We're tangled up in the nets like a kitten in the knitting. All we can do now is to wait for the end.'

As the minutes ticked by, I suddenly became very calm. I knew that if the explosion split us asunder, I would have to relive for a few suffocating seconds the agony I had felt when I had been spewed out of *Starlight*. I knew that even this didn't seem to matter any more. It occurred to me then with startling clarity that I had overcome my fear of the depths, and somehow this consoled and satisfied me, even though I knew I would have to pay a heavy price for the victory.

I glanced at Lieutenant Poole, who was smiling faintly at me, and I knew that he realized something of what I was feeling. Oddly enough, I was almost sure then that his

The explosion hit us with the full
force of a tornado, and the
X craft seemed to swing round.

thoughts were running on similar lines, and this was confirmed when he said: 'It's strange. It's not nearly so bad as I've always imagined it would be.'

Tubbs – dear old stolid, reliable Tubbs – was sitting blank-faced in his seat, as if he was in the cinema, bored and waiting for the lights to go down.

At last Lieutenant Poole said: 'We've got twenty seconds left.'

The explosion, when it came, hit us with the full force of a tornado. The lights went out immediately, and the X craft seemed to swing around in a complete circle several times, like a stone being cast from a sling. Things were falling about me as I crashed around the compartment, and then suddenly I had the strange feeling that we were hurtling through space.

As if from a long way off, I heard Lieutenant Poole calling out of the darkness: 'We've been thrown out of the nets! Get her up, Tubbs! GET HER UP!'

There was less noise now, and I could even hear Tubbs scrambling through the darkness towards the helm. We were still rocking crazily, but I couldn't feel any water coming in, and I thought: we've got a chance. Then I heard the motors start up, and I knew we were going to live.

Shock waves continued to hit us as we rose awkwardly, but by now the force of the explosion had almost spent itself. When we finally reached the surface, Lieutenant Poole flung open the hatch, and we all scrambled out on to the deck. The gust of black smoke-laden air that hit us smelt like nectar.

Standing there together we gazed through the billowing smoke at the battleship. The whole of her foredeck was a mass of flames, and she was keeling badly over to the left.

'It'll be a long time before she goes into action again,' Lieutenant Poole said. He gave me a broad smile. 'All in all I think the trip was worth it.'

I knew exactly what he meant. 'Well worth it,' I said.

THE GOLDEN LAKE
OF CHILIL
by Lee Stone

I KNEW LAZARO WAS GOING TO DIE from the moment when,
working beside me, he suddenly dropped his spade and
crumpled awkwardly on the side of the shallow excavation we
were marking. Lazaro had told me three days earlier that he
was going to die soon. A pure Zapotec Indian, he confided in
me like an old friend, although I had known him for only the
two months I'd been in Mexico. Shunned by the *mestizo*, the
half-Spanish, half-Indians of Yucatan province, and by the
criollo, the Spaniard born in Mexico and rooted in it, the
Zapotecs never had many friends. It wasn't entirely unnatural
that this old illiterate Indian should find a kindred spirit in a
drifter like me: a classics student waiting for his university
place, with empty pockets and a zest for adventure.

'The gods will come for me when the sun is high, very soon
now, *amigo*,' Lazaro had said and grinned toothlessly.

It was impossible to tell with any accuracy, but he must
have been at least seventy. He was employed as a day labourer
on the site of our British Mayan Archaeological Expedition.
His job, for a miserable twenty *pesos* a day, was to shift the loose
earth and stack up the potsherds – the bits of pottery which,
expertly put together, formed the links in the fascinating story
of the Mayan culture we were painstakingly unearthing.

The day Lazaro died we were working together on a lonely
corner of the vast site. There was nothing I could do for him.
From the earth where he lay, small and untidy, he gazed up
with glazed eyes at the hot, blue sky, his lips moving

soundlessly. I crouched nearer to his heaving brown chest, clumsily attempting to comfort his awful last moments.

Suddenly he began to speak, intone rather, with a clarity and calmness that was almost terrifying. 'Go to the mine of Chilil,' he said. 'It lies four miles to the north of Tenajapa. Follow the path through the mountains from Contehuitz till you reach the top of the ravine of Chilil. A huge ravine, much water in the bottom. On the eastern side, two rocks, as big as lorries, guard a slit, the way into the mine. Inside – ancient Mixtec treasure! All the treasure of the Mixtec high priests . . . one thousand years old . . . gold, silver, carved jade, obsidian, crystal . . . all priceless . . . But go *now*, before the rains come.'

His voice trailed away into a convulsive, gurgling rattle. Then his head fell back, lifeless, on to the soft earth.

A stone rattled down the side of the excavation. I looked up and saw Rodrigues crouching at the top of the trench.

'The old devil is dead,' Rodrigues said. He seemed senselessly glad.

As much as I'd always instinctively liked Lazaro, I'd instinctively never liked Rodrigues. He had the oversized nose and thin mouth of his *criollo* race; he was one of that breed you always find at ancient excavations, of whom you are never quite sure whether they are there for historical scholarship or personal greed.

'We must get him out of this heat,' I said.

That night, while Lazaro's body lay mute and shrouded in the local church, I sat by the light of an oil lamp in my tent and recalled his dying outburst. A mine near Tenejapa? An almost inaccessible village, I remembered once reading, peopled by local Indians who spoke languages derived from ancient Mayan. The only way to reach it was by foot or on horseback, and it was the hot, muggy abode of some rather unpleasant wild life.

What was it the old Indian had said about Mixtec treasure? Certainly that area had yielded some exciting archaeological finds in the last fifty years. The Mixtecs, who flourished in Mexico about the time the Normans invaded England, used to bury their dead in deep chambers upon which they lavished all the mastery of their craftsmanship . . .

Mechanically, I seized a note book and wrote down the fragmentary instructions that Lazaro had choked out. Then I packed up my few possessions in my back-pack and set out into the darkness across the flat, half-excavated site, taking advantage of the cool of the night.

At daybreak I had covered almost twenty miles towards the south-east, travelling in the direction of the hilly country that lay towards San Cristobal. I stopped at an Indian café for something to eat. The villagers were exclusively poverty-stricken Indians and I was beginning to attract interested looks. It is dangerous for a European to travel alone in rural Mexico; to the impoverished *peon* life is cheap, especially if it happens to be someone else's.

Nevertheless, I was lucky, for about ten o'clock a battered truck came by and its Indian driver gave me a one-hundred-and-twenty-mile lift along a dirt road through steaming, parched country. By the end of my fifth day's travelling I was entering the foothills of the mountains. Tenajapa, I calculated, was twelve miles away, and it was all uphill. I was wringing wet with the humidity and exhausted by it, so I unwrapped my bed-roll and spread it under a sapodilla tree. I must have fallen asleep at once.

It was light when I awoke. I knew at once that something was wrong and sat up, immediately alert.

'*Buenos diaz, señor!*'

Voice and face blended sharply through my blurred senses. Rodrigues.

'What do you want?' I exclaimed.

It was an absurd question. Rodrigues ignored it. 'Coffee?' he said, thrusting a mug into my hand. He had made a fire and had cooked breakfast in the time I was sleeping, I noted angrily. 'Listen, *amigo*, we both go the same way. So why not we both go together, huh?' His lips parted in a yellow grin. 'These ancient peoples, you know, *amigo*, they had plenty gold, enough for two of us to share and some over, huh?'

He had heard everything that Lazaro had said, of course. There was nothing I could do about that now. 'If you're asking me whether I'd like your company, Rodrigues, the answer is preferably not.' I gulped down the coffee and got to my feet, stretching. 'Still, I suppose you intend to inflict it on me.'

'*Si, si, amigo*. We travel together, plenty good company, huh?'

Throughout that day's trek upwards into the highlands I found nothing likeable in my companion. His manner was so obsequious that every move he made was suspect; when he grinned, which was too often for comfort, it was like a sneer. He seemed to exude evil.

As the sun climbed in the sky, though, I was less in a mood to consider Rodrigues and his many faults, for I became increasingly absorbed with my own discomfort. We were ascending rapidly and sweat was cascading down our faces as we clambered over the harsh rock face, sparsely dotted with cactus, agave and mesquite. I remembered we were in rattlesnake country, a fact requiring a constant look-out, which didn't improve my humour.

We skirted Contehuitz village – a depressing collection of Indian huts topped by a stain of smoke down in a hollow on our left – and worked our way round to the north of Tenajapa, as dreary a place as Contehuitz. What Lazaro had described as a 'path' was a tortuous, scarcely visible ascent through jagged rocks with sometimes a limitless drop on each side; one step out of place and we, too, would be joining the dead Mixtecs.

We must have been several thousand metres above sea level, but even so, the heat was agonizing. I thought, after the next rest we will have reached a distance of roughly four miles to the north of Tenajapa, and beyond that I would not go. The idea of another night spent walking, lost in mountains infested with predators, was not appealing.

But there it was! An unbelievable, awe-inspiring sight, opening suddenly below us like a shimmering mirage. A vast crater – it must have been at least half a mile square – steep-sided, with, perhaps three-hundred metres below where we stood looking down on it, the radiant blue surface of the lake that filled the Ravine of Chilil.

We didn't wait to look any longer. Forgetting our fatigue, we began the descent towards that vast bowl of water, slithering and stumbling down the bare rock, oblivious to our safety. After fifteen minutes of this I had to pause for breath – the air, it seemed, had become as heavy as lead. Another half hour of scrambling and we were on a wide ledge only about a metre above the lake . . .

The eastern side . . . two huge rocks . . . I recalled the words of Lazaro without recourse to my notebook. We were on the lake's southern side, so we turned right and moved along the ledge as fast as the rock face and our newly-awakened enthusiasm would allow us to go.

Once I remembered wondering what geological freak of nature had caused this marvel – like a giant, rough-sided saucepan with water in the bottom. Sometimes the ledge took us right down to the surface of the water; at other times we were several metres above it. We had been going like this for several hundred metres when we saw the two rocks, standing out distinctly from the face of the ravine, 'as big as lorries', as Lazaro had said.

Rodrigues was suddenly like a man possessed. He hurried ahead of me, several times almost missing his footing in his anxiety to reach the sentinel rocks. Then he seemed to disappear into the rock face. When I arrived at the two rocks I saw the narrow slit between them, scarcely wide enough to take a man sideways. It was fifteen centimetres above the water level and the passage inside it sloped immediately and steeply downwards. I could hear Rodrigues stumbling about inside as he descended the passage, and I followed the echoing sounds gingerly, feeling the side of the rock as a guide.

I was only a couple of metres down the passage, still trying to accustom my eyes to the sudden gloom after the harsh glare of the sun on the rocks and the lake outside, when Rodrigues suddenly appeared again in front of me. He had come back up the passage and his eyes were wild with mingled fear and incredulity. In his out-stretched hand was a heap of gold coins that glittered even in that gloomy cavern.

'Gold!' he gasped. 'There are great heaps of gold down there. For me . . . this is not for you professors – it's for me!'

I can't tell you what happened next, because I have no recollection of it. Some minutes must have passed when I discovered myself crawling on my knees towards the opening of the cave. Beyond the slit the sky was dark, and there was an ominous rumbling sound outside.

I can only suppose, with some degree of certainty, that as I looked at the coins in Rodrigues' hand, he attacked me with his knife, determined that there should be no other witnesses to the find. I can remember my head was singing with pain and there was blood on my face and on my chest. As I crawled towards that darkened sky outside I distinctly heard Rodrigues' muffled cries of exultation from deep down below me.

They were the last sounds the *criollo* ever made.

In his outstretched hand was a heap of gold coins that glittered even in that gloomy cavern.

80

There was a flash that lit the ravine with vivid white light, followed by an ear-splitting crash of thunder. The rain was instant and torrential, and it swept into the mine opening with the force of water through a broken dam. Somehow I clung to the edge of the passage, steadied myself and half crawled, half swam to the opening.

If this was rain it was like no rain I had ever seen before. It was more like a waterfall, just as if some giant hand were pouring water into the vast saucepan. Only two minutes had passed since the first flash of lightning and already the lake water was level with the mine opening. A fifteen centimetre rise in the water surface – it didn't seem possible. Then into my mind came the last words of Lazaro: 'Go *now*, before the rains come.' Another minute and I was swimming for my life. Swung round by the force of the water I saw the lake gushing down through the passageway . . . down into the mine where Rodrigues had gone.

And then I saw something that will haunt me until the day I die.

From out of the mine, which must now have been filled to the brim with water, came the limp, lifeless body of Rodrigues. He was lying on his back, with one arm outstretched. Instinct made me lash out to try to hold him; my fingers could only reach his hand. It was icy cold and as I touched it the fingers opened and half a dozen gold coins slipped from them. I managed to grab one; then, all in the same second, Rodrigues was swept away from me by the brutal eddying force of the water.

The rain continued to cascade down and the lake surface was visibly rising. I was sure I was going to drown, for the edge of the ravine was already blurred and indistinct behind the thundering torrent of water. Just when I thought I must be swept out into the centre of the lake, my hand touched a rock. I grabbed, held on, pulled myself up. My head was free of the water and above it was the ledge ascending the side of the rock face.

It is hard for me to remember the agonizing hours it took me to crawl back up the side of the Ravine of Chilil. Several times I was convinced that the thundering rain would wash me back into the lake like some carelessly tossed cork; then, as I crawled higher, I was conscious of the searing, stabbing pains in my chest where Rodrigues must have struck me with his knife.

I vaguely remember reaching the top, crawling, I knew not where, through the night, more dead than alive. I must have blacked out a dozen times and yet I must have had some unerring instinct for direction, for they've since told me that the Indian who found me lived in Tenajapa. I can certainly remember looking up at his brown, impassive face, silhouetted against a dawn sky, as a dead man might look up from his grave, and I can remember saying, '*Estoy enfermo. I am ill.*'

They've since told me that some Indians gave me medicine and bound my chest wounds. They got me to San Cristobal and then across country to Merida, where a plane brought me to Mexico City. The doctors here have been very kind and they've put on my bedside table the magnificent gold coin they prised from my hand. Tomorrow they're going to operate on my lungs; it seems one of them was badly punctured by Rodrigues' knife. As soon as I'm better I intend to go back to the Ravine of Chilil and find that treasure.

But because they say that the operation could be tricky, I've decided to set down this account of the mine and the Mixtec treasure in case anything goes wrong tomorrow. The story of it will therefore only be made known if I don't survive. In that event I feel I have done my duty by passing on the message that Lazaro gave me when he was dying.

In that event, *amigo*, it will be up to you to decide what you want to do about it.

HOUR OF THE
WARTO-WASP
by M. S. Goodall

ON THE PLANET TOXGLO MINOR in the galaxy of Thaarl, another day was drawing to a close. It was the season of Hoarst, when the hours of daylight were short and Toxglo Minor's twin suns glowed feebly above the purple rim of the horizon, like embers without heat.

Far to the north, in a volcanic region known as the Heights of Vuldar, an inner atmosphere collection craft banked steeply between two peaks and levelled out exactly fifty metres above a dusty plain. Retro-jets blasting, the sleek grey and silver ship slowed almost to a hover, her microsonic radar probes constantly scanning the ground below.

In charge of the crew of ten was Spaceway Commander Septin Cragge. Young, tough, experienced and reliable, Cragge had been away from his home planet of Earth for more than a decade. It was now 2081, commonly known as the year of G.A.S.H. – the Galactic Animal Survey Harvest – a project involving fifty teams of scientists and naturalists whose task was to scour a number of the lesser planets in the Thaarl galaxy for unknown species of wildlife. Different types of animals were to be recorded and computerized, and any quadruped capable of domestication was marked down for shipment to Earth at a later date. Septin Cragge was in command of the search on Toxglo Minor, a task with which he was becoming increasingly bored.

'Raise airspeed to thirty knots, change course by one degree to zero-green-zero.' Cragge's voice had a flat, dull quality to it

83

as he turned to face the bespectacled young engineer sitting next to him in the command cabin. 'Any joy from the scanning probes, Bodine?'

The engineer shook his head and gestured to the bank of view-screens in front of him. 'Nothing, Commander. No contact, not even a blip. If you ask me, animal life on Toxglo Minor is practically non-existent.'

'Certainly looks that way,' said Cragge wearily. 'We've been quartering the surface of this planet for more than two months, and all we've found so far is one miserable herd of low-grade Hornosaurs.' Common to many of the planets throughout the Thaarl galaxy, Hornosaurs were placid, unintelligent creatures roughly equivalent in size and demeanour to an Earthly cow. They were farmed extensively for their thick, spike-covered hides, from which a rich form of protein was extracted.

'Shall I change course again, Commander?' Bodine's voice broke sharply through Cragge's gloomy thoughts. 'You never know, it might change our luck as well!'

'All right, lad, give it a try. Three degrees on a westerly bearing, and then –'

'Hold it!' Bodine jerked bolt upright in his chair and stared at the view-screen in front of him with disbelieving eyes. 'I'm getting a scanning probe readout, Commander. Distance twenty miles and closing; course two-zero-red. It's something big. Something airborne!'

'Airborne? Are you sure?'

Bodine nodded, eyes glued to the flickering, dancing images on the screen. 'Normally I'd say it was some kind of freak weather formation, like a whirlwind or a hurricane. But this is too well-defined to be a cloud. Too dense . . . too solid!'

'Okay, let's grab some height and go in for a closer look.' Commander Cragge rapped out a series of orders and the spaceship soared skywards like a silver dart, her main engines trailing parallel lines of smoke above the dusty landscape.

'Distance five miles,' said Bodine calmly. 'Whatever that airborne mass is, our magnification cameras should be within range for a visual sighting.'

'Let's see it,' snapped Cragge.

As Bodine stabbed at a button, a large screen above the men's heads flashed with light, wavered for an instant, and became steady. The view of the horizon ahead was perfect, and as he stared at the enlarged image, Septin Cragge felt his stomach muscles contract briefly in an involuntary spasm of fear.

Moving towards the spaceship, filling the purple sky ahead, was a throbbing, undulating black mass. Bigger than a thundercloud and twice as dense, it travelled through the air at a steady, constant speed, a hundred metres above the surface of the planet. And as the mass moved, it made a sound . . . *the continual, violent vibration of a hundred thousand wings.*

'Ye Gods.' It was engineer Bodine who spoke first, his voice a mere whisper in the sudden silence of the cabin. 'It looks like a swarm of some sort. Giant locusts, maybe.'

'Or even worse,' said Cragge grimly. 'Warn the rest of the crew – all hands to battle stations. I need an information print-out and I need it fast.' As alarm bells clanged throughout the ship, Commander Cragge concentrated on obtaining a speedy assimilation of data from the moving black mass ahead. Unseen micro-sensors probed the throbbing air, testing, evaluating and examining. In less than a minute, every shred of relevant fact had been beamed back to Commander Cragge's onboard computers and fed into the memory-bank system.

When the information feed-back came, the data was worse than even Cragge had anticipated. Three times he checked the snake-like line of white tape as it ejected the facts he so desperately needed; but each time the information was the

same: DANGER! DANGER! SWARM AHEAD MADE
UP OF ASTRO-INSECT TYPE Z-DASH-7. RECORDED
NAME: *WARTO-WASP!* WEIGHT: 200 KILOGRAMS.
WING SPAN: 40 METRES. BITE AND STING FATAL.
INSECT DEADLY – REPEAT – DEADLY!

Showing the slip of paper to the white-faced Bodine, Cragge
leapt to the ship's inboard communication system. 'Attention
all hands, this is your Commander speaking. We have a Red-
Plus-One emergency. The ship is closing fast with a gigantic
swarm of Toxglo Minor Warto-Wasps. Each wasp is almost as
big as this craft, and the insect's bite and sting are fatal. We are
on a collision course with the swarm and too late to take
evasive action. Our only chance of survival is to blast a way
straight through. Laser-cannon crews – are you in position?'

'All cannons loaded, crews in position, Commander.' The
voice echoed tinnily back over the built-in speaker system.
'First aid squad also standing by.'

'Good! Hold your fire, wait for my signal. Over and out.'
Snapping off the intercom, Cragge whirled in his chair and
looked worriedly at Bodine. 'How long?' he asked with a
calmness he certainly didn't feel.

'Thirty seconds,' said the engineer. 'If you intend to blast a
hole through the middle of the swarm, I suggest you reduce
speed. Incidentally, are the Warto-Wasps' bodies armoured
against laser-cannon fire?'

'I hope not, Bodine. If they are, we're done for.'
Commander Cragge took a deep breath and nodded swiftly.
'Okay, here we go. Course steady, reduce power and speed by
fifty per cent . . . now!'

Outside, in the darkening sky of Toxglo-Minor, the
gigantic alien swarm moved onwards at the same constant,
grinding speed. And suddenly, as Cragge's ship slowed down
with retro-rockets blasting, the humans inside felt a typhoon-
like force of wind lift their craft and hurl it from side to side.

86

'It's the vibration from the wasps' wings,' yelled Bodine as he clung hard to the side of his fixed chair. 'If it gets much worse, the whole ship will be shaken apart.'

'Right rudder two degrees,' screamed Cragge. 'All laser-cannons on rapid fire. Start blasting. Give these brutes everything we've got.'

Seconds later, the grey and silver survey craft hit the edge of the swarm. Up in the ship's nose, four banks of short-range laser-cannons fired in unison, and white-hot, deadly disinteg-rator beams flashed again and again into the tightly-packed ranks of Warto-Wasps. The effect was similar to carving a road tunnel through a mountain, thought Septin Cragge. Even as he watched, chunks of armour-plated body discs from those giant insects unfortunate enough to be in the path of the pulverizing beams, flashed past the viewing ports and bounced off the ship's stern. Rolling, hexagon-shaped eyes and shrivelled wings glowed for an instant in the tiny circle of light, and then vanished as the spaceship ploughed remorse-lessly on. From time to time, groups of infuriated Warto-Wasps dived with suicidal ferocity at the slim, silver craft, their enormous, rasping sucker-feet groping for a hold. Time and again, they almost made it . . . but time and again the searing laser-cannons blew them to smithereens.

Slowly, the swarm began to thin. Engineer Bodine stared hard at his control gauges and gave a thumbs-up sign of triumph. 'We're almost through, Commander. Another two, maybe three minutes, we'll be safe.'

'Increase speed by ten per cent,' said Cragge quietly. Then, flicking on the intercom system, he added so that the rest of the crew could hear: 'Well done, crew, I think we're going to make it. Danger nearly over.'

For a spaceway Commander of Cragge's experience, it was a premature and disastrous announcement. On the gun-deck above, one of the younger members of the crew leaned back from the sighting socket of his cannon and grinned across at a colleague nearby. For perhaps fifteen seconds, there was a gap in the protective ring of rapid-firing disintegrator beams blasting from the nose of the ship. Only a few moments in time, but long enough for a solitary Warto-Wasp to turn and pounce.

Four pairs of jointed, powerful legs as big as crane jibs wrapped themselves tightly round the belly of the spaceship. Pincer-like jaws clamped hard round the tapering nose, trying to bite, crush and tear. Inside, Cragge realized his mistake instantly.

'Full power,' he screamed at Bodine. 'One of the Warto-Wasps has landed on the ship. We must try and shake it off.'

The engineer's hands moved in a blur of speed. Twin pairs of throttle levers jerked forward and the craft responded with all the grace and beauty of a shooting star. On hyper-drive plus ten, the ship burst through the outer ring of the swarm and clawed for height, streaking above the surface of Toxglo Minor in a howl of exhaust gases.

But the giant insect refused to budge. As the ship's speed increased, the Warto-Wasp's streamlined body seemed to stretch and elongate, flattening itself into every groove and curve of the metal, enormous wings folded and laid back, jib-like legs wrapped tighter and tighter around the tube-like belly. Cragge knew then, that if he maintained his present rate of speed and climb, his craft would literally fall apart under the enormous pressures.

'Reduce power,' he snapped at Bodine. 'Bring us down to cruise level and hold her steady. If that brute up top won't be *blown* off, we'll have to find a way of killing it!'

'What about the laser-cannons?' asked Bodine worriedly, as he worked the throttles. 'Can't our gunners get the insect's head in their sights?'

'Negative,' said Cragge. 'When that thing jumped us, it

created a major malfunction in the upper gun-deck. All our forward cannons are out of action.'

'Charming,' said Bodine. 'So what do we do now?'

It was a question which Commander Cragge did not have time to answer, for as the spaceship slowed down, the giant Warto-Wasp suddenly made its move. Like some prehistoric Mammoth's tusk, the insect's long, armoured sting drove down and under the ship's keel. Alumino-metal plates burst apart as the tail drove like a lance into the heart of the craft's engine-room. Two members of the crew died instantly as an eddying spray of deadly poison gushed from the tip of the sting and filled the atmosphere with liquid death. Seconds later, the warp-drive rotor blew up and the main generator started to fail.

As damage reports flooded into the command cabin, Cragge knew he was losing power fast. Even with the emergency generator working flat out and the ship's propulsion maintained on hyper-drive, it would be a miracle if they could stay in the air for more than half an hour. His eyes flickering over the dials in front of him, the Commander came to an immediate decision.

'Alert! Alert!' he shouted into the intercom. 'All hands prepare for emergency touchdown in fifteen minutes. Don survival suits and have hand-blaster weapons at the ready.' Clicking the switch off, Cragge whirled to face his engineer. 'How is it going, Bodine? Can you get us down in one piece?'

'You'll find out in approximately fourteen minutes, Commander! Just cross your fingers and keep 'em like that!'

Outside, the huge head of the Warto-Wasp rolled sluggishly from side to side as Bodine eased the crippled ship towards a flat area of the plain below. The insect's jaws were still trying to crush and gnaw their way through the specially strengthened plasti-glass of the viewing ports to suck at the helpless human flesh inside . . . but miraculously the ports held.

'Height twenty metres, landing pads in position. Two minutes to touchdown.' As Bodine's voice echoed calmly through the command cabin, Cragge zipped up his survival suit, snapped his helmet into position and flicked the intercom switch once again.

'Commander to all hands. As soon as we land, exit through the starboard hatch and fan out round the ship in a semi-circle. I'll be right there with you. As soon as I give the word, set your hand-blasters to kill and open up on the Warto-Wasp with a concentrated burst of fire. We must finish the brute before it has a chance to take to the air again. Over and out – and good luck.'

Moments later, the lowered legs of the landing tripod smacked into the dusty plain, and as the starboard hatch swung open, Cragge led the crew out at a fast, crouching run. Above them, gigantic wings stirred and flapped. The Warto-Wasp was already withdrawing its long, curved tail and gleaming sting from the jagged hole in the ship's hull. In a matter of seconds it would be airborne: free to attack again.

'Ready . . . aim . . .' Twenty metres away, Cragge and the crew were drawn up in a horseshoe formation, blasters held steady in the regulation double-handed grip, each weapon aimed at the Warto-Wasp's heaving body. '*Fire!*' It was more of a bark than a word of command, and even before the sound of Cragge's voice had died away, long, controlled bursts of flame were lancing deep into the insect's body. A loud, sighing scream broke from its gaping jaws, the giant wings withered and the mighty head sagged. The Warto-Wasp died just three seconds before its riddled body burst into flames. The battle was over.

Septin Cragge glanced at his watch. From the time they had first encountered the swarm until the death of the lone creature now blazing at their feet, just one hour had elapsed. 'The longest hour of my life,' muttered Cragge wearily.

*Long bursts of flame lanced deep
into the insect's body.*

By late afternoon the next day, engineer Bodine and two of the crew had succeeded in repairing the jagged rent in the spaceship's hull. The warp-drive rotor had been replaced and the main generator was working smoothly again. As the crew prepared to take off, Cragge addressed them cheerfully, a small slip of paper waving in his right hand.

'I think you all ought to know,' he said slowly, 'that I have just acquired some fresh computer data on those alien insects. It appears that no humans have ever survived an attack by a Warto-Wasp before. We're the first . . . and I think we have every right to be proud of it.'

'Hear, hear, Commander!' Bodine grinned and raised a triumphant fist in the air. 'Maybe they'll give us a medal when we get back to Earth. We are going back to Earth now, aren't we?'

'That we are, my friend. It's been a long, long time, but that's where we'll be headed as soon as we blast off today from Toxglo Minor.'

They left at 1700 hours, relaxed and happy. But what they didn't know, as they entered deep Space on a heading for home, was that lying unseen and well-hidden behind a fuel duct in the main engine-room, were fifty gleaming white orbs, each the size of a marrow.

The Warto-Wasp had completed its task. With its armoured sting, the giant insect had pierced the space-craft's hull . . . *and laid its eggs!*

THE MAN IN THE MIST
by Angus Allan

MANY WERE THE LEGENDS that surrounded the group of islands, flung like the small change from a giant's pockets into the chill seas around the north-west of Scotland. Most were uninhabited. Some were the home of sea-birds, and drew naturalists to their barren backs in the summer seasons. Many bore the ruins of crofts, once tenanted and farmed by eager, strong-limbed people, now in their lonely graves. But some were still inhabited.

Such an island was Shant. It lay two miles beyond the mouth of a sea-loch, wind-blasted and desolate. Sheep cropped the harsh grass, and scrawny hens ran around the granite walls of the cottage where Ina MacClure lived. Loneliness appealed to her nature. Her forebears had been here, before the Highland rebellions of the mid-eighteenth century. She often felt that their spirits were still around her – dimly seen in mist and rain-squall. Telling her 'Stay. Stay . . .'

Her husband Hamish was with her, but not constantly. He kept the lighthouse, just three-quarters of a mile from Shant, on the treacherous Vorra Rocks. Like Ina, he was one of those people who choose to live away from their fellows – perhaps to enjoy a closeness to nature that escapes all town-dwellers.

Jeannie came there in her holidays. And relished the same sense of peace as her aunt and uncle. She had been born to Ina MacClure's sister, who had died in the very moment of childbirth. A great-grandfather's dwindling legacy had made it possible for her to be educated in a boarding school far to the south. She was fifteen – fifteen and eleven months, as she liked to say. At the start of the summer recess, she stepped as usual from the ferry, which was a more than grand term for Robertson's rowing boat, on to the sea turf of Shant's shore.

Ina MacClure greeted her niece warmly. 'Come on up to the cottage, Jeannie. I have your favourite meal ready. The terns have been nesting on the north cliff, and there are skuas about.'

As she ate her supper, Jeannie asked about her Uncle Hamish. 'When will I see him?'

'Oh, he's not due back from the Vorra Lighthouse until Saturday. But tomorrow, you can take out the boat and carry his provisions to him. You'll like that.'

'Of course I shall,' said Jeannie. 'You – er – remember what tomorrow is?'

Ina MacClure swallowed hard. Her hands intertwined, and it seemed to Jeannie that her aunt was somehow feeling awkward. 'Yes. Yes,' she said. 'Of course it is your birthday. You are sixteen. Well, we have your present, naturally . . .'

'Oh, Auntie! I wasn't hinting at anything like that,' laughed Jeannie. 'As a matter of fact, I've brought a present for you!' She searched in her bag and drew out a soft-knitted shawl, which she draped round Ina's shoulders. 'All the way from Princes Street, Edinburgh,' said Jeannie, proudly, delighted at the genuine pleasure that shone in her aunt's eyes. 'And I've got something for Uncle Hamish, too. How do you think he'll like this pipe-rack? You know how he's always mislaying his pipes, even out in that lighthouse.'

Jeannie went for a walk after dinner, and breathed deeply of the soft Atlantic air. The silence of Shant was so intense that she could almost – crazily – hear it. As she always did when she came here, she felt totally at home. She pitied her friends who knew nothing but noisy streets and bustling city centres.

She felt at peace as she returned to the cottage, and rested in the deep rocking chair beside the fire that burned, summer and winter, with its iron pot hanging from the dark iron chain. She reached out and took up the black-bound family photograph album from the shelf above, and leafed through its pages, marvelling at the severe faces of grandparents and great-grandparents; of distant second cousins, perhaps twice or thrice removed. Here was her great-great uncle, standing with rifle crooked in his arm, beside his horse somewhere on the Veldt of South Africa. 'He became a Major,' said Aunt Ina, picking at her knitting.

'What happened here?' said Jeannie, pointing at a page where a photograph had been torn away, to leave four shredded corners.

Her aunt's face tightened. 'Now just don't worry about that one, Jeannie. Turn over.'

Jeannie sat back, and for the first time in her life, disobeyed her aunt's command. 'It was of my father, wasn't it?'

Ina MacClure's hands fluttered. The knitting fell to the floor, unheeded. The old woman couldn't have looked more distressed.

'Of all nights you should ask this,' she said. 'Please, my child, do not pursue your questioning.'

'Auntie. What's wrong – you sound so strange?'

'Jeannie, he was not a good man. He deserted your mother. He ran off. He was what I would have called a "bad lot", and he shirked his responsibilities . . .'

Jeannie sighed. 'It was an awful long time ago, Auntie. I don't bear him any ill-will, honestly. There are girls at my school whose parents are divorced – that kind of thing – and it doesn't seem to matter to them. Come on, now. Do you still have the photo you've torn out of the book?'

'No.' Ina MacClure shook her head vehemently. And the blaze of her eyes told Jeannie that it would not have been the thing to pursue the conversation. The girl said: 'All right, Auntie. Don't worry. Do you think I could have a cup of cocoa?'

Jeannie's aunt made it. And her hands were shaking. In the tiny kitchen, she pulled open a drawer and looked, just for an instant, to the tissue-wrapped thing that lay there. She thought: 'what must be done must be done. But why did she have to mention the missing picture . . . tonight . . .?'

At twenty minutes past eleven on the following morning, Jeannie trotted down from the cottage to the landing stage beside the Shant Island rowing boat. She tossed in the package that contained pipe tobacco, her own pipe rack, a couple of tins and a flask of hot soup. She glanced across the strip of water to the Vorra Rocks, where her uncle's lighthouse pointed like a finger at the sky, and unshipped the oars. Deftly, she pulled away, and nodded to her aunt, who stood on the shore watching. 'I did wish you happy birthday, didn't I, Jeannie?' Ina MacClure's voice drifted across to her. 'Twice, Auntie! And thanks again for that lovely jacket you knitted!'

Three-quarters of a mile. A mere three-quarters of a mile between the shore of Shant and the Vorra Rocks. But in that notorious region of the British Isles, nature can move quickly and decisively. The mist swirled in from the mouth of the sea-loch and enveloped Jeannie before she had gone four hundred metres. She paused, resting on her oars, and listened intently, but there was nothing. Not even the cries of the skuas, the screeching of the terns. Biting her lip, she plied the oars again, and concentrated on keeping what she thought would be a straight course.

It was not. In mist, one moves in circles. Jeannie was no exception to the rule, and half an hour later, she realized that she was completely lost. There should have been a guiding blare from the foghorn on the Vorra Lighthouse, but Jeannie didn't know that the thing had gone wrong. Such instruments *always* go wrong at the worst times.

Suddenly, her starboard oar struck something below the surface of the water. She clutched at it – too late. It slipped from her hand and vanished into the murk, bobbing mockingly. Now she was really in trouble! She stood up, and put her remaining oar over the stern, resting it against the cleft in the transom. Furiously, she began to scull, but there was a fierce current beneath her bows, and she knew that, however hard she tried, she was going rapidly astern.

The Rocks of Vorra – the hazard that her own uncle guarded! They'd claim her – rip the bottom-boards from her boat and sink her as sure as death. In this mist there could be no hope. She was sixteen. It was her birthday. And Jeannie knew she was going to die!

It came out of the mist, tall and towering, a trawler whose sea-battered identification letters Jeannie couldn't read. Jeannie staggered as the stern of her boat hit the side of the craft and scraped backwards. The mist swirled thicker than ever, but she must have been on the seaward side, for a rough swell lifted her and pushed her upwards towards the trawler's rail. Panic-stricken though she was, Jeannie saw the man there – leaning out to her. He was swathed in oilskins, and a sou'wester masked all of his face. But his right arm was out-thrust towards her, and she heard his voice.

'Grab hold, lassie! Grab hold, now!'

Flesh met flesh, and Jeannie was hauled to the deck as her boat whirled away from her. She fell on her knees, and the hand that held hers was all she could see. It was a horny, hard hand, that of a man long attuned to the sea. And on the little finger was a ring – a curious ring, of some dark semi-precious stone, inscribed with the single letter 'A', and surrounded by a coil of intricately-worked gold wire.

'You – you saved my life!' Jeannie picked herself to her feet

The trawler came out of the mist,
tall and towering, as Jenny's
boat was tossed by the waves.

and scrabbled after the man. But he was retreating along the deck, his face still shrouded. He held his hands forward, the ring still glittering and dripping water. He said: 'What is done, is done . . .' And then, although it may have been a trick of the ever-present mist, he vanished.

Jeannie recovered her wits and staggered forward to the steps that led to the trawler's bridge. The Captain there, a stolid man named Angus McKay, was surprised to see her. But – a man of little imagination – he said: 'Where the devil did you come from?'

'I stay with the MacClures, on Shant Island,' said Jeannie. 'I was going to my uncle, but the mist came down . . .'

'Aye, him,' said the Captain. 'I ken him well. The idiot's forgotten his foghorn, and it's lucky I'm a master o' the approaches to this loch. I canna see a thing, but I'll put ye ashore at yer Auntie's place.'

'I wouldn't have even been here, if it hadn't been for your deck-hand,' said Jeannie.

'Ma *deck-hand?* Dinna be daft, lassie. I've no people on this boat tonight at all. She's been in the yards for repair, and I've been doing no trawling. I'm taking her in alone.'

Jeannie looked this way and that. 'There *was* a man out there. He pulled me aboard. He spoke to me!'

Angus McKay gave her a withering glance. 'Ye're daft. Like as not, ye dreamed it. If yer boat was in trouble, you jumped out of it and found ma deck. An' lucky ye were. Now bide yer wheesht and let me feel my way in to Shant.'

Jeannie sat down, her mind reeling . . .

The mist was still as thick as ever as McKay, a genius of a navigator, put Jeannie ashore. She was astonished to see that her boat, though with only one oar, was pulled up on the shore. She stepped from the trawler and found herself shouting good-bye to its skipper. He waved a hand and left her standing there, alone on the sea turf.

She walked up towards the cottage, and her Uncle Hamish was at the door. 'Jeannie! We've been so worried! I found the boat tied up at the steps of the lighthouse. I looked everywhere for you, but I couldna find you. I sculled back here to see where you'd gone.'

Jeannie kissed her uncle. 'I didn't mean to upset you. It was just – something crazy. That mist. Well, it's all right now.'

Supper in the cottage was a lively affair. Jeannie told her uncle and aunt of her strange experiences, and they said that Shant and its surroundings were always places of weird and supernatural happenings. Jeannie nodded and smiled, willing to let them believe in the unexplainable. But then her aunt went to the drawer and produced the tissue-wrapped present. 'This,' said Aunt Ina, 'was a ring that belonged to your father. We don't talk about him, because he ran off and did nothing for you. But we thought you ought to have it on your birthday.'

Jeannie unwrapped it. It was a curious ring, of some dark, semi-precious stone, inscribed with the single letter 'A', and surrounded by intricately-worked gold wire. Jeannie felt her eyes fill with tears, but she managed to say, 'Was Dad ever a trawlerman?'

'Yes,' said Aunt Ina. 'Why do you ask . . .?'

KILLING CHANCE
by Kelvin Gosnell

WE CAME IN VERY FAST and very low across Laffan's Plain. Our arrival at the Farnborough Air Display was still a closely guarded secret; in fact very few people had even heard of the Merlin strike fighter let alone seen it, and we wanted to make our entrance as spectacular as possible.

We tore towards the runway at almost the speed of sound; so fast that we would take everyone by surprise. We flashed past the astonished crowd and pulled away in the tight turn that would start our display routine. The routine was specially devised to show off the Merlin's long sleek fuselage and the small delta wings which stuck out, like dagger tips, from the top of that fuselage. The only things which broke up her smooth lines were the big square engine intakes, one either side of the cockpit, and the cleverly recessed jet nozzles, two to each side just under the wing.

The Merlin was like a larger and more streamlined Harrier, and the overall impression the two Merlins (flown by Don Evans and I) made on the crowd was pretty powerful. It went down as one of the most spectacular arrivals of all time at Farnborough. I didn't know it then, but the Merlin was also about to feature in one of the most memorable departures from Farnborough.

The Merlin project had started life many years before. After the success of the Harrier, the world's first vertical-take-off-and-landing aircraft to enter service, it was only natural that someone should think of a supersonic successor to the Harrier. There were many false starts, but when Sir David Shaft took over the project in the early 1980s he realized that our so-called partners in the project were wasting time.

Sir David is one of the best businessmen of all time. He is also a very good liar. The first thing he did was pull out of the project, saying it was 'too expensive', and 'technically unfeasible'. At the same time he secretly brought together a team of engineers and constructors and told them to build the supersonic Harrier in two years, in complete secrecy. Where he got the money from I'll never know, but get it he did. The two Merlin prototypes were built in time for Don and me – the name's Mackay by the way, Duncan Mackay – to fly them into Farnborough and spring them on an unsuspecting public.

Don and I parked our chariots in pride of place, right where potential buyers could get a good look at them, and headed up to the company's chalet for the press reception.

We were utterly besieged by men with cameras and microphones and lights and recorders, and for hours we told them all that we were allowed to tell about the new 'wonder plane' as they insisted on calling it. We told them about the new fuel system which would enable the Merlin's two Spey engines to use any grade of jet fuel, we told them about the perfect performance above Mach Two – we'd only tested her on one grade of fuel and only tried her at Mach One so far, but Sir David had briefed us well!

Some hours later, just as the show was ready to pack up for the day, I actually managed to sneak away to the rest area for a few minutes – Don had disappeared half an hour before.

The third of those minutes was hardly over when Sir David came bounding in. 'Hello, Mac,' he said. 'Taking a blow, old son? Can't say I blame you – is Don doing the same? There's a BBC defence chappie wants a word with him.'

I was just about to answer when the familiar sound of Spey

engines being started groaned across the display area. Don's Merlin was kicking up great lumps of turf as the engines spooled up to full power.

Neither of us could speak for a couple of seconds – we just stared dumbfounded. Sir David broke the silence: 'What the blue blazes does that idiot think he's doing? He's got no right to take off now . . .'

As he spoke, the Merlin staggered into the air very shakily and nearly took the tail off my aircraft as it did so. It swayed off drunkenly along the runway.

'I don't know who that is, Boss,' I said, 'but it certainly isn't Don Evans – he couldn't make a take off that bad if he tried for a week!'

At that moment Sir David's personal phone in the rest area shouted for attention. He grabbed it. 'Yes! What . . .? You must be joking! Well how the blazes can I stop him, pal? I don't know who it is either. Oh, shut up and hold on.' He cupped the mouthpiece and turned to me. 'They've just found Don. He'd been tied up and doped but he's coming round okay. They are politely requesting that we get our aircraft back since it is causing a terrible air traffic hazard. Of all the nerve . . .!'

'Tell 'em we'll do it,' I shot back at him straight away. There must have been something desperately urgent about the way I said it, for he did just as I asked and shot the phone back on its hook. I was already half way out of the chalet heading for his Range Rover when he caught up.

'Drive me down to my plane, Boss,' I said, 'I'll explain my ideas on the way.' I tried my best, but it sounded pretty wild – whoever had taken half of two years' work knew what he was doing. We had designed the Merlin to be uncatchable and our early tests had proved that we were looking pretty successful. There was only one way to get that plane back – and that was for me to give chase in my aircraft. Sir David agreed and punched his Range Rover straight through the crash barrier to drop me right alongside my aircraft.

I grabbed my gear and clambered into the cockpit, inserting and turning the emergency-start key as I did. The engines started to spool up to full power.

'Take care, Mac, and don't bend it unless you have to,' Sir David called up to me and then spurred the Range Rover across the turf towards the control tower.

As soon as I was airborne, I called the tower to see if they could give me a fix on Don's plane – Merlin Zero-one. They could, but it was old news. It had been heading south but had now dropped so low that it was off their scanners. I climbed and started a standard offensive reconnaissance sweep pattern.

Any other aircraft would have been easy to spot, but not this one! If the pilot, who had obviously trained on Harriers and knew his stuff, wanted to land and hide in a wood or under a bridge, then he could, she was such a potent device.

I was just about to give up and come home when Farnborough control crackled into my ears, 'Merlin Zero-two' – that was my call sign – 'We have an unconfirmed report of an aircraft crashing in a service area on the M-3 motorway.'

'Roger, control.' It was the only lead I had. I had to follow it up. 'Give me a bearing to get there.'

They did and I cut in the reheat to get there in little more than seventy-five seconds. From one hundred metres above ground there was no sign of a crash nor of a landed aircraft. The service area is one of those nicely landscaped ones with trees all around so that it does not look like a purpose-built slum. Those trees may have been easy on the motorists' eyes, but they were also easy to hide an aircraft under!

I entered the activating instructions for the Tracker on the weapons computer and waited for the image to come up on one of the cockpit screens.

The Tracker is a very useful piece of kit which can look down at the ground and tell you which bits of it are hot and which are cold – which may sound useless until you remember that aircraft are hot in relation to the terrain around them. You can therefore pick them out even in the foulest weather, or in pitch black night.

With the Tracker fully warmed up and operating, it was easy to see where the other Merlin had landed. It had put down in the trees which backed on to one of the car parks, taxied towards the car park and then the trail stopped. I immediately dropped to the area to find out that it wasn't a car park at all, but a lorry park. Now it made sense – the Merlin was equipped with folding wingtips so that she can, if necessary, be operated from one of the new mini-carriers. With those folded up she would easily fit in the back of a large lorry – which would make a perfect hiding place in which to refuel her and/or spirit her away from the area.

I was just about to throw the aircraft across into a mid-level scan of the motorway when the warning klaxon sounded in the cockpit – I had less than two minutes flying time left so it looked like the chase was over. But then something caught my eye in the service area's petrol station. There was a large pink road tanker just swinging in to refuel – a road tanker full of prime grade paraffin. My engines would run perfectly on that.

I brought the Merlin down right alongside the tanker and then taxied around to the front so that he couldn't try to drive away in panic. I cut the Speys, shot out of the cockpit as quickly as I could and, for all the seriousness of the situation, I just couldn't resist it. You should have seen the look on the tanker driver's face when I calmly asked him to 'fill her up'.

Five minutes, several thousand litres and one bemused tanker driver later we rumbled out of the service station and back into the air again. Now all the time I'd been refuelling there had been a two-seat Hunter jet trainer stooging around the area. I wondered just what he thought he was doing and asked him as such as soon as I was operational again.

I was delighted but astounded to hear Don's voice come back to me. 'You're not going to believe this, Mac. But Sir Dave's ordered me down here to play chase with you on the search. I've got a very worried BBC man with a video camera alongside me – the Boss thought it might make some good publicity shots if I stuck close to you.'

'Stroll on!' was all I could muster, then, 'Okay, Don. Glad you're in one piece and that the knock-out drop's worn off. Try your best to keep up. I've got to scan the motorway for a juggernaut that's hotter than it should be.'

So we went south, me with my eyes glued to the Tracker screen while the automatic terrain following radar kept the Merlin an unwavering hundred metres above the ground and Don sat out to port about a thousand metres away.

Most wagons that appeared in the scope showed up as oblong blue blobs with red blobs at their noses – the red dot came from the heat of their engines. But one, a very big one, showed two large red blobs inside its trailer – the sort of heat generated by a couple of aero-engines takes a long time to die away. Trouble was, now that we'd located the lorry, how did we stop it?

My aircraft was armed, since we were due for a weapon demonstration during the displays, but I could hardly use them on that road with so many private cars about.

All I could do was switch my radio to the police frequency and inform them of the situation – this I did and then sat back circling overhead while we waited for the boys in blue to arrive.

It was while I was waiting, pulling big lazy S-turns over the lorry, that the name of the game was changed. First I saw the big vehicle slow and pull over on to the hard shoulder.

Seconds later the stolen Merlin had been wheeled out of the

Seconds later the stolen Merlin took off perfectly. The game was to be tailchase . . .

truck and was rolling down the road in a short take off which would have looked good in a training film – he learned fast! He stayed very low and I saw the bright orange flicker of reheat from the Speys. The game was to be tailchase . . .

The next ten minutes were the most memorable, exciting and frightening of my entire life: we flew under power cables; we flew metres above river surfaces with their banks rearing up above our heads on either side, we discovered more about the Merlin's flight performance and limitations than we would have during years of the normally very safety-conscious flight test programme – like, for example, that you can turn a Merlin round a street corner at one hundred miles per hour.

Eventually we crossed the coast west of Portsmouth and my target turned right to head out for the Atlantic. He was so positive in this manoeuvre that I think he must have been trying to make a rendezvous with a ship of some kind – they must have planned it as a back-up to the original plan. But all this flying up and down Basingstoke High Street and whizzing over wavetops was gobbling up the gas at a rate far higher than I even cared to think about.

I was in the middle of calling the situation over to Farnborough, in the hope of getting some extra aerial cover, when two things happened: first, Sir David came on the air personally to tell me that under no circumstances was I to allow the stolen Merlin to escape – I was to shoot it down if necessary; and second, the pilot of the stolen aircraft decided to make a stand before his gas ran out too!

He pulled a trick on me that I have never seen before but which has now found its way into the standard combat tactics for the Merlin. If you're pushing a Merlin along at a very low height, and you flick the engine nozzles down for a split-second you hardly change altitude. Matter of fact, there is no reason you should want to do this unless you happen to be over the ocean and wish to blind the guy who's following you – for the downthrust kicks up an incredible splash!

For the ten seconds that it took for my screen to clear I was blind – and in those ten seconds, my target had stopped being a target and become a killer instead.

I saw the Merlin's distinctive shape scamper down out of the sky behind me. The twin muzzle flash of the Aden cannon was all too clear as well. The survival instinct took over. I didn't even have to think about working the controls any more, it all happened automatically. The Merlin became like a part of my body – I didn't feel like I was sitting in it, I felt more like I had strapped it to my back.

I broke away to the right and pulled a sharp turn. My body staggered under the strain of weighing seven times its normal weight.

I couldn't see the killer behind me, but I knew he was there. I knew he would be sitting there, unable to fire because of the fierce rate of turn, just waiting for me to give him that one chance, that one mistake which would be the killing chance that we all look for.

I flicked the turn from left to right. The sudden change in direction felt as if it would drag my brain out – but it didn't.

I killed the turn an instant later – the relief it brought to the body was wonderful. But I only had a fleeting moment to enjoy it – as soon as the force went off, I slammed the engine nozzles straight down to the hover position and opened the throttles wide. It had the same effect as hitting a brick wall – my speed dropped from just over Mach One to zero in ten seconds.

My harness chopped into my shoulders and I was aware of a presence close alongside, to starboard. He had understood what I was doing a fraction of a second after I'd done it and followed suit himself.

When I saw it on the video tape later (Don just caught up in time for everything to be filmed) it seemed totally unreal – the two sleek shapes were exactly side-by-side, juddering to a halt in the sky.

His aircraft hung motionless barely twenty metres from my starboard wingtip. I turned full right to swing my nose round towards him. I hit the cannon without even looking at the computer sight – there was no need at this range. And, as you've probably seen on the video tape, there was no explosion – it was all quite undramatic: Merlin Zero-one just stopped flying. It hit the sea in a cold greeny white splash and disappeared without trace.

The pilot had plenty of time to hit the ejection seat but he didn't – whether it was part of his mission never to be taken alive or whether a splinter from a shell killed him, I'll never know, and the men from the lorry were never caught.

So even now we don't know who it was who tried to steal the aircraft: I'd put my money on industrial spies – it had the flavour of a neatly planned business undertaking to me. It was unimportant anyway – I'd won, that was all that mattered.

I made it back to Farnborough on the last of my fuel reserves and the rest is history now: the dramatic landing when my engines died, out of gas, two seconds after touchdown; and the frenzied reception by my company's team who had watched the entire thing on television. It was all pretty incredible really – the Merlin is the only aircraft in history to have been announced to the public, seen for the first time, flown, won its first combat mission *and* won an immediate production order of two hundred from the Americans, all in one day.

And me . . .? Well, I'm still flying and testing new aircraft, but I tell you one thing – I keep my start-key chained round my wrist now and I am *very* careful about where I park any new experimental types. They say lightning never strikes twice in the same place, but I'm not willing to risk it.

SINFUL SIMON
by John Wagner

SIMON HAD NEVER BEEN NORMAL. He told me a lot of things about himself when he moved into our neighbourhood. Crazy things, like he could just *think* about something and make it happen. I didn't believe him, so he showed me . . .

'See that bottle on the rubbish bin,' he said, pointing to an empty Coke bottle someone had left sitting on top of the yellow bin at the bus stop.

'Yeah,' I said. 'So what?'

'Watch.'

He sort of squinted his eyes like someone looking through a dirty window. The bottle toppled off the bin and shattered on the pavement.

'Aw, anyone could do that,' I told him, though I wasn't sure I could. I thought he must've used some kind of trick, so I went on: 'If you're so smart, why don't you make all the pieces of glass jump back in the bin?'

'Can't,' he said. 'But I can do something much better. See that big bird . . .'

A big old crow was flying over Mr Johnson's house. Simon stared at it and squinted his eyes again – and the crow just stopped in mid-air like it'd been shot. Then it dropped straight down and landed in Mr Johnson's hedge. It sat there, flapping its wings like crazy and squawking fit to burst. That old crow didn't know what'd hit it!

'Fantastic!' I shouted. 'You did that? You really did it?'

Simon was looking smug. 'I can think things to people too,'

Simon squinted at the crow —
and the bird just stopped in
mid-air as if it had been shot.

112

he boasted. 'I can think things to you, or grown-ups or teachers or even anybody! But don't worry. I won't do anything to you, Eddy. You're going to be my friend.'

That was fine by me. Simon seemed like fun.

I took Simon up to meet the gang. It was near the end of summer holidays and we were all going to play football in Hill Park. Robin and Ronnie, the Smith twins, were there. So was Tubby Grover. It was his ball. Big Tommy Frame was usually the leader. He was ten and a bit of a bully. He didn't like Simon from the start.

'You're not getting to play, new boy,' he sneered, pushing Simon quite hard, 'so you can just beat it!'

Simon wasn't very big, but he wasn't afraid. 'Why don't you try and make me?'

Tommy's fist lashed out and hit Simon right in the mouth. Simon fell to the grass, blood trickling down his chin, and Tubby Grover yelled: 'Hit him again, Tommy!'

Tommy stood over him, his fists clenched, and said: 'I'm leader of this gang, you little twerp, and what I say goes. Now beat it before I give you another one!'

Simon just glared right back at him. 'I'll make you sorry for that,' he hissed. His eyes squinted in that funny way I'd seen him do before.

A kind of spooky look came over Tommy's face. Then he turned and ran across the grass and headfirst straight into the old oak tree. He crashed to the ground and started to cry.

We all ran over to him, but Simon got there first. He stood over Tommy and shouted: 'Who's the leader now?'

'Y-you are, Simon,' Tommy sobbed.

'Okay, I won't do anything more to you now,' Simon said. 'Go on – beat it!'

Tommy scrambled to his feet, took one look at Simon and ran off like he'd been stung by a wasp.

Simon turned to Tubby and stuck out his hand. 'Give me the ball,' he demanded.

'Sure thing,' Tubby said. 'You're the boss, Simon.'

'Okay, let's play football.' Simon looked us over. 'Eddy and Robin will be on my side.'

'Hey, that's not fair!' Ronnie Smith butted in. 'Me and Tubby haven't got a chance against three of you!'

Simon didn't say a word, just looked at Ronnie real hard.

'A-all right,' Ronnie said, pretty quickly. 'You're the boss.'

We beat them easily, of course. After the game we all walked down to Tubby's street. Simon said he would treat us and led us into Mrs Bartlett's little shop.

'Five choc-ices, please,' he told her.

Mrs Bartlett fumbled in the freezer and brought out the choc-ices. 'That will be one pound exactly, young man,' she said, handing them over.

Simon gave her one of his looks. He was thinking at her. Suddenly she smiled and exclaimed: 'I've just had a super idea! Why don't I give you nice boys these ices for nothing!'

'Thank you, Mrs B!' we all shouted and got out of there before she changed her mind.

'Cor!' Tubby said as we left him at his gate. 'I wouldn't mind having you around all the time, Simon! I could have all the ices I want, all the sweets and lemonade and cakes . . .'

I told my Mum about Simon that night. 'He's the new kid who's moved into the house at the end of the road.'

'Yes, I've heard their name is Plummer. What's young Simon like then, Eddy?' she asked.

'He's kind of strange,' I replied. 'He can do things just by thinking about them.'

'Oh, can he indeed?'

'Yeah! He made a crow fall out of the sky and he sent that bully Tommy home crying – just by looking at him. He's got some kind of power, I guess.'

'You've been reading too many comics again, Eddy,' Mum said firmly. 'Eat your dinner and stop talking nonsense!'

There's no point in arguing with my Mum once she's made up her mind. I could see she wasn't going to believe me. I'd just have to get Simon along to show her . . .

. . . But when I asked Simon next day, he refused. 'Adults don't understand me, Eddy. They just cause trouble. That's why we had to move from our last place.'

His eyes narrowed and he glowered at me. 'So just keep it to yourself – or I'll think something really horrible for you!'

'Don't do that, Simon,' I said quickly. 'We're friends, remember!'

There was a week left before we had to go back to school, and with Simon in charge the gang had a great time. He got us into the swimming pool three times for free, and once into the cinema. I suppose we all knew it was sinful to take all those things without paying, but we were having too much fun to care. Anyway, Simon didn't use his powers to do really bad things. Well, not very often . . .

One time something bad did happen – on the last Saturday before school. We were all messing around in Tubby's back garden when Simon suddenly announced: 'I'm bored! Let's do something interesting. I know – let's have a fight!'

He held up a gleaming fifty pence piece. 'Tubby, you can fight Eddy. The winner gets this as a prize.'

Tubby gulped. 'I don't want to fight. Eddy's bigger than me. And anyway, I'm no good at fighting.'

'Aw, c'mon, Simon,' I joined in. 'Let's do something else. I haven't got anything against Tubby. I don't want to fight him.'

'*I* want you to fight him!' Simon ordered, and he started squinting at me the way he does.

It was the first time he'd used his power against me. It was horrible. My head felt like it was being squeezed by a giant claw. My thoughts were all mixed up. Only one thing was clear – I hated Tubby! He was spotty and fat and I wanted to hurt him!

I grabbed him, threw him to the ground and jumped on him.

'P-please, Eddy! Let me alone!' he begged. His voice sounded just like a pig when it squeals. I twisted his arm hard up behind his back.

'Porky! Porky! Fat ugly Porky!' someone was screaming, and I realized it was me! But I couldn't stop, couldn't control myself. I twisted and twisted and Tubby was howling and bawling –

Then Mrs Grover was there, pulling me off and holding me back. 'What the devil's come over you?' she scolded.

'I-I'm sorry,' I stammered. Simon had stopped thinking at me and my mind was again my own. Tubby lay there, still sobbing. I felt sick and ashamed of what I'd done. I tried to help Tubby up but his mother pushed me roughly aside.

'You'll be sorry, all right,' she raged. 'I'm phoning your mother about this! Come into the house, William!'

She helped Tubby to his feet and turned to us. 'The rest of you get out of here before I take a stick to you!'

We left the garden and Simon was smirking. Robin and Ronnie Smith looked at him kind of worriedly. I could see they were frightened by what had happened.

'We've got to go now,' Robin said quietly. 'Mum'll be expecting us for dinner.'

They turned and scurried off as fast as they could go.

'Never mind them,' Simon laughed. 'We don't need them – or Tubby.'

'It was wicked, Simon,' I said. 'Why did you make me do it? How am I ever going to explain it to my Mum?'

'Aw, just tell her Tubby said nasty things about her,' Simon said easily. 'Mums like it when their kids stand up for them.'

I wasn't going to lie to my Mum, but there was no point in telling Simon that. I could see he wasn't interested. So I changed the subject.

'What do *your* Mum and Dad think about your power?' I asked him.

'They think what I want them to think,' Simon boasted. Of course, they didn't always. They took me to some stupid doctor once, but I didn't like him so I made them stop.'

'You mean, you can make your parents do whatever you want?'

'Sure I can. Come on – I'll show you.'

We turned off Tubby's street into Victoria Road, where Simon and I lived. There was a big black mongrel dog in Simon's garden. It growled at him as we came up the path. He looked at it hard and it yelped in pain and slunk away with its tail between its legs.

'Stupid dog never learns,' Simon said. 'One day I'll think it dead. That'll teach it to bark at me!'

Simon's mother, Mrs Plummer, was in the kitchen. She was a thin woman with straggly red hair. She looked very old, like my gran, but Mum told me later she was only thirty-five.

'This is my friend Eddy,' Simon announced. 'He's staying for dinner.'

'Er . . . I've really got to go home soon,' I started, but my voice tailed away as Simon glowered at me.

'You're staying,' he said in a low voice.

He sat down in the chair at the head of the table and rattled his plate with his soup spoon. 'I'm hungry,' he snapped. 'Get Dad. Let's get started.'

Mrs Plummer nervously told me to sit down, then went off to fetch Simon's Dad.

He came in a minute later, as Simon's Mum was ladling out tomato soup. He was a tall thin man, wearing a greasy overall.

I noticed as he pulled his chair back that his hands were trembling.

'Sorry I'm late,' he apologized, 'I was working on the car.'

'What do you mean coming to the table like that?' Simon roared.

There was a tense silence. Mrs Plummer turned from the cooker with a frightened look in her eyes. I was red with embarrassment, but one look at Simon told me he was enjoying it.

'I've brought my friend Eddy home to dinner,' he went on, 'and I won't have you meeting him with dirt on your stupid face!'

'It's only grease, Simon,' Mr Plummer said, trying to calm his son down. 'I'll go and wash, shall I?'

'Stay where you are!' Simon bellowed. 'You've come to the table dirty – so you can jolly well wash at the table!'

'Please, Simon,' Mrs Plummer blurted, but one look from her son shut her up.

Simon turned back to his father, and squinted. 'Go on – wash!'

A look of pain flashed across Mr Plummer's face. Then his fingers slowly dipped into his steaming tomato soup. He scooped up a handful and splattered it on to his face. He did it again – and again. Then he was rubbing it in, as if he was washing.

'Grease stains are the very devil to get out, you know,' he remarked pleasantly.

My insides were churning, and Mrs Plummer had her head in her hands, weeping soundlessly. Tomato soup ran down her husband's face on to the tablecloth. Now he was scooping up more and rubbing it under his arms, whistling cheerfully.

Simon was bouncing up and down in his chair and laughing excitedly. 'See, Eddy! I can make them do anything! Anything!'

I couldn't stand it another minute. I jumped up and ran out of the house.

As I turned into the street I heard Simon's voice call after me: 'See you tomorrow, Eddy!'

Mum was waiting when I got home, and Dad too. Mrs Grover had phoned and they were angry.

The whole story just tumbled out: the crow and Tommy and Mrs Bartlett and all the other things Simon had done. Then I told them what he'd made his Dad do, and how his Mum had cried.

My Mum looked at my Dad, frowning. 'Can this be true, George?'

'I've heard some strange rumours about that Plummer lad,' Dad said.

'But that's fantastic!' Mum gasped. 'If it's true . . . that poor couple – and her with another baby on the way, too!'

Dad spoke to me. 'I don't know whether to believe that story or not. But you've never lied to me before, son, so I'm going to give you the benefit of the doubt.

'Whatever the truth of the matter,' he went on, 'I don't want you playing with that Plummer boy again, do you hear?'

'Yes. Stay away from him, Eddy,' Mum chipped in. 'He sounds positively . . . *evil*.'

I managed to avoid Simon next day by going to visit my aunt in Chipping Bruton. It was like a breath of fresh air, being out from under Simon's spell. I hadn't realized it before, but Mum had put her finger on it. Simon was evil.

School started next morning. I was in Mr Clegg's class this year, with Tubby and Robin Smith. Normally Tubby and I sat together, but this time he ignored me and went to join Robin at the back of the class.

I'd been praying that Simon wouldn't turn up. But he strolled in ten minutes late, bold as brass.

'Cleggy' was a stickler for punctuality. 'You're the new boy, Plummer? Why are you late?' he demanded.

'I'm late because I felt like it,' Simon replied.

Nobody spoke to Cleggy like that. He came out of his seat like a wild bull and charged!

Simon just stood there and squinted – and Cleggy stopped dead. He shook his head as if confused, then pointed lamely. 'Oh, never mind. Get to your seat, boy.'

Simon ignored the desk Cleggy had indicated and plonked himself down beside me.

'Hello, Eddy. I came round to see you yesterday, but you weren't in,' he said. 'Never mind. Now we're sitting together. That's the way it should be with friends.'

Over the next couple of weeks I tried to stay away from Simon, but it was impossible. I couldn't tell him to get lost. I didn't know what he might do.

But Simon usually kept his power in check in school. I guessed it was because it had caused him trouble in the past.

Then one morning he turned up in a really foul mood. His mother had come home from the hospital with his new baby sister, and her squawling had kept him up all night.

'I've told Mum she'd better keep it quiet tonight – or *I'll* shut it up,' he said to me nastily. 'I'm dog-tired. I'm going to have a little kip right now.'

He laid his head on his desk top and closed his eyes. Next minute he was actually snoring.

Right from that first day, Cleggy had been wary of Simon, but this was more than he could stand. Three quick steps brought him to our desk. The plastic ruler in his hand chopped downwards and caught Simon a sharp rap across the knuckles.

'Wake up, boy!' he roared.

Simon shot up like a scalded cat, shaking his throbbing hand. 'I'll get you for that,' he snarled at Cleggy. 'You'll see!'

With that he stormed out of the class. He didn't come back all day. Perhaps it was the last we would see of him . . .

No such luck! As I left school at quarter-to-four, he was lurking by the gate. 'Hey, Eddy! Come here!' he called. I was afraid to disobey him.

'What are you doing here?' I asked. 'I thought you'd gone home.'

'Home, nothing,' he rasped. 'I've been waiting around for school to end. I'm going to teach that ratbag Clegg a lesson.'

Just then Mr Clegg's car came out of the school gate and drove past us. Simon's cruel eyes narrowed hatefully.

'I'm going to think Cleggy an accident!'

He squinted long and hard, intense concentration on his face. I could only watch in horror as Mr Clegg's car suddenly swerved across the road – into the path of an oncoming lorry! There was a tortured screech, a cry – and then a sickening impact. People were running, the lorry driver was staggering from his cab . . .

'You – you've killed him!' I breathed.

'Maybe, maybe not,' Simon shrugged. 'But one way or another, he won't be bothering me again.'

He glared at me suddenly. 'You've gone all white, Eddy. What's the matter?'

'N-nothing,' I lied.

'Good. Then we'll walk home together.'

I went with him, docile as a lamb. I was really frightened now, terrified of what he might do next.

He was silent until we reached his house. I could hear the high-pitched cries of a baby from inside, and Simon's face flushed with anger. 'I told her! I told her!' he shouted. 'Come on, Eddy – I'm going to fix it so that that screaming brat never makes another sound!'

'No, Simon, wait a minute,' I started, but he was dragging me into the house and through to the sitting room.

Mrs Plummer was bending over a carri-cot, attempting to soothe her baby girl.

'I warned you,' Simon yelled. 'Now get out of my way!'

'No – I won't! I won't let you harm her!' Mrs Plummer placed herself squarely in front of the cot.

'Have it your own way,' Simon sneered. He squinted and his mother screamed with agony and fell writhing to the floor.

Simon stepped over her and pulled the blankets back from the child. As he began to think at her, the screams died away. She opened her eyes and focused them on her brother.

Then her eyes narrowed to slits – *and she squinted at Simon*.

A look of pain etched itself across his face. He seemed to be struggling, wrestling with some unexpected power greater than his own. Then every window in the room burst open with a crash, and a whirlwind was howling past the cot.

Simon screamed once. The wind lifted him up and spun him through the room like a puppet. His head hit the unyielding tiles of the fire surround with a sharp 'crack'.

Simon slumped to the floor and lay still, his neck twisted at a strange angle.

The wind vanished as quickly as it had come. Then there was only silence . . . and the contented gurgles of the baby.

An ambulance came for Simon, but it was too late. He was dead.

The police asked me a lot of questions. I told them everything I knew, though I could tell they didn't believe me. I was frightened and crying, and they sent for Mum and Dad to come and take me home.

Mum tried to comfort the Plummers, but they didn't even seem to notice her presence. They were standing over the baby's cot, staring down with shocked hollow eyes. I could just make out Mrs Plummer muttering, over and over:

'Oh no! Not her, too . . .!'

EMERGENCY
by Ralph L. Sells

HELENA WAS PLAYING WITH THE DOG in the garden when she suddenly remembered that she hadn't finished polishing her Dad's Bentley, a job she did every Sunday morning. Now her Dad wanted the car, so she ran back to the garage and started polishing.

She was nearly finished when her Dad came out. 'Hurry up if you want to come out today, we've got to be back by lunch time.'

Helena loved cars. Although she was sixteen and so too young to drive on the road, she had driven her mother's Mini two or three times on the drive in front of the house. But she wouldn't dare touch her Dad's big Bentley, although she liked to keep it clean and shining, and day-dream about getting in and driving away.

On Sunday mornings Helena and her father generally went for a drive to the river. Her father had not been too well lately and he was pleased to get some fresh air and relax a bit.

'Is there anything to take with us?' Helena asked.

'Nothing, hurry up,' her father shouted, as he started the engine.

They drove off slowly, Helena watching every move her father made. She was sure she could drive that Bentley, and she would, one day!

They were travelling at about fifty miles an hour and had about ten miles to go, when Helena noticed her Dad had started to perspire a lot and looked very flushed.

'Are you OK, Dad?' she asked. The words were hardly out of her mouth when her father slumped over the wheel, gasping for breath and holding his chest in pain.

His foot was still firmly on the throttle, and the car was increasing speed. Helena started to panic, then she controlled herself and thought: 'I must stop the car, but how?'

Her father's foot was firmly wedged down on the throttle, and although Helena had grabbed the wheel and kept the car running straight, she had to stop the car or they would crash. Helena tried pulling her father's leg, but she couldn't move it. In the end she had to bend down and lift it off, and as she did that, she took her hand off the wheel and the car swerved all over the road.

Helena sat up, grabbed the wheel and soon had it under control again. She managed to put on the brake and the heavy vehicle came to a stop at the side of the road.

She was quaking all over and her leg kept jumping. 'Nerves,' she thought, but she wasn't frightened. 'Phew!' she exclaimed, and looked over at her Dad. She quickly realized that her job was far from over. Her father was slumped in his seat, now almost on the floor and still gasping for breath.

Helena undid her father's tie and belt, trying to make him comfortable, but it didn't do any good, he still lay there, gasping.

'He's having a heart attack,' Helena shouted, but nobody heard her. She pressed the horn, but there was nobody about to hear that. She ran up the road, but there wasn't a soul in sight and Helena realized that if her Dad was to be helped, she would have to do it. She would have to drive the car to the hospital and that was about six miles back up the road.

With all her strength she pulled her father over to the passenger seat, then she sat behind the wheel. Trying to catch her breath, she said to herself: 'It's all up to me, I must be calm and do this properly. Dad's very life may depend on it!'

She made sure the gears were in neutral, switched on the ignition and pressed the starter. The Bentley started at once and Helena touched the throttle. The powerful engine gave an almighty roar and Helena very nearly panicked again. She let the engine quieten down and with her face set grimly she put the gear lever home and the great big car started off with Helena clinging firmly to the wheel.

Her first problem was to turn around, so she had to find a space big enough. This was no Mini she was driving: besides she had never even turned that car round.

A little way down the road she came to a small gated entrance to a field. It didn't look big enough, but she knew she had to try, so she gently turned into it, but she couldn't stop! The car hit the gate with a crash, the gate came off its hinges and locked itself round the front bumper. Helena put the brake on, stopped the engine, ran round to the front of the car and tried to pull it off. She pulled and she pushed, she heaved at the heavy gate; she swore at it and kicked it, and in the end she got it off. The gate crashed down into the field, but Helena didn't care about the damage to the gate or to the car.

She got back in and, wiping the sweat from her face, wondered if she would make it in time, then she said out loud: 'Not this way, not sitting here doing nothing, I won't.' With that she started the car, found reverse gear and backed up on to the road, then twisted the steering wheel round and gently touched the throttle. Almost before she realized it the Bentley was sitting on the road, facing the right way. She started off, changing gear as she went, gathering speed till soon she was in top gear.

That six miles felt like sixty, but at last she saw the hospital, and she kept driving towards it with her hand on the horn.

This time somebody had heard her. As she stopped the car outside the hospital, a police patrol car came tearing up behind her and two big policemen got out. At first Helena was

The car hit the gate with a crash, the gate came off its hinges and locked itself round the bumper.

126

a bit scared, then she shouted: 'It's my Dad, come and help me!'

The policemen came running over and suddenly Helena was crying with relief: 'It's my Dad,' she kept repeating.

One of the policemen put his arm round her and said: 'It's all right, we'll help. Tell us all about it later, but let's get him inside.' With that, they quickly lifted her Dad and carried him into the hospital.

A few minutes later, a nurse came out, and took Helena inside, saying to the policemen, 'Now you leave her alone until she's had a cup of tea and got over the shock. She's as white as a sheet.'

A policeman answered: 'She ought to be, by the looks of that car outside.'

Helena had her cup of tea and the nurse calmed her down. Then Helena asked her to find out how her father was.

'You wait here and relax. He'll be all right, I'm sure. I'll let you know as soon as I can.' With a reassuring smile she went off down the hall.

The two policemen appeared. Seeing Helena they came over to her and one of them said: 'You look as if you've been through the mill. The car outside doesn't look too good either, so perhaps you will tell us just what happened.' He sat down and got out his notebook.

Helena repeated the whole story and the policemen were very nice to her, one of them saying: 'Well done. Your Dad will be proud of you. Now don't worry, he'll be all right here. We'll get a report from the hospital and then we'll get the car home for you. Everything will be all right.'

'I'll wait here, if you don't mind. I must phone my Mum and tell her, she doesn't know about it.'

She phoned her mother, told her what happened and she said she'd come to the hospital right away. Helena had just left the telephone when the nurse came running up the hall. When she saw Helena, she called out: 'He's all right, Helena, your Dad is fine now. He's breathing normally. He's in the intensive care unit, right out of danger, thanks to you.'

As the months passed, Helena's father made a complete recovery, and one morning Helena woke up to realize that it was her seventeenth birthday. She stood at her window, looking out at the rain, and her eyes strayed down to the drive in front of the house. Helena gasped, she couldn't believe what she saw. She rubbed her eyes and looked again. No, it hadn't gone away. It was true! She dashed downstairs, still in her pyjamas, and ran outside; she pulled up in front of the most beautiful white sports car in the whole world! Still not quite believing that it was hers, she touched its glossy sides, she rubbed it; she patted it and went whooping round the garden, shouting: 'I've got a car! I've got a car!'

Of course she woke everybody up, and as her family stood watching her, she opened the door of the car, took out the large white envelope that had been placed on the steering wheel and read the words on her birthday card. All it said was: 'To my daughter, Helena, with grateful thanks, Dad'.

THE SILENT SAVAGES
by M. S. Goodall

THE CLAN LED BY GNARK was one of the smallest in the immediate area. Ten fully-grown males, eight females and seven children; just twenty-five people in all. They were rough-skinned, shambling creatures, with bulging foreheads and hairy bodies. Clad only in worn animal skins, they covered the ground at a steady trot, their splayed feet stamping silently on the hard-packed earth of the forest floor.

Gnark had led his people from higher ground to the north, and as he reached the edge of the forest, he stopped, his sensitive nostrils flaring wide to inhale a sample of the late afternoon breeze. A dozen scents filtered through and into his brain. To the south, the ancient smell of river and marsh; to the east, a hint of rain from a dying storm. There were other odours too, but no scent of danger. Gnark knew then that the way ahead was clear and safe.

With a grunt of satisfaction, he led his people forward once again. Spread out for mile after mile in front of him were the crumbling, overgrown ruins and empty streets of what had once been the greatest capital city on Earth, the city of London. But Gnark knew nothing of the past, and cared even less. He did not know, for example, that during the fourth term of global government – in the year 2120 – an unknown micro-virus had filtered through the upper atmosphere. A deadly disease, it attacked the brain cells of every man, woman and child on Earth and destroyed the intelligence of the human race. Three-quarters of the world's population died within six months. The remainder survived as recognizable human beings, but with a mental capacity only two per cent above that of primeval man.

Cities crumbled, languages were forgotten, technology ceased to exist. Yet the new half-humans like Gnark and his clan were fulfilled and happy. Clad only in skins, communicating by grunts and gestures, they became the silent savages of the new age. Hunting with clubs, wooden spears and crudely-made bows, they ate when they were hungry and slept when they were tired. Wars and quarrels were unheard of. Knowing nothing of the past – or the future – it was an existence of peace and contentment.

But now another cold season was coming. Long dark days when biting winds would scythe the air and drive the leaves from the trees. Gnark was leading his clan to what he had come to know as 'The-Open-Space-Among-The-Tumbled-Stones'. His brain could not form such words, and his lips could not speak them, but if he had been gifted with the power of language, that is how he would have described it.

The open space was in the heart of the ruined city of London, and once it had been called Regent's Park, the home of a world-famous zoo. Gnark only knew that many wild animals roamed there – wild, ferocious animals whose skins and furs the half-humans needed for protection and warmth during the new cold season.

Once again, Gnark stopped and sniffed the air. This time his nostrils flared widely with excitement. The scent he sought was there at last, coming from a tangled patch of shrubbery no more than two hundred metres away on his left. It was rich, pungent, almost overwhelming in its freshness. Gnark estimated there were at least six – perhaps even eight – of the huge claw-toed beasts which they had come to trap.

The rest of the clan had scented them too, and, grunting nervously they began to shuffle forward, tongues clicking rapidly against their yellow teeth, shoulders hunched and deep-set eyes glowing with tension. Gnark silenced them with a wave of his right fist. He knew that if the wild beasts were to be caught, the half-humans would have to move together and work as a team. They had done this many times before, but with the coming of each new cold season, the hunt became just that little bit more difficult, the chase longer and more dangerous because the beasts themselves had become more dangerous.

With a series of short, sharp grunts and his left forefinger stabbing the air, Gnark swiftly arranged his attack formation. First, the seven small, bewildered children moved forward in a close-knit group, shambling innocently out of the undergrowth and on to the exposed terrain of a long-deserted street. The children were unarmed, mere pawns in this crude but deadly fight for survival.

Behind, led by Gnark, came the fully-grown males spread out in a semi-circle, all well-hidden, using cover, dodging from one pile of debris to the next, keeping the children in sight, staying close but not too close, crude weapons clutched tightly in their hands. Finally, there were the females; four on each flank, also armed, ready to act as an instant support team. This was Gnark's way. It was his plan, and he had evolved it slowly over many hunts at the beginning of each cold season. The idea was simple and effective. The children were used as bait. When the huge claw-toed beasts, sensing easy meat, caught their scent and moved forward to attack, Gnark and his clan leapt in to spring their trap. Until now, it had always worked, and Gnark saw no reason why it should not work again.

Once, years before, when the half-humans had been whole humans and the world an intelligent place, the claw-toed beasts had been called bears. Like all the other inmates of Regent's Park Zoo, they had been forced to fend for themselves when the deadly micro-virus destroyed their masters' brain cells. Now, along with dozens of other species normally foreign to Britain's shores, the bears had thrived and prospered. They roamed free in a land that had returned unexpectedly to nature – only Gnark, and half-humans like him, were their enemies, because the thick, fur-covered skins of the bears were vital to the people's continued existence through the harsh and deadly winter. Without the warmth of the furs, Gnark and his clan would surely die.

Now, once again, the hunt was on. Twittering nervously, stumbling and stubbing their toes on loose pieces of paving stone, the children moved uneasily down the street as living bait. A sudden change in the direction of the wind gave the bears their scent. With a concentrated roar, they burst from the tangle of shrubbery in which they had been rooting and lumbered towards the terrified children with bared and gleaming fangs.

As Gnark had suspected, there were eight of the beasts; five males and three females, all fully-grown. The fur on their backs would provide his entire clan with warm clothes for the winter, but first the charging animals had to be surrounded, cornered, and killed.

A loud shriek of command broke from Gnark's curled lips. Instantly, the children took to their heels, scattering like ants as the surprised bears slithered to a halt in the middle of the long-abandoned street. Already the male half-humans had broken cover and formed a circle. At another grunted order from Gnark, ten slim, needle-pointed wooden spears zipped through the air and found their targets. Rearing up on their hind legs, the snarling bears ripped and tore at the protruding shafts, breaking them off, hurling them to one side. But the wounds, although not mortal, had been enough to distract the animals, and too late they saw the flanking females close in from both sides. The females were armed with bows and crude arrows. Shower after shower of the tiny missiles streaked through the air and buried themselves deep in the flesh of the roaring bears.

That was when Gnark gave his final bark of command. As the animals fell and milled in confusion, the burly half-men rushed in with heavy clubs swinging. Long, flashing claws tried to slash at the half-humans' bodies, but Gnark and his companions were too nimble by far. Taken utterly by surprise, the bears succumbed slowly to the fury of the clan's attack.

Then it happened! With a growling roar of rage and desperation, the biggest bear lumbered to its feet and charged sideways through the ring of attackers. A swinging paw caught Gnark on the side of the head and sent him sprawling, momentarily dazed. Even as his vision cleared, he saw the wounded animal lurch in fury towards a jumble of debris and broken paving stones. Behind those stones, two small children were crouching in terror.

'Nuuuuugh!' The sound that tore itself from Gnark's throat was almost a spoken word, a cry of warning. But he had no speech, and his brain would not react quickly enough for the sound to come again. The dying bear reached the children before they could move. Mighty paws swept down to envelop them, and they screamed just once before the final, inevitable oblivion. Next moment, the bear too, died under a hail of arrows – but for the twin sons of Gnark, it was already too late.

Darkness fell. In the shadow of a ruined building, the task of skinning the bears was already well advanced. With small, razor-sharp stones, the half-humans worked quickly, deftly. From the high country to the north, a cold, whining wind was already snaking its way through the abandoned canyons of the long-dead city. Soon, the full harshness of the cold season would be upon them, and the people knew that unless the skins were made ready for their shivering bodies, they would die.

Gnark stood off to one side, alone. With his bare hands, he had scratched a shallow pit in the earth and laid his two sons to rest. Water fell from his eyes and he did not know why. It had been a bad hunt, but Gnark did not blame the anger of the bear. He and his people would be only too glad to leave the animals in peace if it were not for the necessity of having their skins. Those precious skins. That thick, soft, life-giving fur. Warmth. In the dreaded cold season it was as important as food, perhaps even more so. Gnark shook his head and furrowed his thick, bulbous forehead. Warmth! Was there another way to find it? Another, better way of getting it without the killing of bears . . . and through them, the killing of children? Gnark grunted and threw a stone far into the blackness of the night. If there was, it had yet to be discovered.

After the skinning the clan slept, huddled together in a remote corner of the ruined block. It was an hour before dawn when Gnark was shaken roughly awake by Feenor, the young male who had been left to stand guard outside. Feenor's eyes were wide and startled as he grunted softly and led Gnark to a place not far from where the battle with the bears had taken place.

A cold wind was still blowing steadily from the north, and as Feenor pointed excitedly with one hand, Gnark raised his nose to the breeze. Into his nostrils came a scent the like of which he had never savoured before. Sharp, strong and harsh, it seemed to claw at the back of his throat and eddy foully down into his stomach. Gnark coughed and spat upon the ground. Whatever the scent was, it obviously came from somewhere close at hand. It was hideously fresh, too.

Swiftly, Gnark decided on a course of action. Gesturing to Feenor that he was to return to the building, wake the others and bring them along, the clan leader flared his nostrils to the wind and began to track down the source of the scent. With every passing metre, the foul odour grew more pungent.

As Gnark and his people stepped out of the darkness, a warning grunt brought Rokko to his feet.

135

Gnark lowered himself to his stomach and began to crawl – through tangled bushes, clumps of nettles, bracken and thorn.

Then he saw it. No more than fifty metres ahead and partially obscured by the crumbling remains of a stone wall was a pale, yellow, flickering light. Gnark's brow furrowed deeply. It was still dark, dawn had yet to break, but ahead of him . . . *there was light.* Gnark knew that such a thing was not possible. Behind him, the rest of the clan had caught up. They too, were crawling on their hands and knees, tongues clicking softly, eyes staring ahead at the impossible sight of the impossible light.

Suddenly, Gnark caught a second scent which was filtering through 'the-one-that-was-foul'. It was the scent of people. More half-humans like themselves. Another clan. Reassured, Gnark got to his feet again and approached the crumbling wall. Beyond it, on open ground, sat at least a hundred people ringed in tight formation around the source of the light. It was a leaping, wriggling, writhing, *living* light. It came from a large, heaped pile of dead branches; a deep, sunset red in the middle which changed to a pale, muted yellow at the edges. Every now and again a half-human would throw another dead branch on to the pile, and the uncanny light would change colour and disgorge a thousand, fluttering points of glowing red upwards to the sky. Pinpricks of light which would flash for an instant and then be gone.

Off to one side of the circle, Gnark saw a tall, hulking half-human who he had met two cold seasons before. His name was Rokko, and he was the leader of this clan. More confident now, Gnark led his own band forward towards the leaping light, and as he did so, his body was enveloped in a strange, unbelievable sensation. Gone now was the bitter chill of the night air. Without new skins or furs or hides, Gnark felt *warm*. And the source of that warmth was the leaping light. It was the birth of a new era, the ultimate discovery.

136

As Gnark and his people stepped out of the darkness, a warning grunt brought big Rokko to his feet. There was silence as Gnark pointed in awe at the leaping light, and his gestures were plain for all to see. How? That was what he wanted to know. How was it done, how was it made, how was it fed, and what was it called?

Rokko picked up two small sticks and drew himself fully erect. Facing Gnark, he made a violent movement with the sticks, rubbing them together, slowly at first, then more quickly. Suddenly – abruptly – he threw the sticks aside and pointed at the leaping colours beside him. A short, sharp sound burst from his open mouth. Like a grunt, but more than a grunt. A spoken word! 'Fi-re,' said Rokko clearly. '*Fire!*' Then he pushed Gnark in the chest and watched him stagger back into the arms of his people.

Gnark recovered his balance and came forward again. It was obvious that the secret of the leaping light – the thing called 'fire', the giver of warmth – was connected with the rubbing together of two small sticks. Gnark needed that secret for his own clan. All half-humans were friends, so why was Rokko acting so strangely? He *must* have the secret. He must have it now!

But as Gnark reached out the hand of friendship, Rokko whirled, lips drawn back in a yellow-toothed snarl. His sinewy fingers fastened round the smaller man's neck and began to squeeze with a violent determination. Gnark stood quite still, unable to comprehend what was happening. No half-human had ever used violence unless it was to clothe or feed a member of his clan. And no half-human had ever used violence on one of his own kind.

All at once, Gnark felt pain. Under the fierce pressure of Rokko's fingers, his vital air supply was being cut off, and he knew then that this was a time like no other. His dull, slow-moving mind told him that something was desperately wrong.

Told him that he had to fight back . . . for life itself.

Up swept Gnark's right foot. The gnarled, trail-hardened toes smashed into Rokko's shin and sent him reeling off balance. As the fingers released their pressure on his throat, Gnark moved instantly into the attack. A strange new emotion was stirring within him, a fierce and exultant passion that suddenly could not be controlled. Picking up a large rock, he flung himself on Rokko with all the strength at his command.

The battle was fought savagely and without quarter. Ten minutes later, Gnark rose alone, the undisputed victor. Breathing heavily, he turned to face the assembled people. Never before had he felt so strong, so brave, so powerful. All these half-humans were his now, they would follow him without question. And the secret of the leaping light – that too, would be his, because no member of Rokko's clan would refuse to answer so fierce a warrior.

An arrogant sneer crossed Gnark's face, and a short, sharp sound burst from his open mouth. Like the sound from Rokko's mouth, it was more than a grunt, it was a spoken word – and the silent savages were silent no longer.

Language had been born once again among the half-humans of planet Earth. The first word they had used was 'fire'. The second word was 'WAR'!

ARTSAR AND KENDALL

by Andrew Muir

KENDALL SHOOK HIS FIST in anger at the Kryall circling high overhead. Another arrow wasted! It had been an infuriating day for the best huntsman of the Verandi. His catch was much less than usual and his pride would suffer unless he finished the afternoon very well indeed. His task would not be any easier if he continued to scare away the birds!

But Kendall could not concentrate on his hunting today; he had even bigger worries on his mind.

As spring arrived tensions were beginning to mount in the lake-dwelling community of the Verandi. At spring's-end, Kendall and his twin brother, Artsar, would reach their twenty-first birthdays and it would be time for Artsar, the elder by an hour, to become Chief of the Islands. This was the cause of the tension.

With a massive effort of will power, Kendall put all thoughts except hunting from his mind. He moved with great stealth despite his strong, tall frame and chose a new hiding place to await the next Kryall arriving.

The sun was cold, but bright, and very welcome after the long months of winter. The ice was beginning to break around the Lake and soon the spring and summer hunting seasons would begin. Kendall was very glad of this. Weeks of hunting the Kryall were becoming boring to him and he could find little pleasure in fishing, the only winter alternative. Fishing in winter was a slow process of making (or finding) a hole in the ice at a choice spot and then waiting all day for the Trupps to bite. Hunting Kryall at least afforded Kendall some degree of excitement and challenge. The trick was to shoot the bird just as it caught a fish in its long beak. For the better huntsmen, like Kendall, the further aim was to wait until the bird left the ice-break and then shoot it. If the timing was perfect both bird *and* fish could be retrieved.

So far on this particular day Kendall had caught only three birds and one fish.

At the same time as Kendall was having trouble hunting, his father, Chief Travlock, was presiding over a stormy meeting of the leading men from the various island settlements.

Chief Travlock was sitting at the head of a beautiful oak table in the largest room of his dwelling. Seated around the table were the six most respected men of the Verandi, including the burly figure of Chert Dergill, a loyal, but impetuous, man who held great sway among the people, especially in his home island. It was he who was speaking now:

'My Lord Chief, I do not wish to be overly forward but I feel someone must express these feelings. Your time as Chief has only a few months left, as your sons will soon be twenty-one. It is an unusual case for our people to have twin heirs to the leadership, indeed it is unique. Although not wishing to slight Artsar, I myself and my people feel Kendall to be more worthy of the Chieftainship.'

'Dergill! This is an outrageous statement to make before me. If your loyalty was not well proven I should slay you for these words. We have only one immediate heir to the throne and that is Artsar. Moreover Artsar has already shown he is thoroughly competent and has been a great asset to our tribe. Your words are close to treason.'

'Forgive me, my Lord, Artsar's competence and wisdom are well-known and I intended no slight on him. However, it is Kendall who excels in hunting and fighting and who relishes these things. Artsar takes no pleasure in hunting and has even declared himself averse to battle.'

'Artsar is the best fisher as Kendall is the best hunter, and Artsar's wisdom has helped clothe and feed our people through these last harsh winters,' the Chief declared icily.

'Indisputable, my Lord, but is weaving or the storing of foods the concern of a chief?'

'You try my patience mightily, Dergill. Artsar's mind is his own and his actions have been fruitful. Kendall may excel in many things we consider important but Artsar performs creditably enough in those fields and excels in others.'

'But . . .'

'Enough! Artsar is my eldest son and shall succeed me by the ancient laws of our people. Another complaint from any of you, including yourself, Dergill, shall be treated as disloyalty. Artsar will soon be Chief and as such will command your utmost respect and obedience. That is all, the subject is closed.'

Fortunes had changed for the better for Kendall by the time his day's hunting was over. Seven birds and four fish were a good catch even by his standards. The last two hours had turned out more profitably than he could have hoped for.

Dragging his haul home on a sledge he noticed the ice was showing signs of beginning to break up. Soon he would have the freedom of the Lake again. This could be the last hunting trip he would have by the frozen island shores this year.

As he approached the island centre he was greeted by Frelmer, a younger friend who was always eager to share his company. Frelmer was delighted at meeting Kendall and happily examined the catch. 'Seven and four! Well done again, Kendall. I wager Artsar could never catch anything like that.'

A shadow passed across Kendall's face as his hitherto

forgotten worries returned. He rounded angrily on his friend. 'Frelmer, I am shocked to hear you utter such petty thoughts. I am not in competition with my brother. If you care for my friendship you will love and honour him as I do. If you wish to speak with me again you will apologize for your words. Goodbye.'

Kendall strode home, further troubled by the situation he was unwillingly causing.

A few weeks passed during which the ice melted, and any thoughts on Artsar's succession were voiced well away from Chief Travelock or Kendall. Artsar himself seemed undisturbed by the latent feelings in the tribe. He continued in his own individual manner and was now involved with entertaining a visitor to the settlements. There was little he enjoyed as much as learning of the world outside the Lake.

Travellers were a rare phenomenon in the isolated communities of the Verandi. In general the only visitors were sellers of ware or solitary hunters trading their catch for food and lodgings. This particular traveller, 'Eemir', came from a coastal community further up to the north of the Lake, and had a strange tale to tell. He was fortunate that he was talking to Artsar, because the other Verandi would have no time for the man's strange, 'corrupt', speech and customs. His soiled appearance was taken by them as a confirmation of vulgar vagrancy – a charge levelled at all strangers by the insular Lakesmen.

Eemir did indeed look a sorry sight as he sat in the cultivated splendour of Artsar's rooms. But his appearance belied the importance of the news he brought with him. He spoke slowly, trying to find the correct phrases in this somewhat different tongue:

'Artsar, you have shared with me a horn of rich, dark mead. I shall now share my news with you. It is dark news, in the worst sense, but the learning of it should be a rich gift to your people, if they heed my tale. For my tale is a tale of warning. I come from the north, as you know, from the Kamper tribe. If I may still say so; you see, my tribe is no more – I am the last of the Kampers.'

Artsar made a movement to express shock and sorrow but Eemir forestalled him. 'No sympathy please, my friend. You knew nothing of my people so your grief would be for me only. And I am still alive and trying to avenge my people rather than merely grieving.

'We were wiped out two months ago by a raiding force from across the fierce sea to the north-west. A great force of mighty warriors who killed us with the greatest of ease before settling in our town. I was struck by an axe which shattered my helmet in two and I lay as dead for many hours. But the blow had been deflected and I was stunned, not dead. I recovered consciousness to find myself lying in a mound of bodies, the corpses of my people, men and children all dead. The Northerners had already taken what wives they wanted and were celebrating in the centre of our village.'

Eemir went on to speak of his life since the invaders had wiped out his tribe. He had wandered southwards down the coast, warning settlements of the encroaching invaders who were following his path down the shoreline. Many had ignored him and perished; some had prepared to defend themselves and still perished. Others had fled and were drifting in to the mainland over the mountains, their old ways of life lost for ever.

He concluded that the invaders, though less in numbers by now, would sail up the river to the Lake settlements in the forthcoming weeks and urged Artsar to persuade the Verandi to prepare for a fierce battle or they would surely be wiped out.

Artsar was convinced by the man's sorry tale and persuaded his father to call a large meeting to hear the story and plan what must be done. However, the Lakesmen were sceptical of the news. They had lived too long in relative peace to believe this story of an alien invasion. They spoke scornfully of 'doom-mongering' and felt with contempt that the vagabond stranger was trying to attract attention to himself. It took all of Artsar's eloquence to persuade the meeting that new weapons must be made ready and a watch kept on the entrance to the Lakes. He alone agreed with Eemir's sorrowful observation that there was little hope that this would be enough.

It was only thirteen days later that Frelmer, (once more in Kendall's favour), was taking the dawn watch. He cursed his luck for being stuck on this hill in the early hours of a miserable day. There was a fierce wind blowing from the north which sent an endless progression of dark clouds across the sky.

'Here I am stuck on this stupid hill, frozen to my bones, all because Artsar was taken in by a mad tramp . . .' But his thoughts were interrupted by a sight that chilled him more than the wind ever could. A long, dark ship sailed into view through the mist.

Frelmer was so astonished that he stood staring for a moment before grabbing his horn and blowing a loud, long wail. This was echoed down the hills around the Lake. Seconds later the settlements were thrown into consternation by the alarm they had never expected to hear.

Weapons were hastily taken up and the men rushed to the shore of the main island. The women and children assembled fretfully in the central buildings.

Artsar and Eemir were the only people who were expecting an attack. Already dressed and ready, they were first to arrive on the shore. Minutes later, Chief Travelock led the men from the main settlement to join them. 'Well traveller, you were right after all. Let us hope the attack is not as fearsome as you also predicted.'

Frelmer grabbed his horn and blew a loud, long wail.

Soon Dergill and the men from the other, smaller, islands swelled the ranks of the defenders. Dergill was in a happy mood. He roared his orders with a huge, expansive grin on his face. 'Ha! Artsar,' he bellowed, 'I never believed you for a moment, but I relish being mistaken; it is too long since we had real battle.'

But soon there was little time for laughter. The tribes had not arrived in time to prevent the raiders reaching the far end of the shore below them. Chief Travlock would have led his men in a fierce charge down the slope to the pebble beach as soon as his forces were complete.

'No, my father,' Artsar implored him, 'let them come to us. The rush up the slope will take the wind from them. Then *we* charge.'

Travlock looked warily at his son for a moment – the words spoken at the past council table rising insidiously into his mind. But the wisdom of Artsar had been praised before; his eyes were resolute, it was not any lack of courage that held him back.

'Are you sure, my brother?' cried Kendall, eager to prove his worth in the fray. Artsar nodded.

Chief Travlock hesitated a moment, then said: 'We do as Artsar advises.'

The long line of helmeted invaders stood ready on the shore. Too many easy victories had made them supremely confident. Spears and swords were brandished, and they released a great shout – almost as if they expected the islanders to run away in fear.

Then they charged up the slope towards the defenders, hurling threats and battle cries as they came. The impatience in the ranks of the Lakesmen was almost palpable, but the Chief's firm command held the islanders back.

The charging wave was on the last quarter of the slope when it seemed almost to pause – it was the crucial moment Artsar had predicted, when the charge's exuberant rush up the slope left the opposing force gasping for a moment. 'Now! My father,' uttered Artsar grimly.

Forward stepped the Chief in front of his ranks, raised his sword in the air, and bellowed the ancient Verandi war cry. The army of islanders swept down like an irresistible flood. Swords and spears glinted in the sun. Their line of battle hurled itself on the enemy, sword and spear found a place in alien flesh. The invaders held for a moment, then the clash of weapons, the screams of dying men echoed in the air.

The onward rush of the islanders proved too much for the invaders and their line fell back, stumbling over the bodies of those already fallen. The Lakesmen pushed after them; knots of men held for a moment before being broken up as the Verandi threw the men from the north into disarray.

The battle reached the shore. The enemy line looked as if it would break in complete disorder. Then – on the very point of victory – tragedy struck the Verandi.

Chief Travlock somehow became separated from his immediate bodyguard in the confusion of the fray. In an instant three of the fierce invading warriors were on him. Nobly the Chief fought them, and called on his comrades. But the Northerners had seen what was happening and rushed to prevent any help reaching him.

Even so, Chief Travlock held all three at bay though they forced him backwards. Then the chief tripped over a fallen victim as he backed before the onslaught. In an instant the leader of the attackers was on him and a broad blade buried itself in the heart of the Verandi's chief.

The battle seemed to halt for a moment; the fighters looked over to the spot where Chief Travlock had fallen. New heart surged into the invaders, sudden shock threatened to numb the powers of the islanders. It was a desperate moment.

Suddenly the ferocious Verandi war cry rent the near

silence that had fallen, and a figure dashed from a group nearby the spot, straight to the victorious killer of Chief Travlock. In a flash, he had embedded his sword in the warrior's throat. Even before the slain man fell, the figure was attacking the rest of the attackers with a tremendous ferocity, driving them relentlessly back. Artsar (for it was he) beat down the defending sword of one and plunged his own weapon deep into the enemy's breast.

The cry from the Verandi nearly tore the sky in two, and they lunged at the foe with redoubled efforts. No force could have stopped them then, and the edge of the sea grew red with the invaders' blood, until there was only a handful of Northerners left standing.

But still they fought on. Their warrior style of life admitted only victory or death. The Verandi were forced to pick off the remaining enemy one by one. The Lakesmen's lust for blood was incensed and they gleefully hacked away at the small band of surviving Northerners.

Artsar, Kendall and Dergill had disposed of their latest combatants and stood slightly aside watching the bloody, and by now inevitable, fate of the invaders.

Dergill spoke first: 'You are chief now, Artsar, and well worthy of the title. You gave us heart for battle when your noble father fell.'

'Yes, the cost was high indeed,' interposed Kendall with a heavy heart.

'And the vengeance grows bloodier still,' commented Artsar as he watched the hard pressed invaders fall one by one.

The Northerners were clustered around one man, obviously a great fighter. But minute by minute their circle grew smaller until there were only two left standing. A dozen Verandi pressed in and claimed another victim almost instantaneously. Seconds later the last warrior was disarmed and encircled. The triumphant Verandi led him up to Artsar. The

Northerner showed no sign of fear and looked Artsar straight in the face, holding his head high and proud.

'Come here, Eemir, you can communicate with these people,' Artsar instructed. 'Tell this man that he is free to go, to mourn his people and to tell of the might of the Verandi.'

When the words were repeated in his own tongue, the warrior shook his head, and spoke rapidly to Eemir. Eemir translated that the warrior's code demanded that he fight on, for it was unthinkable for him to go on living after a defeat. He would challenge all the Verandi one by one; or, if they had no pride, take them all on at once. He must fight on, to show respect for his fellows who had died.

A brief consultation with Kendall and Dergill made Artsar decide to accept the ways of the foreign warrior. Kendall in particular was, as always, hotly declaring that honour must be seen to be done.

'You speak wisely, brother Kendall. This last survivor must be given the respect of the honest fight he deserves. And in this way we shall also honour our dead and our great chief's memory. We shall match this proud Northerner with our greatest warrior.'

Kendall rejoiced at these words. His brother would step forward as undisputed leader of his people in one-man combat. Confidence in his brother as chief had been assured by his wise defensive tactic and courageous action in the battle. He was now following these actions with a display of honour and bravery. Kendall and the other Verandis stepped back dutifully and respectfully.

'You misunderstand me, my brother.' A wry smile crossed the new chief's face. 'Our greatest warrior is what I said, and our greatest warrior is *you!* Only you can do honour to all sides.'

The people murmured in astonishment. It was unheard of for a chief not to claim the title of their greatest warrior.

'But, my brother . . .' Kendall hesitantly began.

'Do you question your Chief? Of all the Verandi, Kendall, you are the last I would expect to be slow to obey my command.' Artsar's voice rang out with an assured, steely quality that had not been heard from him before. The murmurings were quelled.

Kendall looked at his brother's eyes and was met with an intense, determined stare. His pride and confidence soared. 'You are correct, my Lord, as always. I thank you for the honour and obey your orders in the name of you and our islands.'

The Verandi made a circle on the corpse-strewn shore and Kendall went forward to meet the challenge of the Northerner. He gripped his sword tightly and signalled for the fight to begin. Both men were tired after the battle but it did not seem so when the furious duel began. Up and down the sand dunes they fought, first one attacking, then the other. Every eye was glued on the contest so no-one noticed the pale, pained face of Artsar, which contorted with worry each time Kendall was pushed back. Twenty minutes passed with both swordsmen sustaining slight injuries, and still the battle raged on.

Kendall was on the defensive, parrying thrusts desperately as the Northerner bore down on him. The shouts of encouragement from the watchers turned into groans as Kendall seemed to weaken under a ferocious onslaught. The foreign warrior drew his sword over his head and crashed a double-handed blow to the hard pressed Kendall. Caught off-balance, Kendall met the blow with his shield, and the force of the stroke sent him flying to the ground.

With a roar of triumph, the Northerner jumped forward to finish him off. But Kendall, in a last desperate move, rolled forward, throwing his advancing enemy to the ground. Quick as lightning, Kendall was on his feet and drove his sword through the chest of his surprised foe. A great shout of delight went up from the islanders as they rushed to congratulate Kendall.

There was much feasting and drinking on the main island that night. The Verandi danced and sang their celebrations and blessed the departed chief for the two sons he had given to the tribe.

It was late that night that Artsar made his astonishing speech. 'My people, I rejoice to see you celebrating tonight. Although you grieve my dead father, it is indeed a night for joy. Our victory is the finest parting gift we could give him.'

A roar of approval echoed through the hall.

'Although the time may seem inopportune to those of you who are having difficulty concentrating (*much laughter at this*) I have something of great import to tell you.' He paused to let the hubbub die down.

'I am gratified by your ready acceptance of myself as new chief but I know that there were many of you who had misgivings in the past months!'

A sudden silence fell, and many were ashamed to look each other in the face. Dergill interrupted: 'My Lord, many of us are guilty for misjudging you, myself more than most. I admit my mistake – as I know all others would – and respectfully ask your forgiveness, though I will not ask for mercy. I shamed my position in the tribe by doubting you.'

'Dergill, I do not want you to ask forgiveness and I am most certainly not blaming anyone for doubting me. I understand fully the reasons for the misgivings I am talking about, and, though disagreeing with them, I can respect the motives behind them. I know I am, shall we say, slightly eccentric, compared to the customary behaviour around me.' Some laughter arose, but died out in a mixture of confusion and embarrassment.

'I think it takes more than courage and prowess in battle to make a great chief, it also requires knowledge and wisdom. However, I do not think these qualities need to be within one man; it is well known that my brother and I have different talents. Our people would be best served by having both of us at their head, so I propose that you have two chiefs! Kendall will remain here and maintain your security, and I will travel far with my friend, Eemir. We will learn of other people and their ways, we will make friends and have pacts to ensure that no tribe is attacked in isolation again.'

After a minute's stunned silence, there was a hint of a rumbling disagreement which Artsar quickly quelled by announcing in his sternest voice: 'I have spoken! My last decree as sole chief is to declare that there are now two chiefs; and bravery and fighting skills will be married to wisdom and understanding.'

So dawned a new era for the Verandi – an age which would see them grow and develop, make many friends, and eventually head a strong alliance of tribes to live securely in peace and prosperity.

EXTERMINATORS FROM SPACE
by Alan A. Grant

LEFT – FIRE! FIRE! FIRE! RIGHT – FIRE! FIRE!
FIRE! LEFT – FIRE! LEFT – FIRE! FIRE!

A SMALL CROWD HAD GATHERED round fourteen-year-old Zak
Spencer as he pumped the controls of the latest addition to his
father's amusement arcade – the *Exterminators from Space.*

'Look at that lad go!'

'He's got fifty-five thousand – and no-one else has got past
twenty thousand!'

'Keep going, Zak!'

Zak Spencer didn't even hear the cries of encouragement.
When Zak played, his mind focussed on one thing only – the
game.

LEFT – FIRE! FIRE! RIGHT – FIRE! FIRE! DODGE
THAT PHOTON BOMB – FIRE! FIRE! FIRE!

Ever since it had arrived, the new machine had fascinated
Zak, partly because the tiny alien figures that jerked
spasmodically across its screen seemed to hold a specially
sinister quality – but mainly because of the bright flashing
panel which read: SPECIAL SUDDEN-DEATH
FEATURE WHEN 100 000 SCORED. As yet, no-one knew
what that Sudden-death Feature was. No-one had seen it. No-
one had even come close to scoring the magic one hundred
thousand. But Zak Spencer was the best player in town . . .

Now, beads of sweat studded his forehead and his damp
hands were slippery on the Fire buttons. A line of new

attackers appeared, peeling off in twos and threes, zigzagging towards his Defender, their laser cannon blasting.

LEFT – FIRE! RIGHT – FIRE! LEFT – FIRE! RIGHT – RIGHT – RIGHT –

Too late! Zak's Defender disintegrated into a thousand rainbow pieces as a swooping Exterminator obliterated it. There was a murmur of disappointment from Zak's audience, now twelve-strong with the addition of Willy Mauchin, the arcade attendant.

'Two lives gone – but he's sitting on sixty-four thousand!'

Zak's last Defender – a tiny digital 'man' carrying what looked like a bazooka – was crossing the screen to take up its position in the centre. More of the attacking forces flooded into the top of the screen – and battle was joined once more.

Zak played like an automaton, his fingers welded to the control buttons. The onlookers' excited babble rose as Exterminators perished and Zak's score mounted: seventy thousand – seventy-three thousand – seventy-five thousand . . .

LEFT – FIRE! LEFT – FIRE!

Now catch that troop-ship streaking across. Mystery bonus: one thousand.

'Go to it, Zak,' Willy Mauchin yelped. His own highest score had been just over nine thousand and he recognized a master when he saw one. Zak was oblivious to his voice. Nothing existed but him and the machine.

Eighty thousand – eighty-one thousand. LEFT – FIRE! RIGHT – FIRE! LEFT –

BOOOOM!

There was a loud gasp of disappointment as Zak's last Defender fell to the invading Exterminator hordes. The screen lit up with digital letters: GAME OVER. SCORE 83 800. RATING – HONOURED ENEMY. INSERT COINS FOR NEW GAME.

The small knot of spectators filtered away.

'Hard luck, kid – you nearly made it,' a man said, patting Zak on the back as he passed.

'Cheer up, Zak me boy.' Willy Mauchin's toothless mouth formed a grin. 'At least you're an "Honoured Enemy". Nobody else has done better than "Laser Fodder"!'

Zak didn't reply. He felt exhausted, totally drained, the way he always was after a hard game. And to have come so close . . .

He looked again at the still-flashing HI-SCORE: 83 800. Normally, a total like that would have had Zak buzzing with pleasure – but now, somehow, there was only a deep disappointment.

Zak had wanted to reach the Sudden-death Feature ever since he'd first set eyes on *Exterminators from Space*. Day by day his scores had mounted, creeping ever closer to that elusive hundred thousand.

Now, he never bothered with the other electronic machines in his father's amusement arcade, the Spencer Thrillorama. Each day, as soon as he got home from school, Zak headed straight for the Exterminators – and another stab at that seemingly unattainable special feature.

The clock struck six as Burt Spencer came through the wide swing doors. 'Time to close up, Willy,' he began, then stopped as he saw his son standing with glazed eyes, staring at the machine.

'Probably spent his last twenty pence again,' Burt thought sourly. 'The boy's becoming obsessed with that machine! I'm sorry I ever allowed it into my arcade.'

Right from the start, a certain mystery had surrounded the Exterminators machine. It had arrived one day when Burt was up in London on business. Willy Mauchin had taken delivery, and when Burt had returned it was already installed, hooked up between *Mole-hunter* and *Galazians*.

'I didn't order that,' Burt protested.

'Th-the delivery man said it was on a-approval from the Galactic Games Company,' old Willy stuttered worriedly. 'I hope I haven't done anything wrong, Mr Spencer.'

'No, no, it's okay, Willy. I'll get in touch with these Galactic Games people and find out what this approval scheme's all about.' He glanced over and saw that a queue was already forming by the new machine. 'The customers seem to like it. Leave it where it is for the moment.'

Burt Spencer checked the phone directory that night, and then Directory Enquiries. No number was listed for Galactic Games. Next day, he checked with the Companies' Register; there was no such firm as Galactic Games, or anything even remotely like it.

Curiouser and curiouser, Burt thought.

Out in the arcade, there seemed to be an almost permanent line of people by the *Exterminators from Space*. Burt Spencer was never one to look a gift horse in the mouth. Whoever Galactic Games were, if they wanted to leave a brand-new machine with him, who was he to argue? No doubt somebody would turn up to claim it – until then it could rake in the cash!

That had been a month ago – and nobody ever had turned up.

Now, Burt shook his son's arm to snap him out of his reverie. 'You at that bloomin' machine again?' he snapped. 'So help me, Zak, if you don't give it a rest I'm going to have to stop your pocket money!'

'But, Dad – I've *got* to make that hundred thousand! I've just got to play the Sudden-death Feature!' Zak began, but his father cut him short.

'You'll get sudden death from my hand in a minute, lad! Stop wasting time and get upstairs for dinner. I'm locking up.'

After dinner, Zak's father insisted he do two solid hours'

homework – even though Zak didn't have any to do. 'That'll maybe take your mind off Space Exterminators,' he rapped.

'Have you been at that stupid machine again?' his mother chipped in. 'Honest to goodness, Zackary . . .'

Zak fled to his bedroom to avoid the combined attack. But although he sat with his Maths jotters open on his knee, the figures that danced before his eyes were small and red and green and somehow sinister . . .

His parents didn't understand. The Exterminators were there – and Zak *had* to fight them, had to *win!*

That night, Zak Spencer had a dream – a dream as strange as it was startling. Zak was alone, sitting in complete and utter darkness. Then came a glow, an eerie green glow first a mere pinpoint of throbbing light – then it was rushing towards him, growing, expanding, until it hovered over him, pulsing with menace. It became a huge repulsive shape – with a face that was exquisitely sinister!

'Greetings, Honoured Enemy. I am The Exterminator.' Its voice was an electronic scream that jangled in Zak's brain. 'I have come for you.'

In his dream, Zak fought to tear his eyes away from the evil vision, but to no avail. It was as if he were paralysed, powerless before it.

'Come,' the creature cried. 'The game waits. You can release us. Come . . . Come!'

Zak awoke sitting up. In a daze, he rubbed at his eyes. 01.30, he read on his bedside clock. What a nightmare!

He slid out of bed, crossed to the window, and threw it open to take a breath of fresh air.

Zak's room was on the first floor of the building; below, the arcade jutted out. He stared down through the arcade skylight – and the hairs on the back of his neck stood up.

The *Exterminators from Space* machine was switched on!

Again, that voice seemed to reverberate through Zak's

head: 'The game waits. Come . . . Come.'

Without quite knowing why, Zak knew that he just *had* to go. His slippers were left unnoticed by his bed; his dressing gown stayed where it hung on the door. Clad only in his pyjamas, Zak left his bedroom and crept along the hall to the kitchen.

The house was silent as he eased open the door. There, on the mantelpiece, were his father's keys – the keys to the arcade.

They rattled noisily, and Zak froze. 'What am I doing here?' he thought suddenly. 'If Dad catches me, I'm for it!'

And then the voice – 'Come . . . Come!'

And Zak went.

Moments later, he turned the key in the small door that connected house and arcade. Inside, all was dark – except for the space between *Galazians* and *Mole-hunter*, where the *Exterminators from Space* pulsed quietly . . . ominously.

Zak walked slowly towards the machine. The screen cleared, and then bold digital lettering showed:

CREDIT ONE GAME. PUSH SOLO PLAYER START.

As if of their own volition, Zak's fingers crept along the keyboard, pressed the one-player button. A series of wild electronic whistles issued from the machine – and the first wave of Exterminators jerked on-screen.

Zak's left hand was already skimming over the direction control as his first Defender reached the centre. The forefinger of his right hand stabbed once, twice, three times on the Fire button – and three Exterminators exploded in quick succession.

The game was on.

LEFT – FIRE! FIRE! RIGHT – FIRE! FIRE!

Fire and move and fire again. Never let them home in on a sitting target. Watch out for those photon bombs – they came every sixteen seconds at this stage.

The controls felt good beneath Zak's hands. He was into the

rhythm already, and the Exterminators' numbers steadily dwindled.

Fresh lines of attackers appeared on the screen, their laser cannon seeking him relentlessly. Zak despatched them almost with contempt. Another wave appeared, and another. Zak didn't bother looking at his score. He could feel it in his bones – he was on form tonight.

Nothing could stop him.

BOOM!

Zak's Defender was hit, annihilated. On the screen, a caption flared: TOO COCKY, ZAK. CONCENTRATE.

The machine was speaking to him! Zak bit his lip, focused his entire attention on the screen. Defender number two was taking up position. SCORE – 6050. Not good.

Then they were on him again and there was no more time to think, just react.

The minutes ticked by. There was no-one passing the arcade at that late hour, no-one to notice the green glow of the Exterminators machine, no-one to see the figure of the boy hunched over it, locked in grim battle . . .

Zak lost his second Defender at ninety-one thousand and fifty. His expression did not change. He had them now – he knew it.

As if agreeing with him, the screen flashed: ALMOST THERE, ZAK. WE ARE WAITING.

The Exterminators moved quickly now, almost faster than the eye could follow. Photon bombs merged with meteor streams in an unending assault. The screen was crisscrossed by swarming attackers blazing laser death.

Zak took them in his stride. Ninety-six thousand. He was smiling now, supremely confident. Ninety-eight thousand, five hundred. A large troop transporter weaved across the top of the screen, dropping photon bombs in whirling clusters. Zak's left hand touched the Direction control. His index finger jabbed once –

– and he was leaping in the air in triumph even before his Defender's laser-bolt drove home with a heart-stopping BAM.

One hundred thousand!

The screen seemed to explode in a cascade of glittering rainbow shards. Zak blinked – and when he looked again, there was . . . The Exterminator.

'Congratulations, Zak Spencer. You have truly earned the distinction we bestow upon you.'

As it spoke, the image on the screen leaned forward. Its flickering arms seemed to reach out and encircle Zak's neck.

'I hereby appoint you EARTH DEFENDER, Grade 1.'

Zak looked down, and round his neck hung a heavy metal chain with a brightly-polished medallion. On it was inscribed 'EARTH DEFENDER'. His mouth fell open. 'Wh-what is this? Wh-what's going on here?'

'We are the Exterminators,' the grim face on the screen replied. 'We roam the cosmos, seeking worlds to conquer. You have found the key which unlocks the dimension-warp to your planet. Even now the Exterminator forces gather, making ready for the invasion of Earth!'

'In-invade Earth?' Zak stammered. 'You – you can't!'

'We can and we will – unless you, Zak Spencer, can prevent us.'

'M-me? What d'you mean?'

'We are a fair race. We give our victims one chance.' The grotesque figure on the screen leaned forward again, pointing a pulsating finger at Zak. 'For Earth, *you* are that chance. Go ahead, Zak Spencer – now you will find out what the Sudden-death Feature is all about!'

The Exterminator withdrew again into the screen, pulsing there, menacing. 'Press the Sudden-death button. Win – and Earth is saved. Lose – and your planet dies.'

Zak's eyes were glued to the screen. His mouth hung open

Zak's hand twitched towards the
Sudden-death button. Then he
pressed . . .

with the enormity of what he'd done. Even though it was only a shadow flickering on the screen now, he knew that somehow – incredibly – it was all *real*, frighteningly real.

His hand twitched towards the Sudden-death button.

And pressed.

The screen erupted! Meteors, comets, stars whirled dizzily around him. Zak felt himself falling, spinning, as if the machine had swallowed him up.

It might have been a second later, it might have been eternity. Zak was sitting on a platform whirling in Space high above the Earth. In his hands was the cool metal grip of a laser-blaster. Beneath his feet were a set of delicate pedals – direction controls!

And there, sweeping round from behind the Moon, a formation of Exterminator craft, white streaks of death spurting from their nose-cannon.

Zak stamped hard with his left foot, not knowing which pedal he hit. The platform spun crazily away, and the first Exterminator laser-bolts shot by him.

Then his gun was up and Zak was firing. No emotion showed in his face as the lead craft, in the very centre of the formation, shattered. The game had begun – battle was joined!

The wedge of attackers splintered, whirled, and came rushing at Zak from every direction. A thrill ran through him as a fiery bolt clipped the edge of his platform. He was in his element.

'They might beat me,' he thought, 'but no-one will ever say Earth died without a fight!' Then he was whirling again, dodging, moving – firing, firing, always firing – fighting as he'd never fought before.

An attacker dived by, and exploded in a crimson fireflash as Zak's lethal beams sought it out. Ship after ship swooped past and was destroyed by the Earth Defender's deadly accuracy.

On they came, and on, never giving him a moment's respite. His platform was a blur as it manoeuvred to avoid the lacework of laser beams.

The barrel of his gun glowed red-hot as Zak sent bolt after bolt streaking through Space into the enemy ranks. Thwup! Thwup! Thwup! Another alien craft blew up, then another, and another . . .

Then suddenly they were gone and in their place, filling the heavens, was a gargantuan battlecraft. A dozen photon torpedoes whistled from its tubes; from its forward turrets an incessant rain of fragmentation bombs poured.

Zak sent the platform into an emergency dive. A frag-bomb burst, and shrapnel gashed his face. He didn't notice the pain. He was already training his gun, letting loose with a salvo of laser-bolts that exploded against the giant attacker's forward turrets, ripping them apart.

Still the massive death-machine came on. It was everywhere now, circling Zak. Instinctively, the fourteen-year-old Earth Defender knew he could run no more. Spinning the platform, Zak dived – this time *towards* the looming bulk of the battleship. His finger was frozen in the Fire position, a continuous storm of destruction spitting from its spiral barrel.

Zak's mouth formed a defiant snarl, and he heard his own voice screaming as he plunged: 'Kill me, Exterminators – but Zak Spencer of Earth will take you with him!'

There was a blinding flash, an ear-splitting roar . . . and Zak Spencer knew no more.

It was morning when Burt Spencer found him. Zak lay slumped across the now-silent *Exterminators from Space* machine.

'Blimey!' he exclaimed. 'Young blighter's been down here all night!'

Zak came round in a daze, to find his father roughly jerking his arm and yelling in his ear: 'That does it, Zak! I've had it up to here with you and this machine! So help me, Zak, I swear you'll get no more pocket money for a year! And as for this machine . . .' Burt stopped. 'What have you done to it?'

The screen was blackened and cracked like an eggshell. The plastic casing was charred and melted.

Zak blinked. 'Then . . . I won.'

'What d'you mean – won?' his father roared. 'You've wrecked the bloomin' machine! It's only fit for scrap now!'

'It wasn't me, Dad,' Zak protested. 'There were these Exterminators, see. They came and came, but I fought them, Dad. I killed them all! *I saved the Earth, Dad!*'

'Saved the Earth? You've been up all night playing this blasted machine – and you've ruined it for good!'

Something popped in Zak's mind. He looked around him. Reality. The arcade, chilly at eight o'clock in the morning. The machines silent.

Had it all been a dream?

Zak felt totally dejected. It must have been a dream. There could be no other explanation.

'Now get upstairs,' his father ordered. 'You've cut your face. Get your mum to put something on it.'

Zak turned and shuffled towards the connecting door.

'And while you're at it,' his father went on, 'take that stupid thing off from round your neck!'

Zak looked down. A heavy metal chain hung there. His fingers clasped the badge of shiny metal, twisted it so that he could read it.

EARTH DEFENDER, it said.

His father's angry voice followed him up the stairs: 'When the man from Galactic Games turns up, *you* can explain what happened to his *Exterminators from Space!*'

Zak smiled. He knew no-one would ever come.

SIX-TEN TO TANBURY

by Angus Allan

IT HAD BEEN A LONG DAY for David Fordham. His parents had roused him at five-thirty, and while the newly-risen sun did its best to drive off the dawn mist, the boy made an eager and excited breakfast. His bag had been packed on the previous evening, so there was no need to worry about that. But his father said: 'Hurry it up now, son. We don't want you missing the coach from Castle Dunham.'

'Give a bloke a chance, Dad,' said David through a mouthful of egg, and added, 'Sorry, Mum,' as he saw her frown of disapproval.

'You've got some on your chin, now,' she tutted. 'I can't think what your Auntie Margaret's going to say if you gobble like a pig.'

'She keeps pigs, so she's used to them,' grinned David, refusing to be put down in the first moments of his holiday.

His father took him to the end of the lane, where, as arranged, one of the local farmers picked him up to run him into the market town. 'You take care now,' called Mr Fordham. 'Your mum and I will be down in three days' time to join you, so see you behave yourself until we get there.'

Proud to be allowed to travel on his own for the first time ever, David Fordham kept up a brisk chatter with the farmer all the way to Castle Dunham.

It was still only seven-fifteen when the car drew into the forecourt of the large coach station on the edge of Castle Dunham's main square, and David confidently transferred to the sleek express coach, all shining red paintwork and gleaming chrome. This was more like style! He settled back in a reclining seat, and earned the distinct approval of the old lady next to him by looking behind and asking permission before he worked the lever to try it out. As it turned out, he liked it better upright, anyway, and upright it remained all the way to London, where, for the first time, he really felt on his own, and a bit nervous of all the hustle and bustle. A helpful policeman set him right for Victoria underground station, and a lively ticket collector there saw him on the way for Euston railway station.

The mid-day train to North Wales was already waiting, and with plenty of time in hand, David parked his bag on his reserved seat and strolled up to look at the big diesel at its head. He was too shy to speak to the driver, but was delighted when the man nodded to him and winked an eye. David had the feeling that this was going to be a day to remember.

The guard touched his shoulder. 'Come on, chum. Better get yourself inside. We'll be off in a mo', and you don't want to be left behind.'

'Not likely,' said David. 'Thanks.'

He found that the seat opposite him had been taken by an elderly man with a trim, rather military moustache and a pair of half-moon glasses that kept slipping down his nose. Affably, the man laid aside his copy of *The Times* and smiled at the boy. 'Holidays, eh?' he said, and David nodded, happily. Everyone was being so pleasant. The sun was still shining brightly, and things were going just splendidly. 'I'm off to stay with my aunt on the coast,' he said. 'She's got a little farm. She's got horses, and a goat, and some pigs.' A vague memory made him wipe the back of his hand across his chin.

'Got anything to read?' said the kindly man. 'It's a long trip. I'd lend you some of this' – he flapped the paper – 'but I can't imagine you'd enjoy it much.'

'Oh, that's all right,' said David. 'I've some comics in my bag. But I want to look out of the windows. At least for a bit.'

'Absolutely right,' agreed his companion, enthusiastically. 'Did the same myself, when I was your age. Of course, it was all steam trains then. Great, snorting locomotives and fussy little tank-engines in the sidings. My eyes would nearly drop out of my head while I tried to note down their numbers.' He launched into a long reminiscence, but there was nothing boring about him, and he had sense enough to stop as the train pulled away from the station. 'Back to the crossword,' he said. 'I'll leave you to your train-spotting.'

David was agog as they passed through the cluttered yards outside Euston. There really *was* a lot to see. Bright yellow track-laying units; special coaches used by the engineering department; and long, powerful diesels, the twins of their own loco. Now a long tunnel, and then the increasing speed as they flashed on.

The boy began to count telegraph poles. How many to a mile? He tried to work it out, but gave up. He opened his mouth to strike up a new conversation with the old man opposite, but thought better of it. The man seemed totally engrossed in that crossword of his. Were those half-moon spectacles about to slide off his nose completely? Despite himself, David felt his eyes closing. He *had* been up an awful long time . . .

The train was slowing down. David opened his eyes with a jerk. His companion had gone. Perhaps down to the buffet car? His paper lay discarded on the table in front of him.

Shuddering now, the big train slid into the platform of a small country station. The platform read 'Lower Hawtrey', and there were hanging baskets of flowers on the rather old-fashioned lamp-posts. David found himself standing up, reaching for his bag. He actually had time to wonder, consciously, what he was doing. But something strange seemed to have hold of him – an odd compulsion that he couldn't resist. He walked down the aisle of the coach, the faces of other passengers indistinct and misty, and went to the door at the end. Before he could touch it, the handle was opened from outside by an ancient, whiskered porter in shirtsleeves, a red kerchief round his neck. In the moment that the train stopped, he beckoned David down. 'Hurry up now, lad,' he said.

David – his own voice sounded somehow far away – said: 'But I'm going to North Wales.'

'Course you are, course you are,' said the porter. 'Here. Give me your ticket.' David produced it, and the man, after what seemed like ages of fumbling, brought out a pair of clippers and punched a hole in it. David saw that the mark was in the shape of the letter H, presumably standing for Hawtrey.

'Look here,' he said suddenly, 'I'm not supposed to get off here! Nobody said I had to change! What am I *doing* . . .?'

'You'll want the six-ten to Tanbury,' said the porter, pleasantly. 'Be through shortly, it will.'

'Tanbury? But I've never heard of Tanbury! I don't want to go there!' David's head was reeling. Try as he might, he couldn't seem to focus his thoughts. He turned, as if to jump back into the express . . . and it wasn't there.

He'd had no notion of it leaving. As far as he recalled, there hadn't been a sound. And yet the platform of the tiny wayside station was absolutely empty. In both directions, the line stretched away into the shimmering, sunny distance, totally deserted.

David gulped. Something had gone wrong, terribly wrong. He turned again, but now the ancient porter had vanished, too. The boy ran down the platform, calling. There was no response, and to his astonishment he found the booking office shuttered, the main gate closed and padlocked. The waiting room was empty, and cold, despite the warmth of the evening. A part of David told him that he should have felt panic. But he didn't. Instinct said that everything would come right, in the end. He remembered the porter's words. 'You'll want the sixten to Tanbury . . .'

Then, from afar, David became aware of a small figure stumbling up the track towards the station, arms waving. As the figure drew closer, the boy saw that it was a railway guard, his jacket torn, his trousers muddied. His face was streaked with dirt, so that his wide, feverish eyes stared whitely up at him. 'Come on, boy. We need everyone we can get! It's terrible!' The guard scrambled up beside David and gripped him by the shoulders. 'A crash. Back by Hawtrey Junction Box. The six-ten to Tanbury's been derailed!'

All else fled from David's mind. His bag banging against his hip, he set off in the direction the man was pointing, down the slope of the platform end and along the ballast at the trackside. He was tired no more, and he ran at full speed towards the distant point where the lines curved away behind a cutting. He rounded the bend, to stop short at a scene of almost indescribable chaos!

Milling like ants, people were scrambling hither and thither over the debris of the crash. Carriages lay on their sides; broken glass was strewn this way and that. One carriage pointed up in the air, the end of it a splintered wreck of mangled wood and metal. Driven into the side of the cutting, a tank engine spouted shrieking steam into the sky. It did not occur to David that there was anything strange about this unfamiliar and antiquated locomotive, lying on its buckled side.

Babbling pandemonium filled David's ears as he drew closer. A man lay holding his shin and groaning with the pain of a broken leg. David crouched beside him, thankful for the lessons in first aid that had been part of his previous year's schooling. Deftly, he tore strips from the man's own shirt, fashioned a pair of crude splints from shattered carriagework, and strapped up the damaged limb. Then he found a child, wandering, white-faced and bewildered, and managed, by pure chance, to locate her distraught mother.

Somewhere, ambulance bells were ringing, and from a road above the cutting, skilled men came pouring down to deal with the casualties. A fire-engine arrived, too, turning out blue-clad firemen, armed with axes to tackle the wreckage.

Locals were arriving from the nearest village. Someone yelled to David: 'Can you make tea, young 'un? That's what they'll need – tea! I've got what's needed.'

David said: 'I can do more by helping the injured.' And he set to with a will that gained, even in those hours of toil, admiration from those who spared the time to notice. David was here, there and everywhere – helping nurses, holding instruments for a doctor, calming a woman in hysterics, even seeing to the comfort of the driver and fireman of the shattered engine, who lay like bewildered dummies on the slope of the embankment. The guard – that same one who had appeared on Lower Hawtrey platform – clapped the boy on the shoulder. 'A mere lad,' he said. 'I'm proud of you, son. You're doing your share and more.'

David gulped. 'Was anybody . . .?'

'Killed?' The guard guessed what he had been about to say. 'No, mercifully. It was a miracle. But some of them are serious. Real serious.'

There was one casualty whom David knew he had personally saved from death. A poor farmer with a torn arm. The boy bandaged an improvised tourniquet around it, above the wicked gash. The bleeding stopped, and with a pencil from his pocket, David wrote the time on the man's sleeve, so that the ambulance men would know what time the tourniquet had been put on and when to release it.

David was here, there and everywhere, helping the injured people.

He stood up, gasping, and felt a hand on his shoulder. It was the shirtsleeved porter with the red kerchief. 'Son, you've done more than your share,' he said. 'Come on, now. It's time for your train.'

'But – but I have no train! This was the one you told me about! The – what was it? The six-ten to Tanbury.'

'Do as I say,' said the porter. 'Come along.' All at once, David realized he was terribly, terribly weary. Almost in a trance, he stumbled his way back along the track to Lower Hawtrey. And to his astonishment, at the platform, he saw the gleaming, modern coaches of the North Wales express train.

He tried to say something, but couldn't. As if he were floating, he allowed himself to be urged back into his coach, and almost immediately, felt the slight jerk as the train pulled away.

David opened his eyes to look straight into the amused eyes of the elderly gentleman with the military moustache. The man moved up his slipping spectacles and said: 'Had a good sleep?'

'A sleep! Then – then it was all a *dream?*'

'Oh! You've been *dreaming*, have you? Go on. Tell me. I love dreams.'

David swallowed. 'Crumbs – it was all so *real*. We stopped. At an old-fashioned station called Lower Hawtrey.' He paused. 'We *didn't* stop, did we?'

'Not for an instant,' said the elderly man. 'This is a non-stop express, my boy. And Lower Hawtrey? Why, there's no station there any more. It was closed down in the late fifties, and demolished some ten years ago.' He went on. 'As a matter of fact, I remember Lower Hawtrey well, having always been interested in railways. There was a terrible crash there. Let me see – around 1955, I think. No fatalities, but plenty injured. A local train to Tanbury came off the rails just by the junction box.'

The boy's mouth had fallen open. His eyes were wider than they'd ever been. 'But – but that's what I dreamed!'

'Really? Then you must have read about it somewhere.'

'No. No, I couldn't have done,' said David. His brain was reeling. 'What else happened?'

'Umm. Ah, yes. There was a hero in the event – a boy. Just a little chap, about your own age, I should imagine. He apparently helped out at the scene of the accident, and then ran off before anyone could find out who he was. Curious business.'

David felt cold fingers crawling up his spine. Of course, it *had* all been a dream. And yet how could it have mirrored fact in such a mystifying way? How could it have brought him to events that had occurred long before he was even born . . .?

Eventually, the train rolled into David's destination, and he took his leave of his amiable companion. Swinging his bag, he set off down the platform, and knew that his aunt would be there beyond the barrier to meet him.

He joined the queue and handed his ticket in to the collector at the gate, and the man said: 'Just a moment, son.'

'Yes?' David looked at him in puzzlement.

The collector looked at him keenly. 'What have you been doing to this, boyo?' he said, and held out David's ticket.

'Nothing. What's wrong with it?'

'Oh, it's valid, all right. But how come you've got the station-mark of Lower Hawtrey punched in it?'

David gaped, incredulously. Sure enough, the slip of paper was pierced by the neat incision of a pair of clippers – an incision in the shape of the letter H!

THE ISLAND IN SPACE
by S. H. Lewis

'LOOK, SHEILA! IT'S THERE AGAIN – the faint outline of a face!'

With a gasp of amazement young Tony Jackson pointed a trembling finger at the viewing screen in the control room of the spacecraft 'Alpha One'.

'A human face,' Tony went on excitedly. 'But it's impossible, sis! We're out in Space – in the middle of nowhere. And no life form has ever been recorded in this part of the Galaxy!'

It was true enough. Tony Jackson, his twin sister Sheila, and their parents were returning to Earth from a holiday trip round the lifeless planets of the Delta Zone.

The Jacksons had been away from Britain for three whole months, but even the marvels of space travel in the 21st century could become really boring at times. That's why the twins had switched on the viewing screen, hoping vaguely for something unexpected to happen. And suddenly, unbelievably, it had!

'Yes, you're right, Tony. It *is* a boy's face on the screen,' Sheila said. 'His lips are moving now. I believe he's trying to say something!'

With growing excitement, Sheila began to press the control buttons on the viewing panel. Abruptly the screen went blank. There was a hiss of interference, and then at last the mystery face was clear again, a look of near despair in those tense blue eyes.

'Help . . . please help!' The voice from the screen was husky with emotion. 'We are in danger. Great danger! Our position is Zero 767 – Space Zone 7. Hurry, please hurry!'

The voice trailed away, the image vanished from the screen and the twins looked at each other in utter astonishment.

'Pinch me. I'm dreaming, sis! Or maybe there *wasn't* a face on the screen at all,' Tony went on. 'Perhaps it was just my reflection.'

'No, Tony. It was real!' The twins' parents had suddenly come in through the doorway of the control room. 'We saw that face on the screen, too,' Mr. Jackson added. 'We were up on Deck 4 when we saw that call for help on the extension viewing screen.'

Grim-faced, he moved swiftly to his flight control seat in the forward navigation area of Alpha One. Tiny lights flashed as his fingers tapped the numbered control buttons and the spacecraft banked steeply on a sudden change of course.

'Hold tight, family. We're going to the rescue,' he said. 'This may be just a joke – a fake distress call put out by that joky lot at Earth Control. But somehow I believe that distress call was genuine. So, Space Zone 7, here we come!'

And, with a shuddering surge of power, the Jacksons' spacecraft zoomed forward on its flight into the unknown.

'Gosh! What an adventure!' breathed Tony. 'I only hope we're not too late!'

It was hours later when the Jacksons received their second surprise as they crowded round the viewing screen in the forward control area.

'Incredible!' gasped Tony, almost jumping out of his seat. 'Take a look. There on the screen is Position Zero 767 – Space Zone 7. A chunk of land with trees and things, sort of motionless in outer space.'

'Like a South Sea Island on Earth!' exclaimed Sheila. 'With golden sand and palm trees! An island in Space. I can

175

hardly believe my eyes, Dad. What's the explanation?'

Bill Jackson shook his head. 'The universe is full of strange mysteries,' he said. 'Maybe this island was at one time part of a planet, just like our own Earth. There could have been a catastrophe that sent this chunk of land zooming into outer space!'

Mrs. Jackson nodded thoughtfully. 'You mean, like some kind of atomic explosion,' she suggested.

'Yes. Maybe something like that did happen,' Bill Jackson agreed. 'But one thing is certain: that distress call we heard came from Space Island, and we're going to touch down to see what we can do to help.'

Slowly Alpha One began the descent, banking through the clouds and dropping gently towards the island beach.

'Look. There's a level stretch of shore,' Tony said. 'Ideal for touch-down, Dad!'

'You're right, son,' his father agreed, as he guided the spacecraft in low over the waving palm trees, to the flat, golden sand beyond. 'What a super beach, Tony. Ideal for an old-fashioned game of cricket, eh? And . . .'

'Hey, something's moving down there, Dad,' Sheila broke in. 'And – look! Those enormous prints in the sand are *not* human footprints. What are they, Dad? I'm scared!'

'Me, too,' Mrs. Jackson admitted. 'I heard a sound like the flapping of wings just then and a high-pitched buzzing sound. Something strange is happening down there, Bill. It's too dangerous to land!'

'Mum's right, Dad!' Sheila clutched nervously at Bill Jackson's shoulder as he sat grimly in front of the controls. 'Perhaps that call for help we heard was some kind of trap, to lure us into danger.'

Bill Jackson frowned. 'Maybe you're right. Hold tight then, we're going up again. I'll circle around and contact Earth Control to find out if anything is known about this place.'

176

But even as Bill Jackson spoke, the buzzing sound increased and something brushed against the upper dome of Alpha One.

'We're losing height! We're going to crash!' Bill Jackson tugged frantically at the controls, desperately trying to save the family from disaster.

But it was too late! Nothing could save the spacecraft now!

Spinning helplessly, Alpha One plunged down, tipping over at a crazy angle and half-burying itself in the soft, golden sand. For a few seconds the buzzing sound and flap of wings continued as if the mystery attackers were inspecting their victim. Then all was quiet again, until at last the emergency door in the side of Alpha One opened, and the Jacksons, badly shaken but unhurt, climbed down the escape ladder to inspect the damage.

Bill Jackson was the first to speak.

'The whole dome of the spacecraft has been shattered,' he said. 'Whatever struck us up there has made quite certain we'll never get away from Space Island.'

'You mean – we're marooned, Dad?' Sheila's voice was near to panic now.

'Yes, shipwrecked. Like poor old Robinson Crusoe on his desert island in that tale of long ago,' Bill Jackson admitted. 'Our supplies are buried somewhere deep in the sand.'

The family exchanged worried looks, not knowing what to say or do. Then suddenly Sheila's face brightened. 'Remember the story of Robinson Crusoe, Dad?' she asked. 'Didn't he have a Man Friday to help him? Well, maybe we'll find a 21st century Man Friday on *this* island. Come on, everyone. Let's explore.'

So, led by Sheila, the Jacksons made their way cautiously across the golden sands. After a while Tony pointed along the beach to a distant, towering headland.

'I reckon that's the highest point on the island,' Tony exclaimed, hurrying on ahead, across a chain of rocks. 'Mind how you go, everyone. This seaweed is very slippery and . . . oh my gosh! Just look at that!'

With a gasp of astonishment, Tony had stopped and was pointing to the beach beyond the headland. Here, half buried in the sand, were the remains of another spacecraft, with the name Zuron Explorer printed on the silvery summit of the upper dome.

The craft had obviously come to grief, just like Alpha One. But not a trace remained of its occupants. The huge spaceship had been sliced in half, and all the inner compartments could be seen clearly like an opened doll's house.

'Zuron Explorer, eh?' Bill Jackson kept repeating the words in utter amazement as he joined Tony and gazed round the headland at the astonishing sight. 'Not much left of it, is there, son? Wonder where it came from?'

Briskly he consulted his pocket computer 'Instant Guide to the Galaxies' and, after a while, turned grimly to face the family. Then he explained, 'Zuron is a planet in the Western Galaxy. Its inhabitants are humans just like ourselves, and Zuron Explorer obviously came to this island to explore it, too!'

'And, like ourselves, it was attacked by something unknown.' Sheila's voice was trembling as she gazed across the empty beach at the innocent-looking palm trees, their branches waving gently against the pale blue of the cloudless sky.

But even as Sheila looked at them, the palm trees began to sway and shudder, as if blown by a sudden hurricane. Then the Jackson family saw the Creatures . . . flying ants of gigantic size, mighty crabs as big as army tanks and hideous looking spiders. There were enormous winged lizards, too, and other flying creatures. As the strange army approached, their huge wings flapped with a droning roar and a fierce current of air whistled across the whole island.

178

White-faced, Sheila clutched at her father's arm. 'Those things must have attacked the Zuron Explorer, Dad,' she gasped.

'Yes. And wrecked our spaceship, too,' Bill Jackson muttered. 'One of those flying creatures must have brushed against our ship in mid-air and brought it crashing down on the beach.'

The droning sound made by the Creatures now changed to high-pitched whistles. As they moved slowly forward, the strange army got into V-formation and their huge legs churned up the sand into a blinding, yellow cloud.

'Look out! They're going to attack!' Tony yelled. 'Run for it! Find a hole in the rocks . . . a cave . . . anywhere. It's our only hope now!'

Heeding Tony's advice, the Jacksons fled. But, fast as they ran, the family were no match for the advancing Creatures.

Sheila almost slipped and fell as they scampered over the slippery rocks. Then, looking round fearfully, she saw a gigantic spider, as big as a house, zigzagging towards her, tottering across the beach like some enormous travelling crane.

Suddenly it lifted one of its gigantic legs as if to knock her over.

She screamed, covering her eyes with her hands, not daring to look any more and desperately hoping for a miracle. And then suddenly, amazingly the miracle happened – the spider retreated!

'Fantastic,' she gasped. 'It's not true!'

But it *was* true! Running across the chain of rocks, from the opposite direction, there now came a human figure, a ray gun gripped in his hand.

'Be calm! I will save you all,' he said. And Sheila's eyes opened in wonder, staring in amazement as the young stranger calmly took charge of the whole situation.

Amazed, the Jacksons watched as the boy dropped down on one knee and a hissing ray from his gun forced the Creatures into a retreat. He just stood there, a confident smile on his lips as he watched the Enemy move back.

'There! They have gone,' he said. 'But do not fear! I will stay in case they attack again!'

'Phew, thanks,' gasped Sheila. 'It'll be great to have you around. Just like a Man Friday,' she added with a giggle, 'on Robinson Crusoe's Island.'

'Robinson Crusoe? Man Friday?' There was a blank look in the stranger's eyes. 'I do not know those persons. My name is Mal.'

'Mal? Nice name,' said Mrs Jackson. 'But how did you come to be on this island, Mal? Were you with the others – the ones in that wrecked spaceship, Zuron Explorer?'

The boy nodded. 'All the others – the Zuronites – were killed by the Creatures,' he said. 'I am the only one left. Their message to you was too late.'

'Our spaceship has been partly destroyed, too,' Tony told him. 'Come, we'll show you.'

'Sheila, are you all right now?' Mrs Jackson asked.

'I'm okay, Mum,' she said. 'Just famished, that's all. It's ages since we had a meal. Are there any food supplies, Dad?'

'The whole food and drinks unit was buried deep in the sand under huge piles of wreckage,' he said. 'We'll never be able to retrieve it.'

That's when Mal once more raced into action, speeding along the beach like an Olympic athlete.

'Hey, come back, Mal. Don't desert us now,' Tony called out. 'With those fiendish Creatures around we still need your help.'

'Yes, and you need food, too,' Mal called back. 'This is a task for me. I will get you some.'

With the Jackson family in pursuit, Mal continued running

along the island beach at incredible speed. At last, with no hint of breathlessness or fatigue, he reached the Jacksons' half-buried spaceship and stood there calmly, hand outstretched.

'What's he doing now, Dad?' Tony gasped. 'He's holding a kind of slim rod in his hand and it's clicking like a metal detector.'

'Or maybe it's a food detector,' Bill Jackson suggested. 'Yes, that's it. I believe he's trying to find out exactly where our food supplies are buried.'

It seemed the correct explanation for suddenly Mal gave a cry of satisfaction and began using his hands to dig away at the tangled remains of the spacecraft. Bits of wreckage flew in all directions as he worked.

Within minutes he'd made a tunnel large enough for him to crawl down through the sand and wreckage, to reappear a few minutes later with two large ice-boxes filled with provisions.

'Food! Delicious food,' Tony gasped. 'Thanks, Mal. You're a real hero.'

'We'll have a picnic,' Mrs Jackson exclaimed. 'And Mal must join us.'

But the boy from Zuron had other ideas. As the Jacksons tucked into their welcome meal, he set about repairing the battered spaceship. Almost before the meal was over Alpha One was repaired and looking almost as good as new. The Jacksons' sleeping quarters were ready, too, and Mal advised them all to get a good night's sleep before attempting the homeward flight to Earth.

'Meanwhile I will stay on guard,' he said. 'The Creatures may try to attack again. But if they do, I will be ready for them. Now you Earth people must sleep until morning.'

But Sheila could not sleep. In her cabin, she kept waking up and looking out through the porthole at the distant figure of Mal, standing on a high rock like a sentry on duty, prepared for any emergency.

At last she sprang from her bunk, dressed quickly and let herself out through the emergency hatchway and down the exit ladder to the beach.

Mal was still standing there, on his rocky outpost, as the Jackson girl approached. 'Mal, you must be starving,' she said, 'standing around in the cold all night, without a wink of sleep. Look, I've brought you something tasty in this basket, left over from our picnic. It's delicious. Go on – try it.'

Mal looked thoughtfully at the basket of food she offered, but did not take it. 'You are very kind,' he said. 'But I do not need food. I do not require sleep, either. Listen!' he added, as a distant buzzing sound rumbled across the island. 'The Creatures are stirring again. You must get back to your spacecraft, Sheila.'

At that moment Bill Jackson himself looked out from the hatchway.

'Sheila, come inside, dear. We are ready for lift-off,' he said. 'I have made a complete inspection of the ship. Our friend Mal did a fine job. All systems are in good shape. So let's get started. Hurry aboard, love.'

'Okay, Dad. Coming!' Sheila waved to her Dad and then turned eagerly to the boy at her side. 'Mal, come with us, too. Now you have lost your friends from Zuron you are welcome to join our party instead. Come back to Earth with us, Mal.'

He hesitated, thoughtfully running a slender hand through his hair. 'But I am not one of your people from Planet Earth,' he said. 'You do not understand, Sheila. I came here with a family of explorers from the planet Zuron and my task was to help and protect them. But I failed, Sheila. They all perished and I am to blame.'

For the first time there was a note of self-reproach in Mal's voice, and Sheila felt so sorry for him that she instinctively clutched at his hand. 'But it wasn't *your* fault, Mal,' she said. 'I am sure you did all you could to protect them, as you have helped to protect us, and . . . Mal!' she gasped. 'Your hand . . . it's as cold as steel.'

Suddenly, as realization dawned, she released her grip on his hand and could only stare at him in astonishment as, for the first time, he admitted the truth about himself.

'No, Sheila, I'm not a real boy,' he said. 'I suppose you Earth people would call me a robot – a machine programmed to help the Zuronite family on their mission to Space Island. My name MAL means *M*ale *A*ssistant *L*abourer. And that's what I am – a machine designed to do all the tasks that Zuronites cannot do, to protect and work for them, as I have worked for you. But I failed my Zuron commanders. I am useless . . . a clever mixed up mass of wires and circuits, but a failure just the same.'

'Don't say that, Mal. It's not true,' Sheila gasped. 'You could be a sensation back on Earth . . . do wonders for mankind and . . .'

Her words faded away in mid-sentence as the droning sound grew louder. And then suddenly the Creatures appeared again. Flapping its huge, clumsy wings, one gigantic flying ant came zooming down from the sky, like a dive bomber hurtling down to attack. At the same time an enormous spider, as big as the spacecraft itself, came waddling forward up the beach. Its gigantic beady eye fixed itself on Sheila in a paralysing glare that made her half stumble in horror.

'Help me, Mal. Help me!' she gasped. 'They're all round us!'

She turned her head and shut her eyes, not daring to look.

But her Dad was watching. Framed in the doorway of the spacecraft, he shuddered in dismay as he realized his daughter's plight. 'Quick, Sheila. Run for it!' he yelled. 'Only a little way to go!'

Now he was leaning out from the hatchway, his hand

outstretched, ready to haul her aboard. But Sheila instinctively knew that she could never make it on her own.

The rocket engines of Alpha One were roaring into life. The Creatures were coming ever closer. And Sheila gestured to her father in hopeless despair. 'Leave me, Dad!' she called out. 'Go without me, while there is still time!'

But then, as Sheila resigned herself to her fate, a slim figure threw himself between the girl and the advancing Creatures.

Mal's hand reached for a metal band on his wrist and his finger firmly pressed a button marked SELF DESTRUCT.

A split second later there was a shattering explosion.

One second Mal was there, and the next all that remained of him was a crackling ball of fire and smoke that brought the Creatures to a sudden, mystified halt.

'Quick, Sheila. Run!'

Bill Jackson's urgent call rang out above the crackle of the flames. Then Sheila was safely in his arms and being lifted into the spacecraft. Next moment with a mighty roar it blasted off into space, on its homeward voyage to Earth. And Sheila, staring tearfully through a porthole, waved a sad goodbye to the handsome boy who'd sacrificed his robot life so that she could escape.

'Goodbye, Space Island,' she said softly to herself. 'Goodbye, Mal.'

And, as Alpha One climbed rapidly into the vast emptiness of outer Space, a small cloud of smoke spiralled upwards from the sandy beach below . . . all that remained of Mal . . . the boy who never was!

Sheila resigned herself to her fate as the gigantic flying ants came ever closer.

THE BIG FISH
by Lee Stone

'COME ON! We must stow our things. If we don't start now we'll miss the tide!'

At Bob Stone's urgent command his two companions instantly began to reel in their fishing lines. The sun was low in the west, pinned like a red medal on the sky over Elmsea Pier. Below their perch on Westport harbour jetty, their long-boat had dropped several metres on its mooring – an ominous sign of a fast ebbing tide.

It had been a good day, though. It was Bob who had suggested to Jimmy Hollingsworth and Clive Case that there was some good fishing to be had at Westport harbour and now, with a bagful of dabs and flounders, and a couple of good-size sole, they could be pleased with their ten hours' sport on the jetty.

The three boys, all senior sea cadets, were mid-way through their annual camp at Elmsea. Bob had been to camp at Elmsea twice before and knew the nine-mile long Westport harbour as well as most.

Recalling this as he reeled in his line, Jimmy asked: 'Is there usually this much activity in the harbour? I reckon four Heron class destroyers, two Ajax cruisers and half a dozen submarines have passed us today. And there seem to be a lot more small warships to the northwest.'

'Naval manoeuvres, I think,' Bob said briskly. 'No, it isn't usually like this. They must be trying out some war games.'

The three cadets dropped nimbly into their long-boat,

stowed their fishing tackle neatly and while Bob and Clive took the oars, Jimmy cast off. A wide part of the harbour channel, which they had first to reach and navigate, was marked by a line of poles sticking out of the sea bed. Beyond that half-mile stretch the harbour channel narrowed considerably and was marked with buoys as far as the wharves of Elmsea. On each side of the channel the water was sometimes two miles wide, but shallow and treacherous.

Indeed, Bob was already becoming anxious about negotiating the harbour channel on a falling tide in gathering dusk. True, the channel was well marked and deep enough, provided he could keep to it. But there were banks and ledges on either beam, to say nothing of three or four small rocky islands, presenting after dark a considerable peril to all but the most experienced Westport harbour pilots.

For the first part of the run back Bob decided that they should row hard. When they came to the narrow part of the channel they dropped speed in favour of more caution.

'Keep a look-out for'ard for Temple Buoy,' Bob commanded. 'I don't see its light yet.'

'Nor do I,' Jimmy answered. 'And there's a nasty mist rolling in from the sea. Wait – there's a large vessel making Elmsea ahead of us in the fairway. No, I'm not sure; she may be stationary. I think there's a small vessel directly ahead of her, too.'

'I see her. The one nearest us is on tow; that's a tug for'ard.' Rapidly Bob took in the situation. To pass the vessel – in the gathering darkness she looked like a coaster – on the port side, as he should, would mean cutting in ahead of her and astern of the tug, if that was what it was, in order to keep in the harbour channel. That would hardly add up to good seamanship, as Lieutenant Burns, their navigation instructor back at Elmsea camp, would say. On top of that, he was sure there wasn't sufficient room in the channel to allow him to overtake on the port side. Bob remembered the stony face of Lieutenant Burns again and made up his mind.

'I'm going to pass her on her starboard side,' he called. He estimated that they would pass the coaster more or less at the spot where he expected to find Temple Buoy.

As the crew bent to the oars Bob felt a sudden anxiety. It was clear that even passing the coaster on her starboard side was going to take them uncomfortably close to Temple Island and its adjacent ledge. There was no other choice, however; it was better to do that than to attempt to cut in between the two craft.

Suddenly, just as they were about to pass her, the stern of the coaster swung wildly outwards. Bob was briefly aware of one of her engines being stopped and the other putting on power, making her stern come out to starboard. He heard Clive and Jimmy shout as they were thrown violently off balance. All in a space of a second or two the long-boat came round in a desperate half-circle, missing the stern of the coaster by inches.

Then, in that same fleeting moment, there was an ominous grating as the bottom of the long-boat, shivering momentarily from the shock, came abruptly to rest with her nose poised high in the air.

'Beached!' Bob groaned. For a moment he wanted to lie down in the bottom of the boat and die.

Already Clive and Jimmy were scrambling out into shallow water, holding the boat to prevent it from swinging.

'We've struck Temple Ledge!' Clive gasped.

'I can't understand it,' Jimmy said. 'The light of the buoy wasn't on.'

'I should have passed the coaster on the port side,' Bob said.

'It's a good thing you didn't,' Jimmy replied. 'If you had we would have struck her bows for sure as she swung over.'

'Maybe,' Bob said. He was feeling appalled over his lack of

seamanship. 'Let's see if we can shove her off.'

They slipped off their shoes and rolled up their trousers, squeezing out water in handfuls. It was nearly dark now. The sea mist, the rolling mist that comes down suddenly, had closed in, damp and dense.

'Hang on!' Clive called from one end. 'Don't shove. She's making water aft.' He peered into the darkness of the boat where they had been sitting. 'One of the planks is fractured. I reckon I can fix it with the stuff in the repair box, but only for long enough to get us back to Elmsea.'

'How long will it take?'

'Probably an hour.'

'That means we'll be here until tomorrow morning,' Bob said despondently. He stared around at the dense, swirling sea fret. 'About five o'clock tomorrow morning, I'd say. It's five to ten now. The tide won't turn for three hours and there'll be another three before it's up again where it is now. We can put half an hour more on top of that, at least, before we can get off. That brings us up to half past four.'

While Clive settled down to caulk the leak at one end of the boat, Bob and Jimmy tried to make themselves comfortable at the other. The dank, humid mist and the stark interior of the long-boat promised a dismal night ahead.

When, an hour later, Clive joined them – by which time the boat had been left high and dry on Temple Ledge by the ebbing tide – the three huddled together to get what warmth they could from their chilly predicament.

Only a short distance from where the boat lay, the silhouette of a mass of rocks and boulders indicated that their beaching could have been far more catastrophic.

'Phew!' breathed Bob eyeing the rock-pile. Then he added, thinking aloud, 'We seem to be on a connecting link between the ledge and Temple Island.'

189

'I wish we could light a fire,' Jimmy said. 'I could do with a nice piece of fried fish right now – and we already have the fish.'

'Don't talk about food,' Clive said. 'I'm starving.'

'You know something,' Bob said, still thinking aloud. 'I have a funny feeling about the coaster. Why do you think her stern came out like that right at the moment when we were about to pass her? It's almost as if they saw us coming and deliberately tried to beach us.'

'I'd rather think about that in the morning,' Jimmy said. 'If we survive until morning.'

The Moon was now fairly well up and although covered by a thin film of cloud, it threw a faint light on the water and over Temple Island.

It was then that Bob saw it. 'Look!' he whispered. 'Over there, on Temple island . . . a light flashing.'

Clive and Jimmy peered over the side in disbelief.

'Can't see a thing,' Jimmy said. 'Anyway, no one lives on that heap of rock.'

'There it is again!'

This time all three chorussed their agreement.

'It's Morse code,' Clive said. He was a qualified cadet radio officer. 'At least, it's the Morse system. But it's gibberish. I can't make out a word of it.'

'I think I'll go and investigate,' Bob said. He was beginning to think anything in the world would be better than just lying shivering in the long-boat until first light. And if someone was operating a flashlight over on Temple Island, perhaps they had a boat with which help could be summoned.

He felt the stiffness of cold in his legs as he swung over the side of the boat and was almost glad to be moving again. 'Give me fifteen minutes,' he said. 'Send out a posse if I'm not back by then.'

The long-boat vanished in the darkness behind him as he

moved up the ledge on to Temple Island. The mysterious light – there was no telling in the darkness and the mist how far away it was – still flashed continuously.

Suddenly Bob was aware of a silhouette against the skyline, a man's silhouette from which the flashing light was coming. Instinct made him crouch and proceed stealthily up the sloping rock face. Why, he wondered, should anyone want to send incomprehensible Morse code signals in the middle of the night from the wretched barren rock pile that gloried in the name of Temple Island?

Minutes later he had climbed to the top of the rock face. All around he could sense and hear the sea, but the mysterious flashing light and the human silhouette had vanished as completely as if they had never been there.

'It must have been a mirage,' Bob breathed to himself. 'I've started seeing things.'

Then he was aware of a soft footstep and, before he could even begin to turn, there was a thud like a hammer blow on his head. The pain forced him to his knees with a strangled cry of agony and anger. And above that, he remembered afterwards, there was another cry of anguish, not his this time. He remembered nothing more . . .

'You lost consciousness,' Jimmy said. 'He came round from behind you and clobbered you with a rock. Good thing I decided to follow you, or you could have died of cold up there.'

'Where is he?' Bob's voice was weak with exhaustion. He knew that he was lying in the long-boat again with Jimmy crouched over him. Clive was sponging his head with ice-cold sea-water. His throbbing head continued to multiply questions that were instantly annihilated by stabs of pain.

'Over there, behind you.' Jimmy indicated the other end of the long-boat. 'I clobbered him with another rock when I saw him clobber you,' he added with stark simplicity.

'You hit him?'

'Don't worry about it. He's up to no good, that's for sure. He's carrying a gun – at least, he was, till I took it off him – and he's got papers on him that look very foreign to me. He must have been sending Morse signals in another language.'

Bob pulled himself into a sitting position, groaning as his head exploded with the effort. 'What do you plan to do with him now?'

'We'll row him back to Elmsea with us. I expect Lieutenant Burns would like to ask him some questions. Even if he can answer them all satisfactorily, there's still the question of why he gave you a bump on the head without any warning.'

Bob groaned again and, as if in sympathy, an answering groan came from the huddled figure at the other end of the long-boat.

'Try to get some rest,' Jimmy said. 'I'm going to tie our visitor's wrists to the aft rowlocks, in case he gets aggressive again.'

Several hours later Bob woke from a shivering doze. Clive was crouching over him.

'Tide's coming up fast, judging by the way the stern is swinging,' he said.

'What time is it?' Bob asked.

'Twenty-five to five.'

Bob peered over the edge. Water was swirling round the boat. The sea mist had cleared and the sky in the east was flooded with light. 'Let's go,' he said.

The three cadets sat at their oars. Moments later they were back in the harbour channel. The rising tide was with them and they fairly raced along towards the wharves of Elmsea and the landing stage.

But a mile away from their destination a high-speed launch rounded a bend in the channel and hailed them: 'Pull

Suddenly Bob was aware of a man's silhouette against the skyline.

alongside! Take the rope from our stern!'

'Harbour police,' Bob said. 'Now it's going to be question time.'

'Cadets Stone, Hollingsworth and Case?' said a cheery police inspector as they clambered aboard.

'That's us, inspector. Plus one more, in the long-boat. We'll need to explain how we got him . . .'

'Come below,' the Inspector said. 'I expect you'd like a cup of tea. We had an alert from your cadet camp at midnight and we've been searching for you ever since. Like to tell us what happened?'

Twenty-four hours later, most of it spent in sleeping, Bob, Jimmy and Clive were told by an orderly to report to Lieutenant Burns.

The lieutenant's usual grim scowl was relaxed into a grin. 'Stand at ease,' he said.

'We've just had a report from Westport Harbour police. It's about the chap you picked up the other night. Seems he's from a foreign embassy in Paris and was brought over in a harmless-looking ship to spy on the naval manoeuvres in the harbour. The Admiralty had a new nuclear submarine out there and it's still on the secret list.'

'What on earth was he doing on Temple Island, sir?' Bob said incredulously.

'From Temple you can see the whole harbour. He wouldn't have missed anything, not from there. Seems that a small craft took him off the ship in the harbour channel and put him down near the ledge. For some reason or other he got too involved in what he was doing and missed the tide to take him off.'

'That explains the stationary coaster in the channel – the one that set us on the ledge,' Jimmy said.

'And the small craft that was ahead of her. That was the one that stopped us passing her on the port side,' echoed Bob.

'But why was the light of Temple Buoy not working?' asked Clive.

'Your spy put it out with a revolver shot,' Lieutenant Burns said. 'He's being taken to London today for an inquiry. You may have to go along later today or tomorrow to give some evidence. That's all – oh, by the way, the police think you did a splendid job. The commanding officer has asked me to congratulate you.'

The three cadets saluted cheerfully and outside the orderly office Bob said: 'That was some fishing trip.'

'Well, we certainly caught a rather bigger fish than we expected!' Jimmy grinned.

BARCLAY'S EXPENDABLE
by Angus Allan

MELTED BY THE INDESCRIBABLE HEAT, the launching gantry collapsed like so much limp spaghetti as, with countless tons of thrust behind it, the rocket lifted away from its pad and sped upwards into the sky.

As it tore free from the drag of Earth's gravity, Barclay, strapped into his padded seat in the orbiter module, relaxed. There would be nothing for him to do for a while, and there was the luxury of being truly alone for the first time in nearly a year. How sick he'd grown of Kowalski, the scientist with the pinched, petulant mouth; of Adams the Chief Medical Officer, always fussing, it seemed, over every step he, Barclay, took – every breath he breathed. Mortlake the dietician, Hendrix the physical fitness expert, Bannerman, in charge of those fiendish flight simulators and G-force machines – between them, they'd nearly driven him crazy with their endless modifications to the mission plan.

And the mission was simple enough. A straightforward double orbit of Earth to test the alarmist theories of some professor or other who claimed that space-flight led to minute but significant changes in organs like the liver and kidneys.

Barclay glanced out of the direct-view panel on his left. He had felt the slight jerk as the single-stage rocket had disengaged, and now he saw it, tumbling away behind him – a piece of abandoned junk. Suddenly, as ground-controlled thrusters altered the module's attitude, he saw the bright curve of Earth itself, the Gulf of Mexico clearly visible. Not, however, that Barclay knew it for what it was . . .

A green light flashed in front of him, three times at precise one-second intervals, and in response Barclay leaned forward to adjust a knurled wheel. The light came on permanently – a steady glow to indicate that the orbiter was exactly on its pre-determined course. He settled back again, completely at ease, and with little actual sensation of the weightlessness he was experiencing. There were no video screens in the module, and – deemed unnecessary – no radio links. So he was completely alone, and completely cut off from anything more than instrumental contact with the Launch Headquarters. He *might* have given just a thought to Thomson, though . . .

Frank Thomson was a good friend to Barclay. Right from the start, the young laboratory assistant had got properly acquainted. Frank – good-natured, attentive without being bothersome – had escorted Barclay here and there in the vast Space Ops complex. He had kept him company in the 'spare hours', and a strong and loyal bond had grown between them. Not that Kowalski, Hendrix and the others had approved. The senior staff had seemed to resent the friendship, somehow, and had done their best, at various times, to make sure that Thomson and Barclay were kept apart.

Now, as he gently pushed open the sighing swing door that led into Mission Control, Frank Thomson knew that he would certainly be met with hostility. And he was. Actually it was Bannerman who turned irritably as he came in, and said: 'What in thunder do *you* want, kid? Can't you see we're busy?'

'This isn't an area I'm restricted from, Mr Bannerman,' Frank replied evenly. 'I just wanted to know how Barclay's doing, that's all.'

'He's doing just fine.' Bannerman had obviously decided to be less than informative.

Frank pushed past him, ignoring the man's scowl of

annoyance, and laid a hand on the arm of Medical Officer Adams. 'How do the monitors look, Doc?'

Adams, who was perhaps the least resentful of the team, nodded curtly. 'Okay, Thomson. Nothing unusual at all. I'd say we're in for a very smooth ride.'

'We?' thought Frank Thomson. 'It's Barclay up there – not any of *us*.' He saw Kowalski glance across at him from the main console, make an impatient gesture and lift a telephone, and Frank knew that any second he would be recalled to his lab on some pretext or other. He couldn't help thinking that, for grown, highly skilled men, some of these scientists had the behaviour patterns of petulant infants.

Tracked by monitoring stations all over the world, the module made a perfect first orbit. And all the while, tiny electrodes taped to Barclay's body sent back their electronic, whispered messages to the central computers. Every facet of his physical condition was being studied in minute detail. It wasn't in Barclay's nature to be bored, but they had taken steps to prevent such a possibility. From time to time, more lights would flash. He would reach out to alter course, maintain it until the lights flashed again, and then re-correct. His training had been perfect, and his movements were automatic. It was only when, half way through the second and final orbit, the Sun threw an unexpected and unplanned-for glittering on one of the direct-view screens, that things began to go wrong.

Barclay's brows drew down. To him, the glittering seemed like the flashing of one of the signals, and his right hand fumbled for one of the controls. Astern, a pair of small five-second retros fired, and the module began to spin. Barclay did nothing more, but sat back, his eyes bewilderedly trying to follow the whirl of Sun, Earth and velvet blackness in front of him.

'What the blazes has he done?' In Mission Control, Kowalski was on his feet, his beaky little mouth working with annoyance. 'Who punched through the signal for him to fire those things?'

'Nobody, sir!' An assistant gaped round at him, white-faced. 'We have an unprogrammed self-initiated situation.'

Nobody queried the jargon, which meant no more than that Barclay had done something off his own bat. But then the arguments started. Kowalski rounded on Adams. 'Why did he act on impulse?'

'How in Hades should *I* know? I checked his body out, not his mind!'

'Hendrix?' Kowalski turned to the Physical Fitness expert. 'I always said your programmes were likely to give Barclay delusions of superiority! He thinks he's some kind of super-hero . . .'

Hendrix coloured redly, and shouted back: 'You idiot! You're talking out of the back of your neck!' He in turn spun on Bannerman, who had put Barclay through all the ground-based simulations of the mission. 'This is your doing! You were supposed to make sure he behaved to a pattern at all times!'

Bannerman – a big man with the hottest of tempers – lost his cool completely. The drop-jawed junior technicians of Mission Control were treated to the horrifying spectacle of one of their chiefs lashing out at another with clenched fists! Hendrix cannoned into Kowalski himself, and the pair went over in a tangle of flying arms and legs, Kowalski's voice rising to an infuriated scream of rage!

Mortlake the Dietician and Adams separated them, and then had to indulge in a shuffling, undignified dance to keep Bannerman from getting back at Hendrix. The behaviour of these eminent men would have disgraced a junior form in a primary school.

Frank Thomson, who had come back yet again to the area,

Hendrix cannoned into Kowalski, and the pair went over in a tangle of flying arms and legs.

was unable to master his disgust. 'What are you all doing?' he yelled. 'You're acting like maniacs while Barclay's in real trouble!'

Kowalski gulped, shook the fog of fury out of his brain, and made for the master console. The instruments there were jumping uncontrollably, and the course-control counters were racing backwards and forwards like the line-up on a demented fruit machine. 'Switch to ground command,' he ordered in a strangled voice.

'I'm sorry, sir.' His chief assistant spread his hands helplessly. 'Barclay's been spun around like a top. He must have pressed half-a-dozen more controls. He's managed to put himself totally in command, and we can't over-ride.'

Kowalski sat down heavily on the nearest chair. 'I don't believe it,' he said. 'We've got millions of dollarsworth of hardware up there – an entire research programme. And we have to stick here like a load of dummies and watch the screens while it all goes wrong.'

For once, nobody said anything to Frank Thomson as the young man came to Kowalski's side, his face ashen with horror and dismay. Frank said: 'You can't do *anything* to put right what's happened?'

'No.'

'And all you can think of is wasted *dollars*? Ye gods, Kowalski! What about *Barclay* . . .?'

Kowalski's dead-fish eyes turned on the lab assistant. 'You're crazy, Thomson. Barclay is expendable. He doesn't count.'

Somehow, Frank Thomson stopped himself from hitting the scientist. Teeth gritted savagely, he turned and ran from the tension of the room.

Sick and shaken, Barclay had been subjected to a buffeting that would have punished a giant. And he was no giant. Pure chance had clamped his hands on just the controls that brought the delirious spinning of the module to a halt – at the cost of almost all the fuel in the retro-rockets and positioning nozzles. He didn't know that, on the ground, computers had given a dramatic and ghastly printout – showing that he would eventually depart Earth orbit altogether, and go soaring off towards the Sun. He would have taken little comfort from the fact that he would have starved to death long before frying.

Sagging in his harness, Barclay watched for the flickering lights on the instruction console that would tell him what to do – but nothing happened. He conjured up a vision of Kowalski and his colleagues, and heard himself grinding his teeth in rage. The frenzy only passed when the image of Frank Thomson flickered into his mind . . .

He had a friend in Thomson – and no mistake. A friend practically beyond belief. Ignoring his inferior position in the hierarchy of the Space Centre, Frank had lobbied the Senior Electronics Controller. He had badgered the Communications Chief, and had even burst into the office of the Operational Director himself. He had been threatened with dismissal. Kowalski had even tried to have him arrested by the security division and imprisoned. But Frank's impassioned pleas had sparked results. He knew, bitterly, that it was only the vague chance of recovering the module – the millions of dollars that it represented – that had done the trick. Now the 'Top Men' were losing their sleep and racking their brains to find a solution, but not one of them cared a whit about poor Barclay.

They couldn't have done it, of course, without the aid of the massive computers. It needed the most astute mathematical brains, capable of thinking on three levels at once, to re-programme the sophisticated machines. But working all night, they had done it, and now, one of the senior men – a character who had not actually touched a computer in years – punched out the order that made coloured lights flash (at precise one-second intervals) on Barclay's display.

Barclay grunted, and stretched out his right hand. He didn't notice it was shaking. Astern of the module, a line of tiny micro-adjustment thrusters sparked. They used up the very last dregs of fuel.

In Mission Control, Kowalski sat sullenly. He heard the Operation Director's monosyllabic 'Well?'

At the master console, the white-faced technician turned and said: 'I think it's worked, sir. The module's going to come back into atmosphere. At a steeper angle than we'd planned – but it *could* survive re-entry.'

Frank Thomson felt his nails dig into the palms of his hands. The Ops Director looked at him. 'Satisfied?'

'I'd like to be at splashdown, if that's at all possible, sir,' said Frank.

'That makes two of us, son,' said the boss. And then, to Kowalski: 'The report on your behaviour – *all* of your behaviour here – makes it very clear to me that whatever the result of this mission, steps will have to be taken to subject our senior staff to psychological training.'

'I think that's hardly fair, sir,' blustered Kowalski. He should have saved his breath.

'You behaved irresponsibly in a moment of crisis. What is the point in training subjects like Barclay if *you're* to be found at fault?' The Director's eyes swept the shamed faces of the scientists · and doctors. Kowalski, Bannerman, Hendrix, Adams, Mortlake. 'I'll even undergo examination myself,' he said. 'Come on, Thomson. We've got an aircraft to catch.'

A helicopter put Thomson and the Director down on the deck of USS Louisiana just one hour before the orbiter module, its multiple parachutes streaming, drifted down, blackened and distorted, into the Pacific. Within minutes, a derrick hooked on and lifted it from the bobbing sea, and experienced technicians unshipped the bolts on the exit hatch.

'It seems you've proved you were closer to Barclay than anyone else, son,' said the Director to Thomson. 'Go ahead. Get in there and bring him out.'

'Yes, sir!'

'Wait.' The Director had more to say. 'How come you took to him so strong, boy?'

Frank Thomson frowned thoughtfully. Then he said: 'Because I sensed, I guess, that cold-blooded guys like Kowalski and his pals got up *his* nose as much as they got up mine. Barclay's special, sir. What he'd been forced to do for us makes him so, and he certainly isn't expendable.'

The Director nodded. 'You appreciate that none of this can ever reach the press, Thomson – the public at large? How'd it be if, after examination, we released Barclay from operational duty and turned him over to you?'

'I think we'd both like that, sir,' said Frank, and with a beaming smile all over his face, the young man edged his way into the module.

Barclay greeted him with a joyous yelp, and as Frank released the restraining straps, the chimpanzee who had come so close to doom leaped into Thomson's arms and hugged him wildly. The taped electrodes had torn some small patches of skin from the closely-shaven areas of his body, but somehow, Barclay didn't seem too bothered.

TIME TO THINK

by Andrew Muir

IN DECEMBER, 1982, I was not exactly full of the seasonal feelings. It was six months since I had left school and I still had no job. It was always the same story: 'too young' or 'not enough qualifications'. So I had applied for a place on one of the new training schemes. I was lucky enough to be accepted and, with thousands desperate to join such schemes, it was not a chance to let go by.

Now, however, it was the day of decision, a decision that would affect the rest of my life; which particular training scheme should I enter? I had narrowed it down to two: mechanics or computer programming. Hours later I still had not decided; although there were many mechanics around there was also always a demand for them. I mean, work at a garage may be difficult to get, but people always need mechanics for their cars. I could work on my own, be my own boss. It was a bit risky, but surely I would get enough work to get by on. On the other hand, I was fascinated by computers, and they were, undoubtedly, the 'thing' of the future, the only expanding industry in Britain these days.

I sighed, and decided to take both leaflets home with me. It was hopeless trying to decide anything in the Job Centre or library. All your friends turned up at one time or another and talking to them made it too distracting to think clearly.

Putting the leaflets and forms in my pocket, I went out with Jim and Sheila. We went down town and wandered around the shopping centre. It was warm there and you could hear the

205

latest singles in the record shop. And there was a cheap old cafe where you could still get a hamburger roll and a cup of tea for seventy pence. If you were lucky, while you were inside, someone might put the juke-box on.

On the way home, I spent some time at Jim's. He was going down to London soon, and I wouldn't see him for a while. Jim had nothing to suggest on my predicament. He had enough problems trying to decide what he would do in London.

I was walking home at about half-past eight, in a mixture of sleet and rain, pondering on my problem. As I cut through the fields to the back gardens of my street, I noticed someone coming toward me.

The big day had arrived, November 19th, 2017. I was working on the biggest assignment of my life; sitting at the controls of one of the most advanced computers the world had ever known. No-one could work with this system as fast as I could. And an up-to-the-minute grasp of the situation had never been so important as now.

I was sitting near the centre of a large, circular room, along with a handful of technicians, some of the greatest scientific minds in the world, and a group of top government officials headed by the President.

We were approaching the climax of a project I had been working with for over four years. The most amazing project in human history, and also the most secretive and heavily guarded. I knew a great deal of the scientific detail of my work, but the concepts were still beyond my understanding. The project had been started years before I joined; in fact it had begun in the mid nineteen-eighties while I was just beginning my career in computers. We were developing a system that would realize one of man's oldest dreams – time travel.

The solemnity of the occasion intensified when Dr Aldridge

McKinnon stepped forward to address the President and government spectators: 'Gentlemen, Mr President, this is the day we have all worked towards. The last time you visited us for a demonstration of our progress we were transferring inanimate objects into the past. If you recall, our last action that day was to transfer a baseball bat to the middle of the Arizona desert in the year 2010! As you are no doubt aware, our last information sheets to your committee reported the recovery of this object and with the results of tests proving that it had, "in fact" been there for years.

'More importantly, these tests were followed by experiments with animals – the information on these experiments you have seen already – we trust the animals are busily adapting to their new times!' (Polite, but rather nervous, laughter.)

'Today sees the first trial run in Time by a human being; namely myself. As the principal theoretician on this project it is in the interests of common-sense, not merely vanity, that I make this historic trip. Although the technique seems to have been perfected there are a few concepts that remain mysterious. As far as is known I have never arrived in the past! We wonder, therefore, if this experiment is doomed to failure before we begin. I do not think so. I believe that it is a mystery of Time still to be explained. I intend to make a brief journey into the recent past, thirty-five years ago in fact, and to attempt to leave a definite sign of the success of my journey. This 2017 Decam coin will be deposited in a safety-box at a specified bank, in the year 1982, and, hopefully, Mr President, you will have it presented to you when it is retrieved in a few hours' time. The first time that safety-box will have been opened in thirty-five years in one sense, and the second in a few hours in another. Exactly one week from now, Professor Albie will reverse the process and bring me back from the same co-ordinates I will arrive at today.

'The year 1982 has been selected for several reasons; the clothing presents little problem to duplicate, and I will be able to cope easily with the everyday language and customs. More significantly, in 1982 I was in my nineteenth year and began a college course specializing in the sciences relating to Time Research. It seems an appropriate time to return to and observe my reasons for undertaking that course, knowing what is to follow.

'We will now begin a final, precautionary, check of all our equipment and controls. My assistants will give you a guided tour and explain the workings of each section.'

McKinnon rambled on for a few more minutes – the extrovert, show-man side of him enjoying the drama of the moment. I began running computer checks on all our equipment for what seemed like the thousandth time that day. I must admit the tension and excitement were getting to me also, but even this and the reverently admiring President and government aides watching my computers at work could not really dispel the clouds that hung over my private life.

My control over all the computers in our huge complex had ensured a secret as carefully guarded as the project I was working on. Six months ago I had started to get dizzy spells, and since then I had grown increasingly weak and tired. Not overly concerned at first, I had visited a doctor friend for a private examination. I needed secrecy because my large-salaried job depended on, among other things, a clean bill of health.

Now, months of extensive tests later, I had to face a grim fact. My blood had developed a fatal and multiplying organism that was spreading rapidly throughout my body. Dr Kerr, who knew me well, had decided last week that since there was no possible cure I should be told everything. He told me I only had a few more months to live.

Since that day I had been brooding on the unfairness of it all.

'Why should *my* life be cut short?' I kept asking myself. I thought of all the good times I had enjoyed and I was terrified to think that suddenly there would be no more. Even my awareness of the past was to be wiped out. What had I done to deserve this? I could not accept it. But there was nothing I could do. Unless . . . no, that was too ridiculous, it would never work – yet what had I to lose?

The tests being completed, and our guests waiting as expectantly as ourselves, it was time for Dr McKinnon to become the first man to travel in time. He savoured the moment for as long as possible. I moved forward to join the people watching him.

'Well gentlemen, I shall return in about thirty-five years, or one week as far as you are concerned. Goodbye for the present – as I may say more literally than is usual.'

There was applause as he moved forward to the capsule. The system was activated, and the door opened, by one of the assistants pressing a button on the nearby control unit. Dr McKinnon stepped forward.

'No! It isn't fair. I want to live!' I yelled.

Running forward, I pushed Dr McKinnon to the side and jumped into the capsule.

There was a blast of hot air, followed by a blinding light that lost none of its intensity when I shut my eyes. Staggering under the force of the light I felt a rush of cold air and opened my eyes as the light vanished as instantaneously as it had materialized.

It was November 1982. I found myself in the toilet room that was part of the original, central, buildings of the complex I had just left. Now, that is, in 2017, they were mostly disused subsidiary buildings peopled by some office workers. So, I thought wryly, Dr McKinnon·had selected a toilet cubicle for his transfer position! I felt like laughing at his gamble, but

*Running forward, I pushed
Dr McKinnon to the side and
jumped into the capsule.*

soon realized his reason for choosing this spot. The toilets were being redecorated; what meticulous research Dr McKinnon must have conducted to discover the exact time in 1982 of the refurbishing of the toilets! He knew that there would be no unwanted visitors here at this time. A glance out of the window showed that it was evening.

A month later I arrived at Prestwick Airport after a flight in an antiquated mode of air transport. After an initial period of hiding and confusion, I had sold my thermo-jacket, time-piece and various personal electronic gadgets to an agency too delighted to press me for explanations. I was confident they would accept – after all I knew the company was made world famous for the introduction of the original designs. Also, my previous enthusiasm for boxing and tennis had finally justified itself. I can still remember my lecturers' complaints over the time I spent reading sports magazines rather than text books. If they could only see the money I had accumulated from carefully selected bets that month! My survival was ensured because of those hours spent reading sports magazines and the results I had remembered from them.

Suitably dressed for the period, I quickly – and by now confidently – made my way to my home town. But things grew almost intolerable as I made my way through Scotland. Reliving the times of my youth and remembering to keep up appearances was a terrible strain. Every object, every newspaper, in fact *everything* filled me with wonder and made me want to shout aloud. At the same time I had to concentrate on what I was going to do.

Originally I had intended to present myself at home and explain everything to my parents and let them tell my younger self. I did not wish to have a conversation with myself. It had occurred to me that I had never met myself before, so how could I now without jeopardizing the future? And if I changed the future what would happen to the 'me' that was here now?

The more I thought about it the more complicated everything became. My parents had died in a road crash in '95. Although I was desperate to see them, how could I face them with the knowledge of what the future held in store? I could warn them, but then again I met my wife, then a nurse, because of that crash. If I changed all that I could well be 'killing' my own two daughters! These torturing dilemmas had plagued me since I arrived back in time. I was still totally confused and hoping that some answer would materialize as I approached home. It did not.

As I reached my home street I realized that I could not go on with that plan. I wandered around the neighbourhood in an increasingly distraught state. Everything seemed simultaneously familiar but nightmarishly strange. What could I do? Nothing seemed possible or right.

I resolved to take a last look at my old house (secretly praying for a glimpse of its inhabitants), and then go away to try and think it all out again. I arrived at the house in mid-evening. The curtains were drawn, and the television could be heard outside the front windows. I walked quietly around the house and let myself out by the back garden way. I could not face those familiar streets again.

Tears were falling down my face, caused by an emotion that man has yet to invent a name for. I was walking slowly over the fields, oblivious to the rain and sleet, when I saw a figure striding towards me.

I stood stock still in shock and amazement. A memory rushed back to my mind: the night I decided to apply for computer training! Of course, and the drunk (for so I had thought then) man who had had me wondering what he had been doing behind our row of houses.

Staring in stupefaction, I was rooted to the spot. Desperately I thought, 'I must tell him to take the computer training. I must!'

I was thinking that computers would be a better area to get trained for, when I noticed that the figure coming towards me had suddenly stopped. As I moved nearer to him I noticed he was muttering to himself and there were tears on his face. 'What's that funny old geezer up to,' I wondered, 'why is he snooping around our houses? Looks like he's up to no good, he seems terrified because I've seen him. Oh, there he goes swaying about on his feet, just a drunk I suppose.' I realized I was staring at the drunk and started to walk on again. 'It's funny, I could have sworn he was muttering about computers; I must have computers on the brain!'

'Get a grip on yourself, man, or you'll pass out,' I thought. 'What a morose looking boy I was . . . Oh no, he's staring at me, I must tell him.' Then suddenly I realized – of course he would decide to do the computer training, otherwise I would not be here. He passed by, giving a long, distrustful stare. 'Evening, my boy,' I said, and walked on over the fields to the main road.

I sat in the sleet and the rain by the side of a garage. My mind was in a whirl, but gradually a feeling of elation spread over me. It had worked! Everything was going to be all right. I still had only a few months to live, but in thirty-five years I would have them all over again. Although doomed to die time after time, I had also achieved a kind of immortality.

FIRE, FLOOD AND FAITH
by Lee Stone

STEVE BROCK was crossing Tranquillity's dust-covered Main Street when the six riders came hurtling into town. He didn't even have time to sidestep before they rode him down and sent him sprawling full length against the raised edge of the wooden sidewalk.

Steve picked himself up carefully, turning the warm morning air a few degrees hotter with a string of invectives hurled into the cloud of dust left in the wake of the six riders. Suddenly he was aware that he was being watched. A young cowboy, leaning on the tethering post, was regarding him sympathetically.

Feeling angry and foolish, Steve said by way of explanation: 'They rode me down deliberately!'

'Sure did, mister,' said the cowboy. He spoke with a slow drawl, more like a city man than a rural cowpoke. He eased himself up from the tethering post and sauntered into the sun-lanced street where Steve was dusting himself down. 'Name's Tod Jennings.'

'Steve Brock. I just rode into town half an hour ago.'

'Ah! Then you don't know those ranchers. They're the Saggers gang. Seems they're looking for a feller and they think you're him.'

'Me?' Steve Brock stared back at Tod Jennings in disbelief. 'I told you, I just arrived here.'

The cowboy eased his hat back on his head, grinning. 'Well, mister, they're looking for a stranger who informed on

Charlie Saggers. Young Charlie was caught red-handed by the law, trapping beaver before the season opened. Charlie Saggers is a-comin' up before the Judge tomorrow, and Charlie happens to be his pa's favourite boy.'

For a moment Steve looked aghast at Tod Jennings, then he laughed softly. 'They've got the wrong man, mister, that's all I can say,' he said. 'I'm just stoppin' to git my supplies and then I'm ridin' straight on through.'

As he walked across to the general store, Steve's mind flashed back over the events of the past week. He'd ridden into Tranquillity County from the great ranch, inherited from his father, three hundred miles away in the warm south. He'd been in the saddle for nearly two weeks, riding, riding, and living rough, just to try to erase the nightmare event that had destroyed his ranch and bankrupted him those two long weeks ago . . .

It had happened one morning when, as part of his improvement plan, Steve had rigged up a dynamite charge to blast a big outcrop of rock a couple of hundred metres from his ranch house. The charge had gone horribly wrong and stray sparks had fired the edge of a hot, dusty cornfield. Within minutes the field was an uncontrollable blaze; within an hour it had spread across his entire ranch, engulfing all his father's years of toil. All had been consumed by the raging flames. Steve had saddled his one remaining horse, and ridden blindly northwards.

At last, exhausted and saddle-weary, he had arrived at a prospector's abandoned shack, a ramshackle hut on high ground above a valley. A bend in the river running by gave its name to this desolate vista: River Bend Valley.

Throwing down his saddle pack, Steve had slept for a day and a night. When he awoke and took stock of his surroundings he found his temporary lodging was just a hundred metres from a wooden bridge over the river bend.

Beyond the bridge was a track up the other side of the valley and two miles beyond the summit of that hill was the township of Tranquillity, in the centre of the nation's best beaver hunting country . . .

Inside the general store Steve paid for his order and slung his loaded pack on his back. As he reached the door to go, the storeman called out: 'You thinkin' on leavin' town, stranger?'

'Mebbe. What's it to you?'

'Because Jess Saggers told me to give you this message. He figures you should git out of town. Says it could be unhealthy if you stick around these parts.'

'You give Mr Saggers a message from me, old timer,' Steve said evenly. 'There's a prospector's shack two miles back up at the head of River Bend Valley. You tell him if he wants to meet me, he can come up there any time he figures.'

Outside on the sidewalk, where the hot summer sun cut the street in two, Steve struggled to master his overwhelming anger. 'Mebbe I'll stick around this town a mite longer,' he thought. 'Mebbe I'll even stay right here for good.'

Next evening, alone in the prospector's shack, Steve was gulping down his supper of tinned bully beef and biscuit when he saw the riders coming down the hill from the direction of Tranquillity. Swiftly he bolted the door; then, easing back the bolt of his Winchester rifle, he cautiously opened the solitary window.

The six riders halted in a fold of the hill just above the bridge across the river bend. One of them, red-bearded and massively built, pushed his horse a few metres forward. Steve recognized the man; he must be Jess Saggers, he thought.

'I got your message, stranger,' Saggers called out. 'And here's another one for you. My boy Charlie's got sent down for twenty-eight days this mornin' on account of you, and now me and my friends are gonna teach you a lesson.'

Carefully Steve aimed his Winchester just to the right of Jess Saggers' ear. As the bullet whistled past him, Saggers almost fell from his saddle in astonishment.

For answer, a fusillade of shots whipped into the woodwork around the shack window, throwing out sharp splinters like confetti. Steve ducked. The firing stopped; then, for several minutes, there was silence. Not daring to raise his head again, Steve strained his ears to catch some sound, some clue betraying movement. Suddenly a body hurtled against the barred door, then another, and another. Steve smiled to himself. That won't work, he said, half aloud; whatever else may be wrong about this old shack, that door was built to last.

The Saggers gang evidently thought so, too, for minutes later Steve heard the sound of horses' hooves riding back across the wooden bridge and up the hill. Carefully he raised his eyes to the window ledge. The six riders were vanishing into the fading light.

They would come back, of course; the Saggers gang didn't look like the types who gave up easily. Steve settled down to wait.

They weren't long in coming, but this time when Steve raised his head to look it was dark outside; he could tell they were there more by the stealthiness of sound than the keenness of sight. There came a swish of liquid, the bustle of urgent steps on the dewy grass. Then a burst of light, the sound of crackling, the acrid smell of smoke.

'They've set fire to the roof!' Steve thought.

Even as he drew himself to his feet, gun blazing through the open window into the night, the hot, downward swirling smoke filled his lungs to bursting. Reeling, he lifted the bar across the door, and opened it to a searing wall of flames that seemed to scorch his lungs.

As he plunged through that searing fire Steve knew he was a

sitting target for the six mean ranchers on the other side of the inferno. As he staggered, gasping, to escape the flames, he saw the myriad sparks, felt the all-pervading heat, and heard the rapid bark of rifle shots . . .

A familiar voice said: 'Don't seem I was a mite too soon, Mr Brock, sir.'

Steve's eyes flickered. He lay on the ground. The sparks above him had turned into stars, the white, snapping curtain of flame was a quiet, dark purple sky. He turned his head, recognized the face and, seconds later, remembered the name.

'Tod Jennings. What are you doing here?'

'As I said, seems I just about arrived in time. You see, I work down in Tranquillity for a feller name of Bud Williams, who's one of the Saggers outfit. When Jess Saggers came over to fetch Bud Williams this afternoon, I had it pretty well figured out that they were a-comin' to look you up. So I just thought I'd follow them with a Winchester.'

'But there were six . . .'

'Mebbe so. But in the dark a Winchester can do a lot of talking. Mebbe they just thought the Sheriff was out there with a posse. Anyways, I let off half a dozen shots and they turned tail and rode out of the valley like a bunch of frightened coyotes.'

Steve looked up quizzically at Tod Jennings. Why was he always around when there was trouble for Steve? Then he realized that his silence must seem ungracious.

'I'm sure grateful you happened around, Mr Jennings,' he said slowly. 'Seems you turned up just in time to save my life.' He raised himself slowly from the ground, wincing with the sharp pain that seared through his lungs at each intake of breath. Tod Jennings stooped down, gently offering his water flask.

2 18

'There was a lot of fire,' he said softly. 'Guess your tubes could be a bit scorched.'

Steve looked at the smouldering, fire-blackened wreckage of the prospector's shack. 'Guess I've taken on a bit more than I can chew around here.'

'It's a shame to hear you say that,' Tod Jennings said. There was real sincerity in his lazy, city-type drawl. 'You know, this is government land, free for homesteading. You could just file a claim on it and providing you live on it for a year and a day it's all yours.'

Steve laughed scornfully. 'What'll I do with it, Mr Jennings? It don't seem much like corn or cattle country to me.' He kicked the soft turf, oozing with brackish water. 'A man could scarce raise a goat on this.'

'Well, mebbe you should think about it. Rovin' and roamin', that doesn't always suit a man. Besides which, no one ever stood up to the Saggers gang before. I just got a feelin' you could beat that bunch.'

Steve snorted. 'I got a feelin' that six to one is lousy odds for an unlucky man, Mr Jennings. And you know something? I never informed on Charlie Saggers. I never even heard the man's name until yesterday.'

'I know that,' Tod Jennings said softly.

Something in the calm assertiveness of that reply made Steve's eyebrows arch inquisitively. He said: 'You think they'll be back?'

'Not tonight. You figure on making camp here?'

'Sure do. Don't reckon on stayin' here much after tomorrow, though.'

Tod Jennings swung himself up into his saddle. 'Mebbe I'll just ride by and look in on you,' he drawled.

Steve watched him ride off up the hill. Then his thoughts turned back to his own wretched plight. A lost inheritance, a ruined burned-out shack on a piece of worthless land: that was the sum of his life so far. What the hell, anyway, he said suddenly to himself. I'm finished, done for. But I might at least try to give back as good as I get from this jumped-up rancher Saggers and his cronies. As he turned into his sleeping bag his mind was already half made up . . .

Next morning Steve was up bright and early. He washed in the river, saddled up and rode out of the valley up the hill that led to Tranquillity. As he rode up the main street he was aware of being watched by some of Saggers' men. Undeterred, Steve dismounted at the Land Registry Office, just as Flem Franklyn was opening it up.

Steve leaned on the polished office counter and kept to the point: 'I'm homesteading. Wanna file my claim.'

Flem Franklyn nodded and passed over an official form. 'Fill that in, mister. You can write?'

'Sure can.'

'Know the rules? Identify your spread by drawing a plan and swear you intend to live there a year and a day. After that, Federal law says it's all yours.'

Flem Franklyn watched with growing curiosity as Steve sketched a plan of his spread on the space provided. 'That's River Bend Valley,' he said. 'Ain't no man ever filed a claim there before this.'

'Yep.'

Flem's eyes narrowed. 'You know why, mister? Because that's slough land. It's full of water. It ain't worth a hoot.'

'Depends,' Steve said. 'Depends on what kinda value you put on things.'

He filled in the form carefully, then walked out into the strong sunlight. He was feeling good now. As he rode back down the main street he met and returned unflinchingly the hostile stares of the Saggers clan.

'Mornin', neighbours,' he called, and felt better still.

Some of the elation began to drain away, though, when, back at River Bend, he began the back-jarring task of moving the rubble of the burned-out shack. First he made a pile of useless timber, then, anything that could be salvaged he fashioned into a makeshift camp, with a flat roof piled high with fern branches. You couldn't call it a shack but it would do for a week or so; a man had to have some place, however primitive, that he could call home.

When the setting Sun was colouring the river blood-red, he went down to the water's edge and washed. A couple of beaver were working at their dam, gnawing branches into shape before threading them industriously into the rigid pile of timber. Steve smiled. 'I guess everyone has to have a place they can call home,' he said to himself.

Looking up, he saw a lone rider coming down the hill. Jennings? No, not tall enough, too square in the saddle. Abruptly the rider reined in and regarded Steve soundlessly from afar. Then he swung his mount round and disappeared again.

Steve blinked uneasily, not trusting his eyes. He felt weary from the morning's toil and drowsy in the evening warmth. He lay back on the river bank and regarded the crimson-flecked sky, pressing like a lead weight on his eyelids . . .

The rumble of distant thunder that awakened him seemed incredible, for the night sky was as calm and as cloudless as ever. He shook his head in disbelief and gazed incredulously across the river as a sudden blinding flash lit the darkness like day, followed by a crescendo of sound that rose to an ear-splitting roar.

Steve felt his heart stop still. He knew that sound, knew it too well. It was dynamite.

The roar of concentrated thunder triggered by the triple explosion rolled across the heavens, then stopped ominously leaving an eerie stillness. Slowly Steve was aware of a gurgling sound, growing louder beyond the blackness, a swirling, rushing noise . . . He drew back violently at the touch of cold water on his ankle and jumped to his feet.

Then he was completely submerged under a frenetic torrent of water; picked up, swept off his feet by the stinging rush.

Steve thought, 'I'm going to drown – what happened? I'm going to drown and I don't even know what's happened . . .'

Something cold, wet and spongy brushed against his side, something else, heavy and slimy, was flapping against his legs. Gasping, Steve felt with his hands, his fingers closed around a living body and he drew back in horror. The slimy black living things were all about him, clinging to his arms and legs while the water in his lungs, in his whole body, was remorselessly dragging him down . . .

Down? Suddenly he was aware that his head had broken the surface. The night's blackness had come down to the water, but this was air, he could *feel* it. He took in a gulp of breath that made his head whirl. Instinctively he trod water and began to swim, against the swirling current and against the moving, living objects that were clinging to him, brushing him. Beaver! That's what they were.

His feet touched oozing mud. In a moment more he had stopped swimming and was walking up a slope to higher ground. On a grassy bank he collapsed.

First light streaked the sky when he awoke upon a scene incredible to imagine. As far as the distant hill, beyond which was the track to Tranquillity, the entire expanse of River Bend Valley was filled with water. It was as if the river had been picked up and removed, to be replaced by a huge, instant shallow lake. Nine-tenths of his spread, his useless claim, was covered by this flood.

Steve watched in dazed wonder as hundreds, thousands

*The slimy living things surrounded Steve,
while the water in his lungs was
remorselessly dragging him down . . .*

perhaps, of busy, struggling beaver – the horror of the previous night – swam to and fro on the lake's surface; brown, glistening bodies so active that they turned the water into a constant bubbling cauldron.

Surveying the amazing vista, he looked eastwards to where the river had once entered the valley and now entered the lake and saw at once what had happened. The Saggers gang had flooded his claim by dynamiting the bend and so clearing the river course. The river now flowed straight and the beavers must have been swept with the rushing water, into the newly formed lake.

The footfall of a dismounting rider sounded softly behind him. Startled, he turned quickly. Tod Jennings was standing there, wearing an expression half-way between astonishment and laughter.

'They sure made a good job of it this time,' Steve said bitterly. 'I figure this is about the time I should start to hit the trail.'

'The trail?' Tod Jennings shifted his gaze from the glistening lake to the dejected young homesteader. 'The trail? Are you kidding? Look out there! Those crazy cowboys have built you a beaver ranch, right here on your own spread, and stocked it for you with the best beaver in Tranquillity River. Look at 'em! Thousands and thousands! *Your* land and *your* beaver. You can make a fortune every year from the pelts. You're rich!'

Steve stared at him, slowly realizing the truth of what was being said. He turned and looked at the lake, the struggling mass of beaver already beginning to turn the valley, his spread, into their permanent home.

'How come you know so much about beaver, Mr Jennings?'

'It's time I told you I'm a Federal agent,' Tod Jennings said, grinning broadly. 'Nature Conservation Department. I was sent out here to keep an eye on the Tranquillity River beaver colony because there'd been reports of trapping out of season. It was I who saw Charlie Saggers breaking the law the other day and I who reported him. So I felt kinda concerned when that gang of ranchers suspected you and tried to drive you away. I figured if I could help you out, I would.'

He paused, and surveyed the lake's incredible mass of pulsating water, a surface of perpetual motion covered by busy beaver bodies. Then, grinning, he stuck out his hand. Steve grasped it gratefully.

'The beaver season opens this very day, Mr Brock,' Tod Jennings said. 'And you've got a spread for life here.'

THE RAID
by Adrian Vincent

THIS IS THE STORY OF A RAID . . . 0200 hours: Troops land. 0315
hours: Attack on enemy emplacement. 0345 hours:
Emplacement destroyed. 0348 hours: Attack on harbour
began. 0410 hours: Lieutenant-Colonel March killed. 0425
hours: Invasion barges destroyed. 0435 hours: Wireless
station attacked. 0455 hours: Wireless station destroyed.
Force One withdrawn. 0530 hours: Troops evacuated.

The official report tells little of the courage and heroism of
the troops under fire – nor does it tell you how Lieutenant-
Colonel March was killed.

The code name was HORSESHOE.

The top brass at Combined Operations Headquarters first
discussed it two months ago, and they had all agreed that the
raid should be carried out. Scale models had been made of the
area showing where the harbour defences and batteries lay,
aerial photographs had been taken, the tides studied. Nothing
had been left to chance. The memory of the last, unsuccessful,
raid had to be erased, and it was therefore imperative that
nothing should go wrong.

Unaware of what was in store for them, five hundred
commandos were being trained on the coast of Devon. They
were already crack shots, experts in the handling of explosives,
deadly with the commando knife, and capable of walking
thirty miles a day without turning a hair. When they had
finished here, they would rank as one of the toughest fighting
forces in the world.

Major Hart was their second in command, and the Major was a very perturbed man. He had already been on a number of raids, and he knew that all this training was merely the prelude to another commando clash. Their intensive training also seemed to indicate that they would be going in under a set of particularly difficult and unpleasant conditions. This did not worry the Major. He was, after all, a professional soldier, who was used to taking things as they came.

He had another, more pressing problem on his hands. The problem of Lieutenant-Colonel March.

Sitting at his desk in the stuffy wooden hut which served as his office, Major Hart sighed as he studied the orders for the day. As usual, since March had arrived, the day's training was abnormally heavy, and in addition there were too many needless chores to keep the men occupied in the evening. The men won't keep standing for this, Hart thought. I can see a blow-up coming.

The door was pushed open suddenly and Lieutenant-Colonel March came into the hut. He was tall and thin, and, like Hart, in his middle thirties. Hart rose to his feet.

'Morning, Hart. Anything on your mind?'

Hart looked down at the orders on his desk. 'As a matter of fact there is. These orders –'

'What about them?' March said sharply.

'I can't help thinking you're pushing the men too far.'

'That's for me to decide.' March wandered over to the window and looked out. 'Anything else?'

Hart said doggedly: 'There's such a thing as over-training.' He took in a deep breath. 'The previous commanding officer appreciated that.'

'The previous commanding officer is dead,' March said. 'Killed on an exercise. If the men had been better trained, it might never have happened.'

Hart was silent. The commanding officer had been killed by

a stray bullet and it was the sort of thing that could happen to the most experienced man. A bad night's sleep, a day when the senses were a fraction less alert, a moment of distraction, any of these things could lead a man to his death. He knew there was no point in telling March this. He tried another tack. 'Very well. But is it necessary for the men to have to do all these useless chores after an exhausting day?'

March turned away from the window and looked bleakly at Hart. 'I'm well aware they're useless, Hart. But they're good for the soul. These men seem to think they're supermen. The chores will teach them a little humility.'

For the first time Hart began to have some idea of what was biting March. He had come to the camp two weeks ago from an infantry battalion, and had found himself working with a breed of men who were individuals, and yet were still capable of working together in a manner that was quite unknown to the ordinary soldier. Inevitably, Hart supposed, it did lead the men into thinking they were some sort of élite – not entirely without justification. They were better trained, and they took greater risks than the average soldier. A reasonable man would take all that into account. But not March.

'What sort of man is he really?' Hart thought. He knew that March had been with the British Expeditionary Force, but apart from that he had not seen a great deal of action, except for a brief spell in the desert. He had, however, a reputation for being a strict disciplinarian. Presumably, this was the reason he had been sent here. The real question, of course, was what he was going to be like when they went into action.

'None of this really matters, anyway,' March said. 'We're moving out tomorrow evening.'

Hart was silent for several moments. 'How much do we know about it?'

'Operation Horseshoe,' March said. 'A night raid on the enemy coast. A dispatch rider with our orders came in less

228

than an hour ago.' He hesitated. 'You'd better come to my office and see what it's all about.'

'In the circumstances,' Hart said drily, 'that might be a good idea.'

The weather had cleared miraculously within the last half hour, and the landing craft could now be seen quite clearly as they rose and fell in the swell of the waves, like a shoal of whales heading purposefully towards the shore. A bank of cloud over the moon had mercifully shrouded the two ships that had brought them, but it would be only a matter of minutes before it cleared, revealing them to the shore batteries. Sitting hunched in the first landing craft, Hart tried to review the situation. They were heading for the fishing port of Portard and their main task was to destroy the twenty invasion barges that were moored inside the harbour. In addition, they were to go inland and destroy a wireless station.

The orders had also pointed out that the civilian population still had unhappy memories of the last raid. A spectacular success would revive their morale. It had occurred already to Major Hart that this was probably the main purpose of the raid. It was unlikely now that the invasion barges would ever set out for England, and the wireless station was of no particular importance. It therefore seemed that a large number of men were going to die that night merely to make the civilians happy.

The craft were already nearing the coast. Soon now, they would be landing near the shelving beach, five hundred metres to the right of the harbour, and out of reach of the guns in the cliff emplacement protecting the harbour. If all went well, Force One was to make its way inland to the wireless station, while Force Two dealt with the invasion barges in the harbour. After both objectives had been destroyed, the two forces would join up again on the beach. It seemed a simple enough operation. But there were snags to it.

First of all there was that gun emplacement.

The gun emplacement was capable of pouring a hail of devastating shell fire down on to the harbour. The fact that they would be destroying their own men as well as the enemy would not stop the gunners. It had been decided therefore, that Force One was to destroy the emplacement from the rear before the attack on the harbour began.

Then there were the enemy barracks.

These were situated between the emplacement and the wireless station. The enemy troops in the barracks would be warned as soon as the emplacement was destroyed, and ready to repel the wave of commandos as they swept on towards the wireless station.

All in all, it looked as if it was going to be a bad night.

They landed at two o'clock in the morning. Nervously aware of the crunch of their boots on the gravel, the men gathered in ragged ranks, waiting for the order to move off. Looking briefly out to sea, Hart noticed that the two ships that were to take them back had moved further away from the coast line. The wisps of smoke from their funnels were now little more than tiny threads of black streaking the rim of the clear moonlit sky. Hart turned, suddenly aware that someone was standing at his elbow. It was March.

'Are we ready to set off?'

Hart nodded. 'Is Timms happy?' Lieutenant Timms was in charge of the force that was going to deal with the invasion barges. Both Hart and March were going with the main force on whom the success of the whole affair really depended.

'I've told him to get as close as possible to the harbour,' March said. 'Then as soon as we've knocked out the emplacement, he can move straight in.'

'Then we'd better get moving,' Hart said. 'Thank God there's a path of sorts to the top.'

'We haven't a chance,' March muttered. 'They're going to wipe out the lot of us!' The searchlight from the barracks was scanning the hard, frost-carpeted ground, and a machine-gun kept pace with it, raking each area the searchlight lit. The bullets thudded impersonally into the living, and the motionless dead, who had been mown down as soon as they had come into sight of the barracks. It had happened just as Hart had feared it would. Warned by the destruction of the emplacement, the enemy troops had been waiting for them. A few more minutes in hand, Hart thought, and we would have reached the barracks. Then it would have been a different matter.

As if from a long way away, he could hear the din of battle coming from the harbour. A faint red glow in the sky told him that some of the barges, at least, were alight. He wiped a hand across his face, blackened by the smoke that had gushed out of the shattered emplacement like the expiring breath of some legendary dragon. 'We can't stay here,' he muttered. He winced as a mortar bomb shattered the earth a few feet away from the gully where they were sheltering. 'We must do something!'

'There's only one thing we can do,' March said. He reached for his whistle. 'Retreat!'

Almost without thinking, Hart knocked it from his lips. 'We can't do that!'

'Are you mad?' March was groping wildly for the whistle even as he spoke. 'If we ever get out of this, I'll have you court-martialled —'

Hart said urgently: 'I'm sorry. But if we start retreating we can't even defend ourselves. They'll finish off the lot of us, and then make for the harbour. And that'll mean the end of Timms and his men as well!'

March stared at him in the darkness. 'I'm the commanding officer here —' He had found the whistle now. He stuffed it in his mouth and blew, but some earth had clogged it, and no sound emerged from it. In any other situation, it would have been laughable. 'Curse it,' March said hysterically. He banged it furiously in the palm of his hand, trying to loosen the piece of dirt that had become lodged in it.

Watching him, Hart realized that March's nerve had suddenly deserted him. The fighting around the gun emplacement had been savage, and March had acquitted himself well enough there. But this, on top of it all, had been too much for him. Hart knew that even the bravest of men broke under undue stress, and he was capable of being sympathetic about it. But not under these conditions. He said firmly: 'We have to attack. It's our only chance.'

'I'm not interested in your opinions,' March shouted. 'My orders are that we retreat.'

A stream of machine-gun bullets spattered across the rim of the gully, and they both ducked low. As they crouched there, Hart saw with an awful clarity what would happen if March was allowed to try and carry out a retreat; his men falling like nine-pins, the force at the harbour being taken by surprise and wiped out. After a raid like this, it was even doubtful that the enemy would take prisoners, preferring to kill the commando force. Something had to be done.

When they both stood up again, Hart had his revolver in his hand. He said quietly: 'Lieutenant-Colonel March, if you try and order a retreat, I shall shoot you.'

March stared at him with incredulity. 'You wouldn't dare!'

'Try it,' Hart said. 'I won't mind a court of enquiry. Shooting an officer for cowardice in the face of the enemy is no crime.'

March was silent for a few seconds. Then with a wild, savage cry he flung himself on Hart. The two of them fell into the bottom of the gully. March fought like a maniac. His fists stabbed out a rapid tattoo of blows, and then he was on top of

Hart, his hands clawing for his throat. They wrestled silently in the dirt, while above them the clatter of the machine-gun went on unceasingly. Hart's revolver went off once, echoing in the narrow gully, even above the machine-gun fire, and then he lost it somewhere in the darkness. He shot out a fist, felt it contact briefly with something hard, and then he was free of the intolerable weight on top of him. His eyes were temporarily blinded because of the pressure of March's fingers on his throat, and for a moment or two he couldn't see a thing. When his vision cleared he saw that March was scrambling out of the gully.

'Come back, you fool!' he called.

Ignoring him, March stood up. For a second, no more, he stood there, a wild figure in the bright arc of the searchlight. Then the machine-gun cut him down. He fell back into the gully without a word. When Hart examined him, he could see he was quite dead. Somehow he found the whistle again. Two blasts for an attack . . .

As he came out of the gully, he could see the men rising around him. They had only gone a few yards, when he knew instinctively that they were going to make it.

'Feeling all right in yourself?' the Brigadier asked kindly.

'Yes,' Hart said shortly.

They sat there in silence for a little while in the impersonal surroundings of the Brigadier's office.

'Your new posting,' the Brigadier said, 'I hope it's to your liking.'

Hart ignored the question. 'I don't seem to have read much about the raid in the press. A few paragraphs –' He smiled thinly.

The Brigadier shook his head regretfully. 'I didn't think it was advisable to say too much.'

'All in all,' Hart said, 'the raid was a waste of time then?'

With a wild cry, March flung himself on Hart. They fell into the bottom of the gully, March fighting like a maniac.

'I wouldn't say that,' the Brigadier said easily. 'Any raid is useful to help us plan for the ultimate invasion.' He shuffled some papers on his desk. 'You'll be getting a decoration . . .'

'Less than a hundred men came back from that raid,' Hart said bitterly. 'You can't expect me to get any joy out of that piece of information.'

'I know,' the Brigadier said consolingly. 'But that's the way it goes. A pity about March, too. I understand he was a good soldier.'

'I believe he was.' Hart's face was expressionless as he rose to his feet. 'Is there anything else, sir?'

'No,' the Brigadier said. He stuck out a hand. 'The best of luck, Major.'

Hart went out, closing the door softly behind him. He went slowly down the corridors of the War Office, and it seemed as if the ghosts of four hundred men walked with him.

NEMESIS
by Angus Allan

ADOLPHO MESSINE had been born in Sicily, an island of strange and sometimes sinister customs, where superstition often ruled the lives of the small farmers and shepherds who lived in the interior. His father's father was said to be deeply involved in that most widespread and feared of criminal organizations, Cosa Nostra – known to the world as the Mafia. His maternal grandmother was supposed to have been some kind of witch, capable of destroying those who crossed her with the power of the evil eye.

But Adolpho had left Sicily as a child, and had been taken to America by his parents, who had been tragically killed in a train crash. From one relative to another, he had travelled far. Long before his third birthday, he had found himself in Liverpool, in England. Here he was to be raised by second cousins, who ran a restaurant business. He had been well schooled, and was considered to be a bright boy. He had shown a remarkable talent for art. There were teachers who said that his command of drawing fell only slightly short of genius. At fifteen, he was able to copy, in oils, the works of many great painters, and had mastered styles as different as those of Rembrandt and Picasso. He was, they all agreed, destined for greatness.

But in his late teens, Adolpho Messine had moved to London. There he chose his own future. In crime.

It was not the sort of house that anyone would have wanted to live in. Lonely, dismal, it stood far back from the side road that wound over the wind-torn moorland. Abandoned for years, its shutters flailed depressingly against the broken windows, driven this way and that by the rain-heavy wind sweeping in from the east. Gaunt trees, in the hopeless wilderness of the garden, bent and groaned to that same wind, and their dead branches were like so many clutching, skeletal hands. Funereal laurels, crowding up against the ancient brickwork, dripped sadly on the sour and weedy soil beneath them.

And yet three men had sought shelter from the storm there, that night. There was Tunny Magill, and Dud Bayley – and the one they'd met in the bar of the Red Lion, back in Higher Scranton. They'd never learned his name, and they'd never know it now, for his pockets had yielded nothing. There he lay, his white, dead face upturned from the mouldering boards of the hallway floor, his arms outflung. Well, what did Tunny Magill or Dud Bayley care about his name? All they knew was that their intuition had proved right. And that now they were rich – rich beyond dreams.

'Look at this! Just look!' Magill, fat and squat, threw his hands in the air, and a scatter of tenners sprayed from them.

'Leave it out, Tunny!' Dud capered across the gloomy hall, snatching at the fluttering scraps of paper. 'No sense in flingin' it about!' He was a tall, angular man, with a face like a rat-trap, and the cold, dead-fish eyes of a man totally without conscience.

Tunny said: 'Must be nigh on a hundred thousand.'

'Nigh on,' agreed his partner. 'So let's count it. We ain't about to go anywhere while this rain keeps up, are we?'

Tunny Magill shrugged. He looked nervously over his shoulder. 'Matter of fact, I wish we *were*, Dud. I don't like this place one little bit.'

'Gahhh. You'll be tellin' me you believe in ghosts, next,' sneered Bayley. 'Worried about him, are you?' He jerked his thumb at the corpse.

'Yeah. Matter of fact, I am.'

'Right, then. Say no more, mate.' Bayley got his hands under their victim's shoulders and hauled him into the dark recess of a cupboard. He slammed the door shut, and dusted his palms together. 'Better?'

'Better.' Magill picked up an old-fashioned leather briefcase, stained with rain, pulled it open, and set it on a dust-laden table. Then, methodically, he began to count the ten-pound banknotes into piles.

From the shadows, on the worm-eaten gallery that ran round the hall above the cobwebbed balustrades of the stairs, Adolpho Messine watched, and let out a long, soft chuckle.

'Here. What was that?' Magill looked up fearfully, tenners slipping from his grasp.

'Nothin', you fool,' snarled Bayley. 'Just this lousy old house, with all its creaks an' groans an' what-not.

'You'll be gettin' me at it next,' he added.

It had been three hours previously that Magill and Bayley, warm and cosy in the public bar of the Red Lion, had been sitting enjoying a beer and a sandwich with nothing more on their minds than the fact that they were low in funds. That fact didn't worry them: As burglars, they knew that they could soon and easily remedy the situation. Like all those who steal, they were contemptible wasters, without a thought for the unfortunates whose homes and whose privacy they regularly invaded.

They considered their targets as mugs. Complacent fools who left windows open, and keys under the mat. 'Them idjits deserve all they get,' Magill was fond of saying.

Alone in the pub, they had done no more than glance at the dark-haired man with the bulging briefcase who had come in, soaking and disgruntled, and who had ordered his ale. But

238

Adolpho Messine watched from the shadows, and let out a soft chuckle.

gradually, that briefcase had grown and grown in the burglars' interest. What did it hold? Something worth pinching, maybe?

A good enough actor, Bayley had struck up a conversation with the stranger, summing him up in a glance. Tallish, a bit on the thin side. Not much in the way of muscle. A bit studious-looking, maybe. And his hands were smooth, like a woman's. No trouble if it came to a barney, that was for sure.

'Been on holiday, have you, mate?'

'Me? No. Why do you ask?'

'You look sort of sunburned.'

'Natural colour.' The stranger had pulled a newspaper from his raincoat, and had begun to read.

Not put off, Bayley said: 'On your way to Leeds?'

'That's right. Bit of bother, though. My car's packed up.'

'Couldn't have happened outside a better place. What's wrong with the car?'

The stranger shrugged. 'Damned if *I* know. Machines are a mystery to me. Something to do with the fuel-pump, I reckon. I was just about to ask the landlord if he could put me up. Can't face doing anything else before this blasted rain stops.'

Inwardly, Bayley hugged himself. 'Chum,' he beamed, 'you're in luck. My mate over there . . .', he gestured at a slightly astonished-looking Magill, 'is a mechanic. Now, he'd be pleased to give your motor the once-over. Wouldn't you, Tunny!'

'Er – yeah. Sure.'

Tunny Magill and Dud Bayley had been working so long together, that they could practically read each other's mind. So Magill, putting on an act that was only just inferior to Bayley's, went outside, to return shaking his head and clucking his tongue.

'Bad news, guv. The feed's properly mucked. Tow-away job, that is.'

Bayley tut-tutted. 'Tell you what,' he said to the stranger. 'Me an' Tunny are going on into Leeds. Why don't we give you a lift? You can phone for someone to pick up your car when you get there.'

The stranger hesitated, but only for a moment. He looked calm enough, but in fact his mind was in turmoil. Possibly, by now, Chief Inspector Draffen had picked up his trail. He didn't want to be caught, out here in the open, defenceless. 'That's real nice of you,' he said. It was odd that he didn't sense, with the instinct of all those who tread the same road, that these men were as criminal as himself . . .

Magill and Bayley were playing it by ear. One more drink in the Red Lion, and they went on their way, in their beat-up van, with their passenger sitting in the back.

'Wanna shove that case up front, mate? Looks a bit uncomfortable, there.'

'Er – no thanks. It's okay, really.' The stranger clutched it closer to him.

Ten kilometres out of Higher Scranton, the clutch of the van had gone. Bayley had decided that they would stop well over the moors, near Joynson's Pots. He'd had a notion of clubbing their victim, dumping him down one of the cavern-holes in the ground there, and making off with the case for whatever it contained. Now he had to revise his plans. He swore, briefly. Outside, the rain was still belting down, and there was only the gloomy shape of that old house, up on the skyline.

'Van's leaking. And it's cramped,' said Magill. 'Come on – let's ask for shelter.'

So all three of them had run up the lane, pushing through the dank and weeping undergrowth, to the door of the deserted mansion. A door that had yielded, to the stranger's slight surprise, to Magill's undoubted expertise.

'That was a flaming pick-lock,' the stranger had said, no

sooner than they were over the threshold. And that was when Bayley, reacting automatically, had seized up a heavy, web-hung candelabrum from a rickety side table and brought it smashing down on the man's head. He had fallen without a sound, his case spinning away from him. And as it had fallen, so it opened, to spill out the mind-boggling fortune in ten-pound notes . . .

Neither Magill nor Bayley had bothered about their victim. Dead or alive, what did they care? All they had eyes for was the wealth that lay scattered in the dust . . .

Magill finished his counting. 'You were right, Dud. One hundred grand, give or take a note or so.' He grinned apologetically. 'Might have missed a ten here or there.'

'Cor! A hundred thousand smackers! Come the end o' this storm, we'll nip away from here smartish. Thumb a lift, smack the geezer over the bonce, and be down in Hull before you can say Jack Robinson. I know old Mitchell there. He's got a boat. He'll shove us across the channel for a coupla hundred, and this time tomorrow, mate, we'll be on the jolly old continong.'

'Gay Paree,' chuckled Magill. 'You remember that cove Pierre Lefai?' (he pronounced it 'Luffee'). 'The fence. He'll take this loot an' give us francs for it. We'll be properly in the clear, old son . . .'

But then Magill shivered. He had heard – or thought he had heard – another thin, ghostly chuckle from the shadows above. From the shadows where, unseen, Adolpho Messine was watching . . .

Just before dawn, the rain died off, as suddenly as it had begun. With the money stuffed back into the briefcase, Magill and Bayley set off down to the road. They spared not a glance for their useless van, but began to walk eastwards. They knew that, sooner or later, some likely and luckless driver would pass them . . .

242

They had been gone an hour before Chief Inspector Draffen and Detective-Sergeant Colborne from the County Constabulary arrived at the old house. The dank undergrowth was steaming in the sunshine that had broken out, but the place looked no more reassuring than it had done before. 'It's the van that the landlord of the Red Lion told us about, sure enough,' said Sergeant Colborne.

'Better take it steady, sir.'

'Are you teaching your grandmother to suck eggs, sergeant?' came the icy reply.

Draffen avoided the front door, though it was open, and gained entry at the rear. It took him moments to discover the dead body in the hallway cupboard. 'Must have died instantly,' he said, shaking his head. 'It's him, all right.'

'It certainly is,' agreed the sergeant. 'Those other two . . .?'

'They could've gone anywhere. At any rate, they've taken the case with them.' The inspector stirred his toe thoughtfully in the dust. 'I suppose it's got to be a call for an intensive watch on all ports and airfields . . .'

Then, in the gloom – for even though the sun was stronger than ever, it hadn't penetrated one whit into the gaunt mansion – there came a soft chuckle.

'What the devil . . .?' Draffen spun round, tensely. 'Who's there?'

There was nothing to be seen, but Adolpho Messine's voice came clearly and sibilantly from the ragged banisters of the gallery. 'I shall guide you, Inspector. I shall direct you to the pair of them . . .'

The sergeant had gone white. 'That – that's his voice, sir! Messine's! I'd know it anywhere!'

Draffen felt sweat break out on his forehead. His hands were clammy, and he couldn't seem to grip them. 'It – it's impossible, Colborne,' he whispered. 'Messine's there. Dead. Lying where he was murdered!'

Shaken, the two policemen ran from the house to their car. As he'd decided, Draffen put through the all-stations alert. Then he sat back, and for the first time, took a handkerchief to mop the beads of perspiration from his brow. 'We – we both heard it. We weren't imagining . . .'

Incredibly, to both their ears, came that same, soft, insistent voice. 'Draffen! Move, man! Drive! Their plans are astray! I *see* them . . .'

Like a man in a trance, the Inspector, his complexion ashen, moved into gear and obeyed. His sergeant sat beside him as rigid as a statue. And all the time, the ghostly voice of the unseen presence behind them kept up its urging . . .

Magill cursed roundly. Nothing had come down the road. Absolutely nothing. Not in either direction. 'You and your bright ideas,' he snarled at Bayley. 'Here. You carry this damn thing for a while. It's heavy.'

'All right, all right,' said Bayley, testily. 'Give it here. Hang about a mo! Bayley turned, his free hand cocked to his ear. 'At flamin' last! Something's coming. Get ready with your thumb, Tunny!'

Putting on his most innocent look, Magill stepped into the verge and raised his hand in a hitch-hiking gesture. But his face went through several stages of gradual dismay as the car that sped up to them revealed its contents as Chief Inspector Draffen and Sergeant Colborne. There was no running. Both sides of the road were protected by high estate fences, far too high to jump or climb. Besides, the enormity of their murderous crime and the crushing certainty of capture held both the burglars rooted to the spot in horror.

'That's the case, sir,' said Sergeant Colborne, snatching it from Bayley's hand. Bayley had time to notice that the younger policeman's voice was curiously shaky. Come to that, the senior rozzer didn't look so good, either . . .

Draffen read them their rights. And then he charged them with the killing of Adolpho Messine. Neither Magill nor Bayley resisted. The car drove them off. And there was no room in it for the wraith who, unseen, but with one final, triumphant chuckle, melted into the hedgerow, his slaying avenged. For a ghost, his haunting of this earth had been short, but decisive.

One day some years later, in Sicily, a member of the Messine family turned up some long-forgotten records written by an old woman who had widely been regarded as the family witch. In them, she had written a kind of prophecy, about a boy called Adolpho. Vaguely, it said that he would travel far and wide; that he would never return to his native land; that he would excel in his chosen profession, bad though it was, and come to his end at the hands of assassins. But he would be able to pause between the grave and Hell to destroy them.

Magill and Bayley went to prison for life. Their dismay was only made worse by what came out at the trial. The man they had so callously killed was one of the most skilful forgers the world had ever known. He had been a master of his art, who had created a small fortune in counterfeit tenners as his last gesture against authority. 'I have to say, though,' Chief Inspector Draffen had told the court in evidence, 'that the ten pound notes *would* have been detected as forgeries, thanks to the new and secret methods of marking employed at present by the Bank of England.' Magill and Bayley both groaned.

Neither of the policemen ever mentioned the strange guidance of Adolpho's spirit. Perhaps neither of them really believed it. And throughout all their lives, Draffen and Colborne never realized a curious but somehow significant fact. The letters of Messine's name made an anagram.

It was – Nemesis: the ancient word for fate and vengeance.

THE LAST LAUGH
by Alan A. Grant

THE *Andromeda Star* WAS THREE DAYS OUT from Pluto Base when I reckoned it was safe to bump off Limpy. It wasn't that I didn't like the guy – he'd been crewman on our space truck for twelve Earth-years, and if he wasn't exactly Buck Rogers at least he was tolerable. But I had a big-money scheme in hand, and if it was going to come off I couldn't afford to have any witnesses.

'I'm down in the airlock now, Mr Ryker.' Limpy's space-worn face appeared in my control console vidscreen. He'd been working the space lanes most of his life, and somehow he'd ended up with me and Kovaks. He didn't know it, but this would be his last trip.

I didn't really know how to tell him. All I could say was 'Sorry, Limpy' and 'Goodbye'. I jabbed a button on my console and the oxygen started to hiss out of the airlock. For a moment, the old guy's brow furrowed in puzzled shock – then he gasped and clutched his throat.

As his lungs sucked desperately for the fast-vanishing air he rasped: 'Gee, boss . . . You d-didn't have to do it . . . n-not this way! I-I wouldn't have talked . . .'

I flipped off the intercom. I didn't want to hear any more. I felt bad enough already.

'Is – is it over?'

I looked up as my partner, Ernie Kovaks, came on to the flight deck. The little man's chubby face was smeared with the

246

same grease that stained his engineer's coverall. But underneath the grime, I could see his features were pale with worry.

'Yeah, it's over. Old Limpy won't ever limp again!'

Ernie's eyes were riveted to the vidscreen. 'It – it's horrible! He was such a harmless old guy. I just wish it hadn't been necessary.'

'You think I wanted to do it?' I shot back at him. 'You know the trouble Ryker-Kovaks Haulage is in – we're in debt up to our eyes, Ernie. And in case you'd forgotten – we're already criminals.'

Ryker-Kovaks Haulage had been losing money steadily for months. Our ship – the *Andromeda Star* – was on its last legs; we needed a new one, one of the latest meso-drive models, to keep up with the competition. But our capital was spent and our creditors were closing in fast. That's why I came up with my scheme . . .

It was one I'd used before, back in the old Luna-haul days, but this time it was on a much larger scale. It was embarrassingly simple: you contract to carry a cargo, then sell it off on the black market and pocket the cash. Then you arrange for your ship to have a very nasty 'accident'. Of course, the insurance company pays up for both your cargo and your ship!

In this case the cargo had been *zipote*, a rare gas used to freeze people in suspended animation tanks, putting them in a state of half-life. It was normally used with the sick and dying. That's why zipote was so valuable – people would do anything to keep a loved one in suspended animation until science could come up with a cure for the illnesses.

We'd sold the zipote for a fat profit to black marketeers soon after we'd landed at Pluto Base. Now all we had to do was arrange the 'accident' for *Andromeda Star*.

'I still don't like it, Ryker,' Ernie muttered. 'Why stop at one murder? Why not kill *me*, too, and double your profits?'

I put one great hairy arm round his stubby shoulders and beamed at him. 'Aw c'mon, Ernie. We're partners – pals. We're in this together.'

I ushered him gently towards the hatch. 'Now go give that escape pod its final check. We're going to need it as soon as I can find us a decent meteor storm!'

Ernie waddled off down the gangway. Suspicion was written all over his face. But that didn't matter. I'd handle Ernie – when the time came.

My scanners picked up the asteroid storm three Earth-hours later. It was a big one, Force seventeen on the Patmoor Scale. More than a billion tonnes of hurtling, iron-hard destruction. Any spacer in his right mind would cut off his arm to avoid it. I wasn't in my right mind. I was crazy . . . crazy like a fox!

I blipped the engine room. Ernie wasn't there. I tried the airlock, and the little ball of fat that was his face came up on-screen.

'I've located our storm,' I told him. 'It's perfect for the job. Is the escape pod ready?'

'Just putting the final touches to her now, Ryker. I'm ready when you are.'

I could trust Ernie to have everything working perfectly. He was only a tubby little guy with the courage of a mouse, but he was the best engineer this side of Alpha Centaurif. It was going to be a pity to lose him.

'Stay there, Ernie. I'll be down in a jiff!'

I set course for a direct collision with the heart of that storm. I jammed all safety systems – I didn't want the ship's computer playing hero and ruining the whole scheme.

I took one last look round my flight deck. It had been home to me for more years than I cared to remember. I wasn't sorry to be saying goodbye.

I ran down the gangway as if my life depended on it. It did!

When I reached the airlock Ernie was waiting, the escape pod hatch open and ready. Limpy's body lay where it had fallen; Ernie had covered the face with an old oil rag.

'I – I couldn't stand it, Limpy staring up at me like that,' he began, but I cut him short.

'Get in! We've got less than a minute to blast this pod out of here!'

We ran to our seats and strapped in. I could hear the crackle and whine of the approaching storm on the pod's sensors.

'Forty-five seconds!' I yelled.

'Pod hatch secure,' Ernie squeaked, his voice high-pitched with tension. 'All systems GO.'

The outside airlock hatch slid open. I punched the GO-code, and we were forced back in our seats as the pod burst free from the *Andromeda Star*.

Through the pod's viewscreen we could see those bright pinpoints of cascading death up ahead, close now. The pod's forward momentum was carrying us on a parallel course with the doomed *Andromeda Star*.

'We're getting too close, Ryker! We've had it! We'll never get clear in time!'

I just laughed and jammed on the retro-engines. I'd been a pilot long enough to judge distance to a metre. I knew we were safe.

'You can open your eyes now, Ernie,' I scoffed. 'We missed the storm by more than a mile! Say your farewells to the old tub.'

Through the viewscreen we saw *Andromeda Star* plunge headlong into the onrushing storm. A small meteor, no bigger than a fist, punched a hole clean through the starboard hull. Another followed . . . then another, and another, till she was riddled like a Swiss cheese.

A lump of rock the size of a small island whirled across the screen. There was a blinding flash as the fuel tanks exploded

. . . and the *Andromeda Star* was suddenly just so much junk. Someday maybe they'd find it, a piece here, a piece there – but that's all. They wouldn't expect to find even a trace of the cargo.

I punched the Emergency Distress, and its powerful signal lanced through space. Help would soon be on its way. Me and Ernie were home and dry. At least, I was!

Ernie was mopping beads of sweat from his brow with an oily rag. He smiled weakly at me. 'I – I suppose the worst of it's over now . . .'

'You bet it is, Ernie boy! From here on in, we're on Easy Street!'

I broke out two shampagne tubes from the pod locker. I'd been saving them specially for this occasion. It was Moet & Luna '99 – one of the best vintages the Moon's vineyards had ever produced. I handed one to Ernie.

'Let's drink to our success, pal,' I grinned.

Ernie hesitated. I bit the short plasteen teat off the tube, and squirted a jet of the bubbling liquid into my mouth. It frothed in the back of my throat and slid down smooth as honey.

I smiled. 'You're not drinking, Ernie.'

He laughed nervously, then de-capped his own tube, sucking deeply on the wine. 'Boy, that's good!' Relief lit up his face like a beacon. 'You know, Ryker – for a while there I thought you were going to kill *me*, too! I really thought you were.'

I looked hurt. 'You do me an injustice, Ernie. We're pals, ain't we?'

'Pals?' He gave the word a bitter twist. 'We're shipmates, Ryker – partners. But pals? No, you've never been my pal.'

He took another deep swig of shampagne. I could see it was getting to him. Normally, Ernie wouldn't say 'Boo' to a Xanuthian goose.

'Oh, you're all pally on the outside, Ryker – but underneath you're selfish through and through. Always calculating the odds, always out for Number One – and heaven help anyone who gets in your way – like poor Limpy!'

He took a third gulp from the shampagne tube. 'What I can't figure is why you didn't kill me, too. One less witness and double the profit – that's your style, Ryker. I was really sure you would do it . . .'

A sudden stab of pain flashed across Ernie's face. His hands clutched at his chest, and he sagged to the floor.

'No, Ryker – the . . . shampagne!'

His body twitched once. I didn't need to feel his pulse. Ernie was gone.

I looked at the time. Exactly one minute and forty-four seconds since Ernie took his first swig. That's how long zipote takes.

I'd saved a little of the cargo we'd sold to the marketeers. Not much, just enough to inject into Ernie's shampagne tube. Strange stuff, zipote: at sub-zero temperatures it's fine for paralysing the heart. At normal body temperatures, it's like being hit in the ribs with a sledgehammer – from the inside. A surefire heart attack you could set your watch by – and no trace of gas in the body afterwards.

I don't know why I chose the shampagne. I wanted the little fellow to go out in style, I guess. After all, I didn't have anything against old Ernie. But it was like he said – one less witness, and double the profit!

His hand was resting across my foot. I pushed it away. Poor old Ernie, the shock of the meteor storm and our narrow escape had been too much for him. Least, that was going to be my story. And Ernie? He wasn't talking to anybody!

I sat back and swigged the last of my shampagne – the untainted stuff. Pretty soon I'd be drinking it whenever I wanted. I was no mug. I had no intention of buying a new space ship. That was just a story to get Ernie to play along.

If a man spends long enough in space, he gets to be like old Limpy was – washed-out, hollow-eyed, a walking vegetable. Well, that wasn't the future I saw for Mrs Ryker's little boy!

I had the cash from the zipote rip-off sealed to my body under strips of plasti-skin. I looked a little chubbier than usual, but not enough so's anybody would ask questions.

I'd be rescued, tell the authorities my story, put in an insurance claim on the ship, then sit back and wait. It might take six months, a year even. So what? I could afford it. After that I'd be on Easy Street for the rest of my life – and I'd make sure it would be a long one.

'Hi, Ryker. Remember me?'

I nearly jumped out of my skin. It was Ernie! But – his body was still lying there, stiff as a board.

The voice came from behind me. I whirled – to face the pod intercom!

'This is a recording, Ryker. The fact that you are hearing it means that I am dead – that you've murdered me, just like I thought you would. Make yourself comfortable, Ryker – you've got a shock coming.'

My mind was racing. What in space was going on here? I could only listen as Ernie's squeaky voice continued:

'I knew you would get me, just like you did Limpy. So I made plans, Ryker. All that time you thought I was checking the escape pod, I was busy working on them.'

I thought he'd taken too long on the pod. An engineer of Ernie's calibre could have done it in his sleep.

The voice from the grave went on: 'I made a few changes in the escape pod, Ryker. I started with the pod's heat-sensors – rigged them so that if my body temperature dropped below ninety-two degrees, they'd trigger off the rest of the sequence. That has just started.'

I noticed a sudden chill in the air. The bulkhead vents were frosting over. Ernie's squeaky voice seemed to gloat: 'The next stage in the sequence is now in operation. The pod's temperature is dropping to below freezing. I want you to be as cold as I am, Ryker! Cold, but not dead. Not yet.

'I'm giving you a chance, Ryker – more than you ever gave Limpy or me.'

I shivered, and mouthed a couple of silent curses. Ernie was a superb engineer – whatever he'd cooked up for me, it was sure to be good.

'I've hidden a bomb aboard the pod. Just a simple device – two phials of fuel taped together with a time switch. Small, but enough to blow the pod to dust – and you with it. You've got thirty minutes to find it and defuse it, Ryker –' Ernie's voice broke into a chuckle even colder than the air. 'Of course, I must warn you – there are one or two boobytraps along the way. Better start looking, Ryker – your time's running out.'

'Damn you, Ernie! You can't do this to me!' I blurted – then realized I was speaking to thin air. *Cold* thin air.

I cast my eyes desperately round the pod's interior. The kind of bomb Ernie had described wouldn't take up much space – there were a thousand places he could have hidden it.

I ignored the obvious ones, like the lockers and the survival stove. I started ripping off the bulkhead panels with an Anderson wrench. There was nothing there – and five minutes were gone!

I pulled off the computer casing – and drew another blank.

Think, Ryker, think! Another three minutes gone . . . but now I was beginning to get my composure back. Ernie had given me a chance. But he'd misjudged his man. Nobody made a fool out of Ike Ryker! I'd find his bomb . . .

Adrenalin pumped through my veins, and I hardly felt the cold. The rubbish chute – of course!

I snatched up a lason torch and bathed the mouth of the chute in its green light. Yeah! Something there all right –

I stooped, stuck my head in to get a better look – and the whole world seemed to explode!

'My eyes! *Aaaaagh*!' I staggered back, rubbing crazily at my face.

Then Ernie's taunting voice was back to mock me: 'Sorry, Ryker – that wasn't the big bomb. That was just meant to handicap you a little.'

I couldn't see a thing for blood and splinters, but I bit back the pain. I had to keep searching – or Ike Ryker would be losing a lot more than his vision.

I started taking the sleeping cabin to pieces, feeling my way like a blind man. I had to hand it to that Ernie – he'd done his usual meticulous job.

I ripped off the light casings, and then the air vents – and that's when boobytrap number two hit me. A low hiss told me that oxygen was escaping from the pod.

'Things get tougher from here on, Ryker.' It was Ernie's voice again. 'The oxygen content of the air you're breathing has just been reduced by fifty per cent! From now on every breath will be torture, the slightest effort totally exhausting.'

He wasn't joking. I was down on my hands and knees panting like a long-haired dog on a hot summer day. I couldn't see, I could hardly breathe, and my limbs were slowly turning to ice. That Ernie was some joker!

I stumbled painfully back into the pod's main chamber. Maybe I should have tried the obvious places first.

I felt my way to the stove, slotted my freezing fingers into every opening. Nothing. Same story with the lockers – not a thing.

I didn't know how long I had left. Ernie supplied that information.

'Three minutes, Ryker! Your last three minutes alive!'

I lost all control. I scrambled across the floor struts and grabbed at my partner's limp body. I shook it like a ragdoll.

Ernie had the last laugh

'Blast you, Ernie!' I grated. 'Blast you for a double-crossing rat!'

Then it hit me – and I almost laughed. Of course – the most obvious place of all. The bomb was hidden on Ernie's body!

I ripped at his coverall like an animal, and there it was, in his inside tool pocket, wrapped up in a grease-stained rag.

'The pod's light sensors indicate that you have found my device, Ryker. Congratulations. Now I will tell you how to defuse it.'

This was it. I'd made it. I was free! Ernie had had his fun, but now it was over. I listened carefully as his voice squeaked on:

'On the front of the timing device, you'll see a five-figure combination lock. All you have to do is work out the right combination. You've always been a calculating man, Ryker – I'm sure you'll manage it. Goodbye . . . and good luck!'

The voice tape snapped off with a sinister finality. I was alone with the bomb, but I wasn't exactly straining myself with cracking the combination. There were a hundred thousand possibilities on a five-digit combination . . . and I had approximately one minute left to find the right one.

I'd nearly killed myself trying to find an escape that wasn't there. Ernie had meant me to die all along.

I threw back my head and laughed like a madman.

But Ernie had the last laugh – and it was on me!